The Cowboy's

Hidden Bride

By Cora Seton

Author's Note

The Cowboy's Hidden Bride is the third volume in the Turners v. Coopers series. To find out more, look for the rest of the books in the series, including:

The Cowboy's Secret Bride (Volume 1)
The Cowboy's Outlaw Bride (Volume 2)
The Cowboy's Stolen Bride (Volume 4)
The Cowboy's Forbidden Bride (Volume 5)

Also, don't miss Cora Seton's Chance Creek series, the Cowboys of Chance Creek, the Heroes of Chance Creek, the Brides of Chance Creek, and the SEALs of Chance Creek:

The Cowboys of Chance Creek Series:

The Cowboy Inherits a Bride (Volume 0)
The Cowboy's E-Mail Order Bride (Volume 1)
The Cowboy Wins a Bride (Volume 2)
The Cowboy Imports a Bride (Volume 3)
The Cowgirl Ropes a Billionaire (Volume 4)
The Sheriff Catches a Bride (Volume 5)
The Cowboy Lassos a Bride (Volume 6)
The Cowboy Rescues a Bride (Volume 7)
The Cowboy Earns a Bride (Volume 8)
The Cowboy's Christmas Bride (Volume 9)

The Heroes of Chance Creek Series:

The Navy SEAL's E-Mail Order Bride (Volume 1)
The Soldier's E-Mail Order Bride (Volume 2)
The Marine's E-Mail Order Bride (Volume 3)
The Navy SEAL's Christmas Bride (Volume 4)
The Airman's E-Mail Order Bride (Volume 5)

The Brides of Chance Creek Series:

Issued to the Bride One Navy SEAL
Issued to the Bride One Airman
Issued to the Bride One Sniper
Issued to the Bride One Marine
Issued to the Bride One Soldier

The SEALs of Chance Creek Series:

A SEAL's Oath
A SEAL's Vow
A SEAL's Pledge
A SEAL's Consent
A SEAL's Purpose
A SEAL's Resolve
A SEAL's Devotion
A SEAL's Desire
A SEAL's Struggle
A SEAL's Triumph

Visit Cora's website at www.coraseton.com
Find Cora on Facebook at facebook.com/CoraSeton
Sign up for my newsletter HERE.
www.coraseton.com/sign-up-for-my-newsletter

Chapter One

"**S**TAY AWAY FROM my sister," Liam Turner growled.

Lance Cooper turned away from the saddle he was oiling, wishing—not for the first time—he lived in any other century except the twenty-first. He'd gladly trade his jeans, T-shirt, boots and cowboy hat for homespun infantry blues if Liam was wearing regimental reds and they were meeting in the middle of a Revolutionary War battlefield.

Then he could shoot the bastard.

"I'll dance with Maya any time I want." Just because Liam's dad and grandfather had been deputies, and his brother was a parole officer, that didn't give him the right to issue orders. Especially after the fact.

He'd asked Maya, a sweet, fun-loving, brunette beauty, to dance at the wedding they'd all attended a few days ago. Liam's older brother, Noah, had married Lance's younger sister, Olivia, much to the chagrin of both families. Lance had partnered with Maya to get a rise out of Liam, but he'd ended up enjoying himself far more than he'd expected. Ever since then he'd had a hard time shaking her from his thoughts.

Still, she was Liam's sister. That made her off-limits.

He couldn't remember a time when his family hadn't sparred with his neighbors. The Flying W—Liam's family's spread—lay directly across Pittance Creek from Thorn Hill, the ranch that had been in Lance's family for well over a hundred years. He and Liam had known each other all their lives. Had competed hard on the football field, Liam as quarterback and Lance the star receiver at Chance Creek High.

They'd squabbled over those assignments. Lance should have been quarterback, and Liam damn well knew it. Lance should have been captain, too. Liam had taken both positions as if he'd been born to them, just because his father had played quarterback a generation earlier. Everyone else went along with it; after all, everyone knew the Turners were one of the prominent families in town, while the Coopers—

Lance didn't care what anyone thought of his family.

"She liked dancing with me. Really liked it," he taunted Liam, then wished he hadn't when he considered what Maya would think if she overheard him. Maya wasn't anything like her brother, and she didn't deserve his disrespect. She was a Turner, though, he reminded himself. If he was smart, he'd stay clear of her.

Even if he'd like to get a whole lot closer.

What had being smart ever gotten him, anyway? Once he'd thought he was on his way to a better life. Back in high school he'd secured a scholarship to Montana State. A history degree would have set him up to teach—and eventually to take over running the local historical museum and archives.

Hell, if he'd managed it, he'd be one step from that job right now. Everyone knew Warren Hill planned to retire in a year or two. Warren had been the one to help him get that scholarship, and he'd have been more than pleased to pass down the job to him. Maybe it didn't pay a lot, but as a supplement to a teaching salary, he could have made a living from it. Lance liked his work on his family's ranch well enough, but he'd never planned to be in charge of it, let alone run it practically single-handedly. Steel wasn't pulling his weight these days, and their few part-time, low-paid ranch hands could barely take up the slack.

He wished his father was still alive and running things, keeping the family's spirits up with his irreverent humor and oversized personality. Somehow everything had gotten done when Dale was around, even if he skirted the law as much as he obeyed it. In a perfect world, Lance would be the one helping out here and there, instead of being swallowed whole by the ranch.

The Turners had botched it all for him. Torn up his family, sent his father to jail, his mother running into another man's arms. Left him responsible for paying his sisters' way—

"Maya only danced with you because she's too damn nice to say no," Liam retorted. "She's better than you'll ever be, and she doesn't need to slum around with a Cooper—"

Lance's fist connected with Liam's face, and Liam staggered several feet back, crashing into one of the posts that held up the roof. He regained his footing and came for Lance. "You're going to regret that, Cooper—hey!"

Lance straightened in surprise when Liam's brother, Noah, burst into the barn, collared Liam and shoved him toward the door.

"Get home. Get your chores done. You left the toolshed a mess." Noah turned to Lance while Liam stood glowering behind him. "I need a word with you."

Lance, unprepared for this turn of events, watched Liam bunch his fists, start forward again, hesitate, turn and stride out the door.

Noah glanced over his shoulder and nodded when his brother was gone. Looking back to Lance, he said, "Let's talk about supplies."

"Supplies?" Lance repeated.

"Now that I'm married to Olivia, I propose we gang up and put in our families' orders together. Feed, antibiotics, you name it. We'll save cash. What do you think?"

"What do I think? I think you're out of your mind. Shouldn't you be on your honeymoon or something?"

Lance still couldn't believe Olivia had married him, or that the happy couple had moved into a cabin on Cooper property. He couldn't believe Noah thought he had the right to any say in the running of Thorn Hill.

Was the world spinning backward?

Sure felt like it.

Noah's mouth pinched into a thin line. "I'm not leaving the Flying W in this drought. Things are too precarious, and you know it. Look at the way things are around here. Thorn Hill is in bad shape, and it's a miracle your family still owns it at all after the years you were away and Dale was—"

"Watch it." Lance wasn't about to listen to Noah badmouth his father. Maybe Dale had gotten in trouble—multiple times. Maybe he'd landed in jail and died there. Lance had been as surprised as anyone else to find out he'd managed to hold on to the spread during the years the rest of them had gone to Idaho. He'd never forget the phone call from the lawyer who let him know he and his siblings had inherited the place.

At the time he'd been happy to come back to Chance Creek.

Now the spread felt like a prison with its endless rounds of work and repairs. There was no time—or money—to pursue the twin careers he'd once thought were in his grasp.

"Let's sit down and go over the numbers," Noah argued.

"Can't." It was nearly five. He was due at the history museum for a Historical Society meeting in a couple of hours, and first he needed to shower, then go get a burger. Tonight's planning session would focus on the Revolutionary War re-enactment the group did every year on July Fourth, and it was about the only thing getting him through the day right now. He'd taken part every year since he'd been a kid—except the years his mother, Enid, had taken them to Idaho and left them there with her sister. It was one of the best things about returning to Chance Creek.

"Can't or won't?" Noah demanded.

"Got somewhere to be."

If he'd known Noah Turner would be trying to boss him around on his own ranch, maybe he'd never have come back.

"You're blind if you can't see what's coming." A muscle worked in Noah's jaw. "Maybe you don't want me interfering, but this is still Olivia's home. My home now, too. Like it or not, I've got an interest in how it's run."

"How would you like it if I told you how to run your ranch?"

"We're not talking about the Flying W."

Of course not. The Flying W probably had plenty of money. It was probably raking it in hand over fist. The Turners always did everything right.

"I don't have time for this." Lance put away the saddle and wiped his hands on a rag.

"Fine. I'll talk to Steel." Noah headed for the door, his impatience evident.

"My brother's not going to say anything different," Lance called after him, but Noah was already gone. He was right about one thing: this drought was taking its toll, and there was no rain in the forecast. The temperatures had been baking since the beginning of May. Now it was June, and there was no relief in sight.

That didn't give Noah an excuse to try to ride roughshod over them, though. He might think his marriage to Olivia gave him control of Cooper land, but that wasn't the way things worked.

And he wouldn't give Liam the satisfaction of taking orders from Noah, either.

Lance paused. Speaking of Liam, he didn't get to dictate who he spent time with. Maybe he should stop and see Maya on his way to town.

After all, Liam had hit on Tory at the wedding. Lance hadn't seen his sister in years before she arrived for the celebration, and he knew damn well Liam hadn't been harboring some secret crush on her. Liam had done it to get back at Lance.

He'd get what was coming to him.

Lance wouldn't mind one bit spending more time with Maya Turner, anyway. Unlike her pain-in-the-ass brothers, she was funny and kind and seemed to have a good head on her shoulders. If their families hadn't been at each other's throats all the time, they might have been friends. But even though Noah had married Olivia, their families were as estranged as ever. Ever since the Founder's Prize had been announced, the rivalry between them had come to a simmer. Both families wanted—needed—to win that prize, a vacant ranch that abutted the northern end of their properties. Whoever controlled the Ridley property controlled Pittance Creek, a vital commodity for both their spreads. Especially in a drought.

His family had taken a big step toward winning when they pulled together a bid to upgrade Chance Creek High—with the help of Carl Whitfield and his wealthy friends. Unfortunately, the Turners had countered by raising money to save the town's library—and were doing most of the renovations themselves.

They were tied for the prize. As if that wasn't bad enough, Noah had offered for Olivia's hand, and Olivia had accepted.

Since their wedding everything had been off-kilter. Lance had no idea what else they could do to win the Founder's Prize, and he dreaded the day when the Turners made their next move and left them behind.

If hanging out with Maya drove Liam around the bend, he'd be glad to do it more often. She ran a fruit and vegetable stand at the end of the lane to the Flying W. He'd heard a rumor she was selling baked goods, too, these days. He could grab a slice of pie to go with his burger. First, though—

He needed that shower.

Thirty minutes later he was heading for the front door.

"Be back later," he called to the house in general, not knowing or caring if anyone heard.

"Where are you off to?" His great-aunt Virginia appeared in the entryway to the living room, stiff but erect as she surveyed him with a sniff.

Lance reluctantly slowed his pace. "Town," he said shortly. No way he was telling Virginia his plans. She hated the Turners worse than the rest of them put together.

"You're up to trouble," she pronounced. "You should be up to winning us the Founder's Prize. What's taking so long?"

"I'm working on it," he lied and kept going.

"Work harder," she shouted after him.

IN THIS HEAT even her pies were wilting.

Maya Turner sat in a metal folding chair behind the large table that made up her family's farm stand. She'd set it up under a white awning early in the morning and had been stuck here all day selling her wares. The table groaned under an array of vegetables, fruits and berries, but the real draw these days was her cooking: fresh bread, muffins, tarts, cookies and pies of all varieties. Normally she was proud of the display, but the temperature had hit ninety degrees by ten this morning and was only getting higher. Beads of sweat kept tracing down the back of her neck under her thick hair. The awning's shade did little to cut the heat, and she'd have to be careful getting up from this chair the way she was sticking to it.

She kept having to wipe her hands off on a towel she'd brought for that purpose in order not to ruin the handstitched lace cap she was working on between customers. It was based on one she'd seen in an illustration in a Revolutionary War history book, and this was the only time she got to work on it without her family members picking on her for it.

Her brothers and sister rarely came out to the farm stand, and when a customer came, she could easily shove it into her workbasket before they managed to park their vehicles and exit them.

She wasn't ashamed of the project; she'd always

managed neat stitches and was an expert at re-creating patterns. Still, Stella rolled her eyes at the frivolity of her hobby. Liam made fun of her for wanting to live in the past, and Noah got that pinched look he always had these days.

At least now she knew why that was. This morning she'd overheard him talking to Stella when they thought they were alone in the kitchen.

"The price of beef is down," he'd said bluntly. "This drought isn't going to help our prospects. We need more money."

"We're all doing the best we can," Stella had told him.

"We need to do more."

"Maybe if you spent more time here instead of hanging around your wife's ranch—"

"That's not fair. I'm not working any less here; I'm just working more all around, and you know that."

Stella had sighed. "You opened up a can of worms when you married Olivia—"

"I expect that kind of talk from Liam but not from you."

"I'm on your side, okay?" Stella had said. "You've taken on too much. You're already working as a parole officer. And you should lighten up on Liam. His new plan could be the answer to all our problems."

"Certifying the ranch as organic? It's an interesting idea, I'll grant you that, but it's kind of a long shot, don't you think?"

Maya knew what he meant. She'd looked into the

process after Liam had brought it up the other day. Turned out he'd been looking into it for nearly a year, which went a long way to explaining why he was always so cranky lately. Getting the ranch certified would take a long series of steps, but at the end of it they'd be positioned to enter a niche market. It wasn't a bad idea. But it would be a lot of additional work.

"I think it's a good idea," Stella had said to Noah. "He's going to need your help, though. He's already stretched thin running the ranch. I've got my secretary job, and Maya runs the farm stand."

"Maybe if Maya spent less time fooling around sewing useless stuff and more time cooking those pies, that stand would be worth the trouble."

Maya had slipped away before she heard any more, afraid if she'd stayed she would tell Noah where he could stick his ideas. The drought had been hard on her garden, too, and at his insistence, she was working marathon baking sessions before each of her three farm stand days a week. She only had a single, conventional stove to cook with. There weren't any double ovens or commercial-style appliances at the Flying W.

She wasn't fooling around, either. She was pursuing a passion when she sewed. Maybe she wasn't a costume designer like Alice at Two Willows, who sold her creations to theater and movie companies. That didn't mean what she did was useless.

Except it was, she admitted to herself, letting her lace-filled hands drop into her lap. She'd never tried to sell one of her creations and wouldn't be able to charge enough to make it worth it. She labored over each one painstakingly, followed her whims, designed and executed whatever item of clothing she wished for at the moment. It was a quiet hobby that kept her out of trouble and filled the hours she sat out here at her stand. She'd always loved historical clothing, and it wasn't like she'd ever get her hands on the real thing, even if she itched to.

Maya still remembered her first field trip to Chance Creek's tiny historical museum when she was in grade school. While the other children weren't too impressed by the faded items in glass cases and couldn't read the old-fashioned cursive writing on the explanatory cards, Maya had been fascinated by it all. She'd been already reading every historical novel she could get her hands on at the Chance Creek library, and the museum had struck her as a kind of time machine that could whisk her away from her boring life into the much more exciting past.

The clothing had interested her the most, and she'd gazed at several old-fashioned dresses until she'd realized everyone else had left the building, and she was alone. She'd had to force herself to follow them, wishing instead she could get past the barriers into the exhibits and touch the pieces and examine the stitches that held them together. She'd lost count of the number of times she'd returned to the museum.

Over the years she'd daydreamed about turning it into a full-on historical re-enactment center. A place people could come and experience history in a hands-on way. If they could wear the clothes, eat the food, try the handicrafts, they'd understand the past so much better—

But that was before her mother had run out on her family. Before she and Stella had struggled to fill Mary's shoes, taking care of the house, getting food on the table, helping with chores, working to help pay the bills.

The last time she'd gone to the local museum, the exhibits that once had fascinated her now horrified her. All the old displays were crumbling with age. The same three gowns she'd studied longingly as a child had yellowed and looked like they might disintegrate if they encountered a whiff of fresh air.

The museum deserved so much better, but like everything else in this town, it needed an infusion of cash.

She had none to spare. Nor did anyone else. And Noah's derision stung.

It also stung that he'd crossed the line between their families and blurred the boundaries between them. Maya still didn't know what to make of his marriage to Olivia, if she was honest with herself. She wasn't like Liam, who'd been full of anger toward the Coopers ever since high school, or like Stella, who held herself rigid whenever they came near. Maya kept her distance from the Coopers because once she'd been friends with Olivia.

But not for a long, long time.

Not since she'd inadvertently got Olivia's father arrested and jailed.

Maya stared down the dusty road, the past defeating

her like it always did.

As children, she and Olivia had been warned against each other, their families at odds for generations before either of them was born, but they'd grown up next door to each other, and early on they'd figured out how to sneak back and forth across the creek to play—and soon realized that if they met on the Ridley property— the long-abandoned ranch that lay to the north of both their spreads—no one would bother them.

Olivia had always been a spitfire, and she'd spiced up Maya's rather dull existence. Her wild stories and vast imagination matched Maya's and made her forget the arguments and silences between her folks back home. Olivia was made of far tougher stuff than Maya was, but she had a tender heart, and both of them had escaped into the stories and pretend scenarios they'd acted out on the Ridley property.

Sometimes Maya's imagination and tender sensibilities got away from her. She'd never forget the time they created an entire alien world, complete with two rival civilizations, the Firimar and the Thrack. Olivia had played a Firimar knight. Maya had been a royal Thrack princess. The story they'd spun out had mesmerized them for weeks—

Until a war broke out between the two empires, with hundreds of thousands of casualties, destroying civilization as they knew it on the planet.

Maya had become distraught when it was clear the two sides were evenly matched and everyone was going to die. She'd broken down in tears as Olivia recounted all the casualties in gruesome detail, overcome with desolation at the scope of the destruction, especially when all the characters she'd grown to love succumbed to horrible deaths one by one. Olivia, suddenly realizing she'd gone too far, had turned the narrative on a dime with some quick thinking.

"I'm not a knight anymore," she'd proclaimed loudly, taking Maya's hand. "I'm Loreor, the Firimar angel of peace. And you're... Ladlea, the Thrack angel of peace. Together we can stop all this and heal everyone. We can turn back time, and it will be as if none of it ever happened! All we have to do is work together." She'd scooped up a stick and brandished it. "Angels of Peace, unite!"

Maya had grabbed a stick, too, more grateful than she could say, and still holding hands, they'd rushed onto the imaginary battlefield and attacked the combatants. They'd swung their sticks, disarmed the armies and then uttered healing incantations that went on and on until all the dead had come back to life. By the time they were done, Maya had been exhausted—

And happy.

That was Olivia to a T. A rebel with a heart of gold.

Maya knew people had been surprised when her parents split up, and she'd been surprised, too, but in hindsight she knew she shouldn't have been. Her mother's disappointment with her father was longstanding, based around the fact that she wanted something better than a small-town ranching life, and her father couldn't conceive of any other existence. Mary would have left them sooner or later, no matter what.

Maya had missed Olivia bitterly when their friend-ship came to an end.

She'd never admitted that to anyone. It wouldn't have done any good. Both of their families had fallen apart at the same time—and she was to blame.

Olivia's family had splintered as soon as Dale went to jail. Olivia's mother, Enid, had rushed her kids out of town to escape the shame, dropped them with her sister, Joan, in Idaho, and run off chasing another man—a married man—before she settled in New Mexico.

Maya had been plagued by guilt for years for her part in it all. She was the one who'd set that chain of events in motion. Thank God no one knew that.

Except Olivia.

And sometimes these days, she suspected Noah knew, too. He hadn't said anything, though.

"I thought I'd find you here," a voice said from be-hind her.

Maya turned and shaded her eyes with her hand. "Uncle Jed? What are you doing out here? Did you walk all the way from the house?"

"I'm not a cripple, you know. I used to keep law and order in this town, just like your dad and granddad. People should remember that!" But her great-uncle Jed was leaning heavily on his cane, and she moved the other folding chair in his direction so he could sit down. She quickly poured him a cup of cold lemonade from the cooler she kept under the table and passed it over.

She watched him drink.

"Is something wrong at the house?"

"Something's wrong with the world." He set the cup down on the table. "My nephew is married to a Cooper, and we haven't won the Founder's Prize yet. William must be turning in his grave."

Maya sighed. That damned prize. She swore it was the start of all their current troubles. "We're restoring the library, Jed. I think that's going to help our chances. I think Dad would approve of that."

"We have to do something more," Jed said.

"Like what?"

"I don't know. I'm making it your job to figure it out." He drained his lemonade, stood up again and turned to head back as she struggled to find an answer.

"You walked all this way to tell me that?" Maya finally managed.

"Yep. Get on it. I look forward to winning the prize."

Maya watched him shuffle off and shook her head. What more could they do to help the town? Fixing the library was proving enough on top of everything else. Noah and Liam had been up on the roof fixing leaks, and they'd all helped to prep the interior for painting. None of them had time for the extra work, but they were making it happen anyway. They'd raised money for the job by hosting a day-long river tubing event on their ranch a few weeks back. They were all dedicated to making the project a success.

Sometimes Maya wondered why they bothered.

Would ownership of the Ridley ranch really change anything? Jed and Liam were set on it, afraid that if the Coopers won, they'd divert Pittance Creek, but Noah was married to Olivia now. Surely he wouldn't let her family hurt theirs. She couldn't say what Jed's real motivations were, but she was pretty sure for Liam it had a lot more to do with his old football rivalry with Lance than anything to do with Pittance Creek. Lance had gotten him thrown off the team their senior year, taken over his position as quarterback and then gone on to win the championship.

Maya never could make heads or tails of that story. Her father had always been chummy with the football coaches. Coach Latham, who'd been in charge when Noah was a star running back, had dinner with the family once a month back when her mother was around. Coach Andrews, who'd moved to town and taken over the team when Latham retired at the start of Liam's second year in high school, hadn't been as close, but still knew her father well. Liam said Lance had lied to get him booted off the team. Back then she'd believed him. These days she wondered if the truth had something to do with their long-running rivalry. They'd both been hotheads when they were younger. Still threw down from time to time. Liam had always been stubborn enough she could see him doing something to Lance that had backfired.

Best to leave the past in the past.

She picked up the lace again and tried to find where she'd left off making tiny stitches to join the ruffle to the cap, but she was far too distracted to do good work. Why on earth would Jed think she could come up with another plan to clinch the prize? She wasn't the mover and shaker in this family.

She was just quiet, well-behaved Maya. The one who did everything right. The one who made sure everyone else was happy. The one who gave up her dreams as soon as they were inconvenient. She'd never gone to college. Never even brought it up again after mentioning it once a few years back. She'd been reading a book about a woman who worked at the Smithsonian Institution, wishing a career like that was available to her. She'd never forget Stella's exasperated look.

"You think you're the only one who wants something they can't get?" she'd snapped. "We need to make money, not spend money."

Maya had never uttered another word.

She wouldn't bring it up again now, either. Things had gone from bad to worse these past couple of years. There was no room in the budget for school.

She'd simply keep sewing.

She had just pushed her needle into the fragile material, still mulling over Jed's demands, when a truck pulled off the road and parked nearby.

Maya let the cap fall into her lap again.

What was Lance Cooper doing here? Never in all her years working this stand had a Cooper stopped by.

"Afternoon," Lance called out as casually as if he came by all the time.

"Afternoon." Maya was dismayed at the butterflies

in her stomach and the uncertain tone in her voice. She couldn't help remembering dancing with him at the wedding. The way he'd held her like she was something fragile.

Something valuable.

It had undone her more than she'd care to admit. She'd felt his strength, rested her cheek against his chest as they'd moved. She'd never been so close to him before.

Hadn't realized what a man he'd become.

Lance had simply been her neighbor up until that night. Now she couldn't think of him without feeling all unsettled inside. It wasn't right.

Toward the end of the number, he'd leaned closer, pressed his cheek to her hair and breathed her in as if wanting to memorize her scent. She didn't think it was a conscious move, and the intimacy of it had shocked her.

So had her reaction. She'd wanted to kiss him. To run her hands over his body. To pull him closer.

Lance was a Cooper. Why wasn't he keeping his distance?

He stopped in front of the table and perused the pyramids of vegetables and stacks of baked goods. He was tall, with the muscular build and tanned skin of a man who worked outside with his hands all day. His chin was covered with dark stubble that matched his thick, dark hair. His gaze ran over each item before he lifted it to meet hers. His gray eyes marked him as a Cooper.

He was good-looking, she had to admit. Far too

good-looking for his own good.

"Help you with something?" she asked.

"Hope so." His low voice with its country twang sent a shiver of awareness down her spine. "What's that?"

Too late she remembered her sewing. Lance reached right across the table and took it from her before she could react.

"Hey!" Maya leaped to her feet. "Give that back!"

He held it out of reach and examined it, making a face as he turned it around.

"What is this thing?"

"Nothing. Give it back!" She moved around the table and reached for it, but Lance lifted it higher, leaving her dancing around him, jumping to try to get it out of his hands.

"This looks like a cap," Lance said. "Like an old-fashioned cap. Revolutionary War era," he mused, turning it over in his hands. "Good workmanship." He seemed to remember who he was talking to. He grinned down at her, a feral grin that left her breathless. "For a Turner."

"What do you know about it?" She tried to grab it again. Failed.

"I know a lot about it."

"Give. It. Back!" This time when she jumped, her fingers tangled in the lace, and as she landed, a loud rip made them both wince.

"Aw, hell." Lance held up the bit of cloth he was still holding.

Maya looked down at the rest of the cap in her hands. To her chagrin, tears stung her eyes. That was days of work—ruined. And the lace he held in his hand had been from an estate sale.

Not cheap.

"Heck, Maya—I didn't mean to do that." Lance's cocky grin was gone, replaced by true concern.

"Yes, you did." She blinked back her tears before she completely humiliated herself, covering her frustration with anger. "Should have expected a Cooper to do something like that. Get out of here. Go!"

"Hey, I said I was sorry—"

"Do I have to call Noah?" She pulled her phone out of her pocket. She didn't want him to see her like this. A minute ago she'd been longing to kiss him. Now she was frustrated and confused. No one valued her workmanship. Not Stella, Not Noah—

Not even Lance Cooper.

"No." Lance jammed his hands in his pockets. "It's just—hell. Forget it." He turned on his heel. A moment later, he peeled out of the turnout.

Only then did Maya realize he'd made off with the other piece of lace he'd torn from her cap—a bit of the ruffle. She could have tried to sew it back on.

Now she'd have to start over.

Coopers.

Chapter Two

LANCE WAS STILL kicking himself for his clumsiness when he got to the Burger Shack. Taking his place in line, he saw a familiar figure ahead of him. He'd known Bart Lawson since grade school, although they'd never run in the same crowd. Something about the set of the man's shoulders made Lance hesitate to say hello, but Bart generally attended the Historical Society meetings, and it would be awkward if he didn't.

"Hey, man," he said when Bart turned to scan the restaurant. "On your way to the museum?"

"What? Oh, right—there's a meeting tonight."

"Something wrong?" Lance wasn't sure how far to press things, but Bart focused on him like he'd been waiting for the chance to talk with someone.

"It's my dad. He passed away a week ago."

"I'm sorry to hear that." He was. Bart's dad had been in and out of the hospital these past few years battling cancer. He was sure it had been hard on the family.

"Yeah. We knew it was coming, but still—"

"It's never easy."

"No." He looked like something else was troubling

him. "Fighting with Maggie, too," he added, his gaze dropping to the ground.

"Fighting? About what?" Bart and Maggie Lawson's marriage always seemed rock solid. They were both practical country folk, with a four-year-old daughter. Bart worked at a construction supply company. Maggie stayed at home with Katie. Lance knew they lived in a small, self-contained suite in Maggie's parents' basement. Bart had told him once they were saving for a down payment on a place of their own. The goal was to buy a house when Katie was in kindergarten and Maggie was back to work. It was hard to get too far ahead these days on only one salary.

"I'm ready to move out right now," Bart said. "I want to buy a house. Start living. You never know when you're going to go—right?"

"I thought you were saving money."

"Maggie could go back to work now. She doesn't need to wait another year."

"Isn't Katie too young for school?" Not that he had an opinion on the matter. He was parroting back all the things Bart had said a few months ago when they'd talked about it.

"Maggie's parents would watch Katie in a heartbeat." Bart sighed. "She keeps saying one more year. Just wait for kindergarten. But what if she wants another year then, and another?"

Lance didn't know what to say. He'd had a couple of long-term girlfriends but nothing serious. He'd never even thought about kids. He was still trying to sort out his own problems.

"I'm thirty-three," Bart went on. "My dad had his first bout of cancer at thirty-eight. Time's passing, man."

Bart's mother had passed away early, as well, Lance remembered. No wonder he was struggling.

"Come to the meeting tonight. It'll take your mind off things. Sounds like you aren't going to solve the problem today anyway."

Bart looked like he had more to say, but he just nodded. "Yeah. Better than going home and arguing again."

Time *was* passing, Lance thought as the line shifted forward. He was thirty-two. A man his age ought to have his life planned out. More to show for it than a struggling ranch. Maybe he should—

"Lance, Bart, did you hear the news?" Sean Riley, a wiry man in his late forties, rushed up to them. He was in the society, too. "Just heard it myself."

"What news?"

"The historical museum—it's being torn down."

"Can I take your order?" the woman behind the counter said to Bart, but Bart was too busy staring at Sean, just like Lance was.

"Torn down? What do you mean?"

"I mean LeRoy Devlin's planning to build a four-plex there with his brother-in-law. He figures he can get four times the rent—you know we pay him pennies."

"Excuse me, can I take your order?"

Bart, looking as baffled as Lance felt, finally turned to face the counter. "Cheeseburger and fries."

Lance didn't know what to say to Sean. The town's museum had sat at the same intersection in the same old building since before he was born. He knew Devlin nominally owned the property, but he'd made it available to the Historical Society for so long, Lance had never considered he might change his mind.

"What are we going to do?"

"I don't know. We're going to talk about it at the meeting," Sean said.

"But the re-enactment—"

"We'll talk about that, too, I guess, but the museum closing takes precedence, don't you think?"

"Yeah." Bart stepped aside, and Lance made his way to the counter. He placed his order automatically. Of course it took precedence. The only problem was he had no idea what they could do about it. The museum didn't rake in a lot of cash. Finding another building to house it wouldn't be easy. And the exhibits needed updating badly. Most of the them had been put together decades ago. Kids these days didn't want to take the time to make out handwritten descriptions. He'd seen school-groups file in and out of the place so fast he doubted anyone learned anything from the exercise.

"We should just start over if we're going to move the museum somewhere else. Make new exhibits. Spiff it all up," Bart said, echoing his thoughts. "That whole place needs an overhaul. Kind of like my life," he added bitterly.

Sean exchanged a surprised look with Lance.

"Woman trouble," Lance murmured.

Sean nodded. "Gotta order. See you two at the meeting."

"That's what I keep saying to Maggie. We need to start fresh. Try something new. Don't get me wrong; I appreciate her parents, I really do. But I'm thirty-three," Bart said again. "And I'm living in my wife's parents' basement. There's got to be more to life than that."

"I guess." Lance wished he could be in charge of rebuilding museum. It'd be right up his alley to take on a project like that—if they had the cash to do it. Sounded a lot more fun than working on the ranch all week and then spending another Friday night at the Dancing Boot.

God, now he sounded old.

For some reason Maya Turner flashed into his mind, and Lance shifted uncomfortably, slipping his hand into his pocket and feeling the scrap of lace there. He should have given it back to her, but he'd been in too much of a hurry to escape.

"Your food's up." He nudged Bart and pointed. "Go grab a table." There was a cap just like the one Maya had been stitching on display in the museum. He wondered if she had copied it or gotten the inspiration somewhere else.

Why was she making such a thing?

Was Maya a history buff, too?

And why the hell did that turn him on?

"THAT'LL BE SIX-FIFTY," Maya said, popping a pie into a bag for Megan Lawrence. An earnest young woman who had recently become a real estate agent, she stopped by about once a week for some of Maya's baked goods.

"I'm looking forward to this," Megan said, handing over the money. She was still in the skirt and blouse she wore for work, but as she'd gotten out of her car, she'd unclipped her light brown hair and run her hand through it. Now it haloed her face in loose curls. "I know it's a terrible habit, but I eat when I'm nervous."

"Is everything all right?" Maya asked. She'd known Megan forever and had always liked her.

"It's nothing. I was just in Silver Falls to show a house. Did you hear the news?"

"That someone was murdered?" Maya nodded. Murder was rare in small-town Montana, but this was the second unexplained death in the past year in the nearby community.

Maggie nodded. "I'm probably making a mountain out of a mole hill being afraid. Who'd want to do away with me? But I showed houses to those men who attacked the Reeds last year, you know? What if they'd killed me when they had the chance?"

"You shouldn't be showing houses alone," Maya said.

"Like Sharon's going to waste her time coming with me." Megan rolled her eyes. Sharon was a senior agent at her firm, and not a particularly helpful one as far as Megan's career was concerned. Privately, Maya thought the older woman was threatened by Megan's aptitude for the job.

"Well, I'm glad you're back safe. Enjoy your evening."

"You, too."

Megan left, and Maya returned to her stitchery, musing over the strange events in the next town over. People were whispering about drugs, since the men who'd attacked the Reeds a while back had been involved with trafficking. They were all either dead or in jail, though. Everyone had assumed life would calm down now, but with this latest death, that didn't seem likely. Maya hated to admit that people in her neck of the woods had problems—and even turned to crime— but it happened here, like everywhere else.

She was reworking the ruffle of her cap with a new piece of lace she'd bought in town. It wasn't nearly as satisfying as the antique lace she'd been using before, but she didn't have enough of it now.

She still couldn't fathom why Lance had stopped at her stand in the first place, or why he'd grabbed her cap right out of her hands. She would have said he'd done it to tease her, except for the way he'd turned it over and examined it—like he'd found some important specimen from the past. How had he known it was a Revolutionary War–era cap?

As she thought it over, a memory surfaced of Lance at last year's Fourth of July re-enactment. He was a part of the group who staged it each year, wasn't he? She had a vague impression of him in uniform.

Maya rarely watched the actual battle. She tended to roam the encampment set up nearby. She liked to talk to the women who tended campfires and worked at 1700s-era crafts. She'd been shy about joining in herself so far, though. No one else in her family participated. Her mother, when she'd still been around, had looked down on the festivities the way she'd looked down on most small-town affairs.

Maybe this year she should give it a try, Maya mused.

She looked up from her project a little later when Maggie Lawson parked her truck and approached the stand. She waited for the woman to make a purchase, but Maggie didn't seem to know what she was looking for. She kept picking things up and putting them down again.

"Can I help you with anything?" Maya asked finally.

Maggie was in her early thirties, with a mop of curly auburn hair and a sweet smile. She was quite a few years older than Maya. They were acquainted but not close.

To Maya's surprise, her eyes filled with tears. "Probably not."

Concerned, Maya shoved the lace cap into her workbasket and forgot about Lance as she leaped up and came around the table. Offering Maggie a paper towel in lieu of a handkerchief, she touched her arm. "What's wrong?"

"Oh, it's Bart. We keep arguing. His dad died, you know."

Now that she thought about it, she had heard that Bart's father had passed away. She should have offered her condolences. Determined to make up for that, she said, "I'm so sorry to hear that. You both must be having a hard time."

"Bart certainly is, but he won't let me comfort him. He won't talk about his grief. He just says, 'Time's passing. We're missing out. We need to take chances. Let's go buy a house.' But we have a plan." She turned a beseeching look on Maya. "Why can't we follow it? We can't afford a house right now, but Katie goes to school in a year, and that's when I'll go back to work. We're not having any more kids—"

"Bart's come face to face with his mortality?" Maya guessed.

"And he's taking out his fears on me. It isn't fair." Maggie dried her eyes. Maya led her to the second folding chair behind the farm stand table and poured Maggie a glass of ice-cold lemonade. It was her day for company, it seemed.

"He wants a house?"

"Right now." Maggie sighed. "Which means he wants me to go back to work right now."

Maya nodded.

"I want this last year with Katie. I'll never get this time back, you know?" Maggie shook her head. "I'm sorry for dumping all of this on you. That's not fair."

"That's what friends and neighbors are for. Have you been able to tell him how you feel?"

"Over and over again. He won't listen."

Maya thought she might cry again, but with visible effort, Maggie pulled herself together. She took a sip of her lemonade.

"Tell you what. How about you and me grab lunch tomorrow?" Maya asked. Maggie seemed lonely, and she could use an excuse to get off the ranch for a little while. Tomorrow wasn't a farm stand day.

They exchanged numbers, and Maggie headed off. Maya settled back to her work. The heat was making her sleepy, but she kept at it, not wanting to nod off. The lace cap reminded her of Lance again, and now she was alone, she could let her mind wander back over the memory. He'd apologized for ripping it. He'd almost seemed like he meant it.

"Are you going to wear that to the re-enactment?"

Maya jumped and put a hand to her heart. "Ethan Cruz, you scared me to death!" She hadn't even seen the man pull in and park his truck. Too busy daydreaming. Thank goodness no one could read her mind.

"Sorry. You were woolgathering." He cocked his hat back and grinned down at her.

"You're right; I was."

"Autumn sent me to grab one of your pies."

"Are you serious?" Autumn was a wonderful cook in her own right. Maya couldn't imagine her buying a pie instead of making one.

"She got caught short-handed. We've got a B and B guest who loves pie. Ate half of one by himself last night. Autumn didn't have time to bake another."

"Well, I've got several. Take your pick." She pointed out the different varieties. "What did you mean about the re-enactment?"

"Looks like you're making a costume for it." He

pointed to the lace cap. "Are you joining in this year?"

"I don't know." She'd only just begun considering it. "I don't really know anyone who's involved." Most of the ladies—and men—who took part in the re-enactment were in their forties and older. Would she fit in?

"I'm going to be in it."

She looked up at him, squinting in the afternoon sun that was lowering behind Ethan's back. Ethan Cruz wasn't exactly old. "Really?"

"Really. You should check it out. In fact, if you're interested in that kind of thing, you should come to the meeting tonight. The Historical Society meeting," he clarified. "I know some of the ladies from Two Willows are planning to join in. I think the women from West-field Manor are coming, too."

"They are?"

He made a face she couldn't quite interpret. "I'll confess I used to think only old people got involved," he admitted. "Guess that makes me old."

"Guess that makes me old, too. It sounds like fun," she said.

"We're meeting at the museum tonight at seven. I'll see you there." He paid for his pie and returned to his truck, leaving Maya to consider the invitation. Why shouldn't she go and check it out? She didn't have to get involved unless it looked interesting.

And she didn't have anything better to do.

Chapter Three

"LANCE? LANCE—HOLD UP."

Lance bit back a groan. He had just pulled into the museum's parking lot, and he waited by his truck for Olivia to catch up, jogging from the direction of her own vehicle. "What are you doing here?"

"Looking for you. I knew you were coming for the meeting, and I was in town. Noah said you two talked today—"

"Is that what he called it? Seemed more like he dictated and expected me to listen."

She frowned. "He's trying to help." Olivia was blonde, short, and energetic, and it didn't pay to underestimate her. He'd teased her a lot when they were kids, but she'd generally gotten her own back when he least expected it.

"He can help by looking after his own ranch. We don't need him at Thorn Hill." He bit back the rest of his angry words. Noah was Olivia's husband after all. "You knew what you were doing when you married him," he added.

"Yeah, I did. But I expected you and Steel to grow up at some point and accept the fact that we're together—and Noah's not going anywhere."

"Well, you expected too much." He pulled his door open. Had she really thought he could give up thirty-two years of hating Turners overnight? "He spends a few days on our spread, and he thinks he knows more than all the rest of us? That's bullshit, and you know it."

Olivia bit her lip, and for a split second Lance wished he'd taken a different approach. But why pussyfoot around the truth? Noah had always been a bossy do-gooder.

"I don't think he's trying to boss you around," she said softly. "I think Noah likes order. When he sees something out of place, he wants it back in place. There's a lot out of place at Thorn Hill."

Lance couldn't deny that, but Olivia was a traitor if she'd admit it to a Turner. He opened his mouth to tell her as much, then spotted Tory climbing out of Olivia's truck and heading their way.

"We're going to dinner," Olivia explained. "Girls' night out."

"In exciting downtown Chance Creek," Tory drawled, joining them.

Lance chuckled. Their little town must look mighty tame after her years in Seattle. As soon as she'd been old enough, she'd ditched the rest of them and moved on. Never looked back, either. She'd headed for Washington, became a massage therapist and opened her own practice.

"What's going on?" Tory asked, looking from one to the other of them.

"We're talking about Turners," Lance said. "No-ah—"

"Never mind, forget I asked." Tory headed back toward Olivia's truck as quickly as she'd come. Lance could only shake his head. She might be back in Chance Creek for the time being, but Tory had made it clear she had no interest in getting embroiled in the local drama again, let alone settling down here. It wasn't clear how long she was staying, either. She'd arrived for Olivia's wedding at the last minute and so far hadn't divulged her plans.

Lance decided he was done with the drama, too, at least for the moment. When Olivia started to speak again, he waved her off.

"I've got a meeting to get to." He started off for the museum. "Tell Noah we've got it covered," he threw over his shoulder.

Olivia let him go, but when he glanced back, she was still standing where he'd left her. Lance swore under his breath. He didn't like to hurt his sister, but he didn't like it pointed out they were letting things slide at the ranch. He and Steel were doing their best with little help—

Which didn't mean he wanted any help from Noah.

His father had tolerated the Turners, but Aunt Virginia had always hated them. "Never trust a Turner" was a phrase he'd heard dozens of times growing up. "Those damn Turners" was another one he'd heard as a kid. They were always interfering in Cooper business.

It didn't help that Dale had liked to slip over to the

wrong side of the law sometimes, and that William Turner—Noah's father—was a sheriff's deputy. Dale had shored up the family finances by a number of means others might not have approved of. He never hurt anyone that Lance knew of. Just smuggled some goods here, sold some illicit spirits there, poached deer out of season when times were tight. More than once he'd heard William telling his father off.

Olivia had been the one to innocently lead the law to Dale that last time he'd poached, but Lance was pretty sure it was William who'd put the law on their father's scent to begin with.

The years they'd spent in Idaho after Dale went to jail had been some of the worst of his life. He'd struggled to forgive his mother for dumping them with her sister and taking off with another man. Leaving Chance Creek had devastated him, since it meant losing his chance to attend Montana State. When he'd found out that Dale hadn't sold the ranch after all—and instead had hired someone to watch over it until his kids were old enough to run it themselves—he'd thought maybe his life was finally about to turn around.

That was before they'd come home to Chance Creek and found the property and buildings in their current run-down state. The place had never been that prosperous to begin with, but it had never been this bad, either. Lance was beginning to feel like the ranch was simply a drain for flushing money away. Something had to change.

But letting Noah Turner boss them around wasn't

the answer.

He entered the museum to find the meeting just getting started. Turnout was somewhat larger than usual, whether because of the upcoming re-enactment or because of the news of the loss of the building that housed the society and the museum itself, he didn't know.

He nodded at Warren Hill, a jowly man in his seventies who ran the museum and was the chairman of the board of the Historical Society, and at Sean Riley sitting with Mark Bugle—another stalwart member of the group. Ethan Cruz waved from a corner of the room, and Bart, who'd driven over separately, indicated an empty seat next to him.

Lance made his way over to it and was just sitting down when it occurred to him what was different about this meeting.

There were women present.

Lots of them.

"What's going on?" he asked Bart under his breath, jutting his chin at a gaggle of women bunched together on one side of the room. Among them was a coterie of older women who ran the encampment year after year, but he'd never seen so many young women at a meeting.

"I'm not sure." Bart shrugged as Warren called the meeting to order, but Lance didn't notice. He was too busy staring at a very familiar face across the room.

"Hell, what's she doing here?" He nudged Bart and indicated Maya.

"She showed up with Ethan Cruz."

Maya looked up, as if she'd heard them talking about her. She'd changed from earlier. She wore a scarlet T-shirt and a pair of high-cut jean shorts with her cowboy boots. Her hair was in two sassy pigtails. She should have looked silly. Girlish. Instead she looked— hot.

She met his gaze steadily and raised an eyebrow when he didn't look away. There was no way he'd look away first, but he was unnerved by the effect she was having on him. That cool gaze seemed to look right through him—like she could divine every one of his secrets, including the reaction his body was having to her.

He shifted in his seat. She finally nodded, turned to Ethan and said something to him. Lance wished he was close enough to hear her. Hell, he wished he was in Ethan's seat.

"What's wrong with you?" Bart's question pulled him back to the present.

"What do you mean?"

"You're staring at Maya Turner like she stole your puppy."

"Am not," Lance growled at him.

Bart chuckled.

"Gentlemen, we're getting started," Warren said loudly.

Lance nodded at the man. "We're listening." He shot Bart a dirty look.

"First, let me say how happy I am to see such an

enthusiastic turnout tonight. We've been working behind the scenes on the re-enactment since about July fifth of last year, as usual, but this is when we throw open our doors to newcomers and take stock. We'll get to the re-enactment in a moment, but first I'm afraid I have some bad news."

Lance could tell there were many people in the room who hadn't heard about the society losing its museum, and as the room quieted down, he braced himself for their reaction.

"LeRoy Devlin, the owner of the building we're sitting in and the land underneath our feet, has long given the museum, the Historical Society and the archives a very generous deal on rent. Unfortunately, that arrangement will come to an end in just a few short months."

"LeRoy's raising our rent?" Ethan asked.

"LeRoy's kicking us out," Lance answered, his temper getting the better of him. "He's tearing down the museum. Building a four-plex."

Murmurs of surprise and disappointment swirled around the room.

"You got the jump on me, Lance," Warren said. "But that about sums it up. LeRoy's found a better use for the property. We'll need to move to a new location, and frankly—I don't know where it's going to be."

Warren looked every bit his age, and Lance felt for the man. He'd had a long tenure as the head of the society and the museum, and Lance believed the rumors that Warren wanted to retire. He probably hadn't been prepared for something like this to happen.

As the meeting descended into a half dozen or more individual conversations, in which people offered up possible solutions or shot them down, Lance found himself meeting Maya's gaze again. To his surprise, he saw true concern there. For someone who'd only just bothered to get involved, the loss of the museum property seemed to affect her. He remembered the cap she'd been sewing. Remembered he still had that damn scrap of lace. It would be ironic to find out the proverbial *girl next door* was as interested in history as he was. He'd already been surprised enough she'd grown into the kind of woman he couldn't seem to tear his thoughts from.

"If we need to move to another property, we're going to need money," Lance said loudly. The other conversations died out, and everyone looked to see who had spoken.

"That's the crux of the problem," Warren agreed. "But where are we going to get it?"

"What about the admission fee to the museum? Hasn't that added up over time?"

Warren shook his head. "You've heard the treasurer's reports all these years. You know we spend every bit that comes in—and more. My salary eats up most of it. When I retire, that won't be a problem," he quipped, "but I imagine whoever takes my place will want to get paid, too." His gaze held Lance's for an extra beat. Lance knew why; Warren had always wanted him to take the position next, but he knew damn well he didn't have the credentials.

A murmur of conversation was rising again around the room, and Lance knew what would happen. People would lose interest in the problem. They'd hope someone else would step up and solve it for them. This was the biggest crowd they'd ever had at a meeting, as far as he could remember. They needed to strike while the iron was hot.

"Bart? What do you think?" he asked, as loudly as he'd spoken before. They needed to have a single, cohesive discussion—not a lot of chit-chat on the sidelines.

"Huh?" Bart blinked. He'd been staring at the ceiling. Probably revisiting his argument with Maggie.

"I said, what can we do to raise money?"

"We're doing the best we can," Mark Bugle cut in. A grandfatherly man, he wore thick eyeglasses that made him resemble a large, befuddled insect.

"I know you are, Mark. But we need some new ideas." And they most likely needed to come from younger members of the organization.

"I don't think anyone likes history anymore. Too busy playing video games." Sean rested his elbows on the table.

"We need a way to make history more interesting. More fun," Lance said.

"We could do a bake sale…" one of the older women suggested.

Lance sought the right choice of words. "A bake sale alone isn't going to cut it, Sarah. We need to think of something that will bring in a wide audience—especially young people."

Sarah's shoulders slumped. "I don't what we can do."

Lance could tell he was losing people. Except Maya, who was sitting bolt upright. She shot a hand into the air, like an A student who knew she had the right answer.

"Maya?" Warren acknowledged her. "Do you have an idea?"

"I think so. You already have a built-in fundraiser with the re-enactment you do every Fourth of July, right?"

"Sure, that makes a little profit," Warren said.

Maya lifted her hands, as if to embrace everyone in the room. "Why don't we scale it up? Make it a really big deal?"

Lance sat back. It was already a big deal—the highlight of Chance Creek's Fourth of July celebration.

"Right now it's interesting, but it doesn't appeal to a very wide audience, and over the years it's gotten a little... stale."

"Stale?" Bart said, loudly enough for everyone to hear.

Lance found he'd balled his hands into fists. Trust a Turner to manage to insult everyone in a room at once.

"The re-enactment is great," Maya backtracked. "What I mean is—this is a new era. We're all used to incredible entertainment available to us on our TVs, our computers, our phones—twenty-four hours a day. I think you need to rev up the drama at the re-enactment if you want to compete with that. Make it more exciting, that's all."

"More exciting than the war that made our country what it is today?" Lance spoke up. "How the hell do you propose we do that?"

If Maya was taken aback by his language, she recovered quickly.

"Let's give people something new. Something they've never seen before. Let's suck them into the drama of the Revolutionary War with a story they can relate to!"

"What do you mean story? Like… a play?" Bart was paying attention now, that was for sure. So were most of the women in the room. In fact, they'd perked up the moment Maya had started talking.

"Something like that. A play that happens right on the field. A series of scenes that sets the stage for the battle you men will re-enact. Scenes that tell us about some of the individuals who will be fighting—and about their families. That's where we women could come in."

"Women don't belong on the battlefield," Lance said. "Don't get all revisionist history on me."

"Not the battlefield." Maya's cheeks pinked, but she held her ground. "Right now you keep women on the sidelines, but they were just as affected by historical events as the men were. In our new re-enactment, we'll tell people who they were and how the outcome of the battle affected them, too."

Lance noticed the older women who ran the encampment exchanging glances. He had a feeling they liked the idea.

"Right now we have two sides," Maya went on. "One side is supposed to win, and one is supposed to lose, but what about the individuals—the men who fought that battle? Who were they? Did they have families? Girlfriends? Sisters? Wives? What were they fighting for?" She looked around the room as if to check that everyone understood. "Here's the thing. I watch TV and movies. I've seen dozens of battle scenes. Men shooting other men is… boring… unless I know who they are. Why they're there. Who they'll leave behind if they die. We need to take the Revolution and make it personal." She took a deep breath. "We need to make it sexy."

"Sexy?" Lance wasn't the only one in the room to echo the word.

"The Revolutionary War isn't sexy. Never has been, never will be," Mark declared sternly.

"And that's your problem," Maya retorted.

"Problem?" Lance said. "But—"

"Maya's right." Summer Hall stood up. "I want to know more about the men who are fighting—and the women who stand behind them. I want to see what's going on in their lives before they get on that battle-field."

"Me, too. We could set up several storylines. If we do it right, we could make our audience cry when the shots ring out," Mia Matheson said.

The meeting was spiraling out of control. Women

all over the room were chiming in animatedly about costumes, scripts, rehearsals...

Suddenly Sarah's bake sale plan didn't seem like such a bad idea.

Lance looked at Warren, afraid the old man would be close to a heart attack, but to his surprise Warren seemed... interested.

Well, he wasn't interested. The re-enactment was a tradition that meant something, and Lance wasn't willing to let a Turner—even a pretty Turner—change it on a whim.

He stood up. "I vote we adjourn this meeting until next week when everyone has had the chance to think about what they really want from the re-enactment. We have a long, strong tradition we don't want to mess up. Meanwhile, we need cash, and I say we're all responsible for that. I want everyone to think of ways they can personally raise funds for the museum—starting today."

Warren turned a look on him Lance couldn't quite interpret. True, he was hijacking the meeting, but hadn't Warren been hinting a few minutes ago he should take over his job?

Or had he mistaken that look?

All Lance knew was that he wasn't ready for the re-enactment to change. He'd used these meetings to get him through a tough spring and early summer. He was clinging to this one piece of the past because his future—

Well, he didn't know what his future held.

"Like how?" someone called out. "How are we supposed to raise money?"

"Like... a bake sale or a garage sale. Some kind of sale," Lance said lamely. "I don't know. We just need to sell... whatever we can." An idea wiggled to life in his brain. He could sell some of the furniture he'd built over the years. He'd gone a little crazy with it at one point, and after gifting all his siblings with bookshelves, end tables and rocking chairs, he still had leftovers that crowded up his workshop.

Could he sell those?

Warren rescued him. "Okay, folks—I know my announcement came as a surprise, and it's going to take some time to understand what we're up against. I'll work this week to come up with preliminary numbers for the cost of moving the museum and so on. Meanwhile, Lance is right. We need to concentrate on raising funds. We'll meet back next week and issue a report. Bring all your ideas then, and we'll vote on them."

"Should we make a list of our email addresses so you can notify everyone ahead of time what's going to happen at the meeting?" Maya called out. "There are a lot of us newcomers here tonight."

"That's a good idea. I should have thought of it," Warren said. The bags under his eyes spoke of his worries, and Lance knew that losing the museum would crush him. He vowed then and there to keep that from happening. Warren had believed in him once upon a time when no one else seemed to be able to notice his efforts to carve out a different path from the one his father had taken. He'd almost sprung Lance from the confinement of life on a ranch in Chance Creek.

The meeting broke up soon afterward. Lance couldn't help but watch Maya chatting with her friends. He wished he was a part of that happy, sociable group instead of over here with Bart, who looked about as happy as a tomcat who'd just been dunked in a lake. Tapping aimlessly at his phone, he hadn't left his seat. Before Lance could ask him about his plans for the night, Warren crossed the room to them.

"Lance. Bart."

Bart just grunted without looking up. Warren sighed and turned to Lance.

"I've been meaning to speak with you. Wondering if you contacted Montana State yet like we talked about? It might be too late to get in for the fall term, but it's never too early to express interest for next year. I told you they have scholarships for mature students—"

"Haven't had time, but I'll look into it," Lance lied. He had no time for school now. No money, either, and what college was going to spend its scholarship dollars on someone who'd stocked shelves, tended bar and whatever else he could back in Idaho before coming home and working his family's ranch? Any college administrator was going to take one look at him and see his fate. He was a rancher. He'd always be a rancher. End of story.

Lance pulled himself together. It wasn't that he didn't love the ranch. He did. It was as much a part of him as a Montana sunrise, and the work was as second nature to him as... well, as turning the leg of a chair on a lathe in his workshop. It simply wasn't his calling.

"That's what you said last time. This time I hope you mean it," Warren said. "You know I want to pass on the museum to you—" His voice broke, and to Lance's horror, the older man blinked rapidly and cleared his throat. "If there is a museum."

"There'll be a museum," Lance assured him quickly, knowing all too well there probably wouldn't be. He felt like a heel letting Warren down when the man was losing the most important thing to him. "I'll call Montana State. See what they have to say. It's just hard to—"

"I know," Warren said. "That's life, isn't it. Just— hard."

Lance bent toward him, really worried now. "Did you see all the people in this room tonight? Did you see how interested they were in the re-enactment? For some reason the idea has caught fire this year, and that means we can raise funds. We're going to do this." He wasn't sure if he was speaking for Warren's benefit or his own. All he knew was that he couldn't let Warren see his life's work disappear.

The man was a widower, Lance recalled. What did he go home to after these meetings? Did he at least have a dog—or a cat?

"I'm heading to the Boot for a drink. Want to come along?"

Warren shook his head. "My drinking days are long over. I've got a cup of tea and an old movie waiting for me at home. I'll be in touch over the weekend. Better ask your friend for that drink, though. Looks like he could use some cheering up."

Still worried for Warren, Lance glanced at Bart, who'd dropped his phone in his lap and was staring into space. "All right. Talk to you over the weekend," he said to Warren. "Bart, you all right, man?"

"Yeah, I'm fine." But his slumped shoulders told another story.

Lance stifled a sigh. "Why don't you come out with me to the Boot? We can forget our troubles for a while."

"I THOUGHT YOUR idea last night was really great," Mia Matheson told Maya. She was seated at the kitchen table at the Flying W while Maya worked on making the baked goods she'd sell tomorrow at her farm stand. Despite her resolve not to let Noah's words get to her, she'd doubled the number of pies she planned to bake, which meant she'd gotten up even earlier than usual, and she was low on energy.

"I'm not sure any of the men liked it." Lance certainly hadn't. She recalled his flushed face and angry expression with chagrin. She'd thought he would appreciate her contributions to the conversation. Instead he'd acted like she'd attacked him personally.

Not that she cared what Lance thought.

Except she did, she admitted to herself. As crazy as that was. There was something about Lance. Something different from the other men she knew in town. She had a feeling he wanted something more, like she did. She couldn't believe she hadn't realized he shared an interest in history—and in the town's museum. One of the older men at the meeting told her Lance had taken charge of the re-enactment the last few years. Still, he was prickly. Defensive. Afraid of change, apparently.

"Men never like ideas that aren't theirs," Mia said. "They'll come around, though."

"You think?" Maya wasn't at all sure about that.

"With a lot of persuasion." Mia watched her roll out another pie crust and thought a moment. "You know, you're right; if we wait for their approval, it'll never happen. We need to forge ahead."

"How?"

"By writing a script. And making it so good, no one will be able to shoot it down. We could bring it to next week's meeting. They'd have to go along with it."

Maya bent to her task. It wasn't enough to simply make more pies; they had to be good ones. "Are you a writer?" she asked Mia.

"No. But you are."

Maya stopped working. "What are you talking about?"

"I'm talking about that play you wrote when we were kids. The one you performed with your friends. It was a hit."

"*Giselle's Revenge*?" Maya hadn't thought about it in years, and she blushed just remembering the performance she'd begged, nagged and pleaded her friends into participating in—including Olivia, who of course got one of the leading roles.

They'd been in sixth grade. In fact, it was just a

month or two before everything had fallen apart with her family. She'd gone through a stint of binge-reading old Gothic novels and had loved the melodrama, twists and turns, and outrageousness of the plots. One day she'd sat down and written a play of her own that included three heroes, four heroines, five deaths, a poisoning, a ghost, a hanging that was a little too realistic and a couple of passionate make-out scenes that had scandalized some of the mothers in the eventual audience.

"It was great," Mia told her.

"You saw it?" They'd eventually performed the play in Karen Sumner's basement, on a slap-dash stage her father built in front of rows of mismatched folding chairs they'd gathered from their families.

"Everyone saw it. What else was there to do that summer?"

It was strange to have her past brought up so unexpectedly. They'd done three performances, if she remembered right. "It was pretty… melodramatic."

"Granted, but drama is exactly what we want for the re-enactment. We want big, exciting, juicy stories. We'll focus on five or six people—oh!" Mia's eyes grew large, and Maya knew she'd had an idea. "Five or six people on either side of the war who actually participated in a single battle. We'll dig up their histories. Look for the good stuff. Act it all out!"

"Do you think we can find information like that?"

"We can find out anything online." Mia waved off her concerns. "Just like you said at the meeting, we'll do vignettes of their lives before the war and then follow-up vignettes to show what happened afterward! It will be heartbreaking!"

Mia was getting a little carried away. "That's a lot of research," Maya cautioned her. "The re-enactment is a month away, and the committee obviously planned to do exactly the same thing they do every year."

"Ah, don't worry about the research." Mia waved a hand, her long ponytail bobbing emphatically. "We'll just ask your uncle Jed; he was around during the Revolution, right?"

"Don't let him hear you say that!" She pretended to look around for him, although she knew Jed was in town playing cards with some of his friends.

"You know, I used to love to come and watch the re-enactment when I was a little girl," Mia confided, "but I never felt like I could be a part of the action. I didn't want to cook over fire pits and sew things. No offense," she added.

"None taken," Maya said cheerfully. "That's the frustrating thing, isn't it? Women's work makes the world go around, but everyone thinks it's so boring. I say we show what was happening on *and* off the battle-field, to men *and* women."

"I like that idea," Mia said. "I can't wait to see what you come up with. Gotta get back to work, though. Happy baking!"

"Wait—what *I* come up with? You just said—" Mia was already at the front door.

"Call me, and we'll brainstorm," she said and

slipped outside.

Maya grumbled over the trap her friend had laid. She had to admit writing the script intrigued her, but if Mia wanted historical accuracy, she'd better be ready to help research the details.

An hour later she was still mulling their conversation over when Mary called. "Maya? It's your mother," she said when Maya picked up, just like she always did. Maya had tried in vain to convince Mary she already knew that because her name showed up on her phone's screen.

"Hi, Mom." She felt a familiar tightening in her gut. Things had been strained between them ever since Mary had left Chance Creek. She'd eventually divorced William and had married again, acquiring two stepchildren, who were far younger than her own. Maya knew none of her siblings were on easy terms with their mother. Sometimes she felt a twinge of pity for Mary. Sometimes she didn't. She was the one who'd left. Maya couldn't imagine running out on her own kids, no matter how bad things got.

"How is the ranch? I've been hearing about that horrible drought you're going through. I can't imagine. It's bad enough there when times are good."

"Mom." Maya bit back her impatience. This was par for the course. "We're getting by." Mary never let an opportunity pass to let them know what she thought about Chance Creek. A year after she'd left, safely married and settled in Ohio, she'd called to ask Maya and her siblings to come join her there. None of them had taken her up on it. They'd all felt a loyalty to their home—and little trust in the woman who'd disappeared from their lives without any warning. Maya wouldn't give her the vindication of knowing how shaky things were getting in Chance Creek.

"And I heard about those murders, how awful!"

"That's in Silver Falls, Mom," Maya said. "Chance Creek is doing great. I'm helping organize the Historical Society's re-enactment this year. It's going to be better than ever."

There was a pause as Mary digested this news. "That's… wonderful!" she said a little too brightly. "Liz has taken an interest in history, too. She's enrolling in AP History this fall."

"That's great." Maya tried to match her mother's carefully upbeat tone. Unlike her siblings, who'd all been adamant about refusing Mary's offer, Maya had wavered back when her mother had issued her invitation, and for a long time after that she'd wished she had joined her. She wished Mary had fought harder for her, if she was honest. "Mom, I've gotta run. I'm swamped with baking for tomorrow's farm stand."

"You never have time to talk," Mary said. Her wistfulness nearly undid Maya, but that was one of her mother's tricks. Make her feel guilty, and then go in for the kill when Maya softened. She couldn't handle a conversation like that now.

"Soon. Bye."

Several hours later she met up with Maggie in town outside of Linda's Diner. It was only noon, but she was exhausted, and she had a lot more baking left to do when she got home. She'd taken a quick shower, but she was already hot again. The sun was relentless, and she'd be glad to get into the air-conditioning.

When she caught sight of her friend, however, she forgot all about her mother. Maggie's eyes were shadowed with dark circles.

"Hey, are you all right?" she asked in concern.

"I'm fine. I had another big fight with Bart last night. It was so stupid," she confessed miserably.

"Oh, Maggie. Let's get a booth, and you can tell me all about it. Where's Katie today?" she asked as she herded Maggie inside. That was better. It had to be twenty degrees cooler in here.

"She's at a playdate with a friend, thank goodness. I'm no good to anyone today."

When they were seated, they took a minute to look at their menus, and a waitress came to take their order, but when she was gone, Maya pushed for more details. "What were you two fighting about?"

"Bart stayed out past midnight last night. Drank too much at the Dancing Boot. Came home and woke up Katie. I'm sure he woke up my parents, too. What is he thinking? We're not teenagers anymore!"

"He's taking his dad's death hard, huh?"

"He is, but honestly, Maya, it's time for him to get himself together and stop taking out his grief on all of us. Do you know how embarrassing it is to have to explain your husband's behavior to your parents? The people making it possible for us to save up to buy a house?"

"I can only imagine." But Maya wondered if that was part of the problem. Was Bart feeling embarrassed to live with his in-laws at his age? Was he angry on some level that they were still alive while his own parents were gone?

"I'm at the end of my rope," Maggie said. "I'm serious, Maya," she added, looking up. "I was ready to throw him out of the house last night."

"I'm sorry things have gotten so bad." Everyone was hurting this summer, it seemed.

"If it gets any worse, I don't know what I'll do."

Chapter Four

"**M**AYA TURNER MIGHT be onto something," Ethan said when he and Lance met at Linda's Diner for lunch. They found a booth near the front of the restaurant and settled in. Ethan had called earlier that morning and asked him to meet and talk more about the re-enactment.

"Not you, too." Lance had already been stopped by Melvin Crane in the drugstore, whose wife had convinced him it was a spectacular idea to include more story elements in the re-enactment. *Maybe it won't be its usual yawn-fest,* Melvin had quoted her. Lance's mind was still reeling. Their re-enactment featured real historical weapons. There was nothing yawn-inducing about that.

"Attendance at the re-enactments has been down," Ethan pointed out as they perused their menus. "Attendance at the museum is even worse. Warren asked me for help with the Historical Society's accounts, so I spent some time this morning with Matt Underwood going over them. Something's got to give."

Lance knew Matt donated his services to the society. "You think Maya's play idea is going to change that?" He looked for their waitress. It was busy here today.

"Stop thinking of it as a play. You know that television channel with all the history shows? At first it only showed normal documentaries, and then suddenly it started airing historical dramas about Vikings, Tudors, you name it."

"Yeah. So what?"

"So people actually watch those series. They don't just want dry facts. They want blood, gore, violence, betrayal—sex."

"Sex?"

"Yeah, sex."

Lance thought about it. Ethan was right; he watched some of those shows.

"We're not going to make the re-enactment R rated."

"No." Ethan grinned. "Wouldn't that make people sit up and take notice, though?"

Lance grinned back. Would serve some of the more uptight members of the town right.

He remembered this was all Maya's idea. Not that he minded Maya having ideas. But Maya was Liam's sister, and Liam was a big pain-in-the-ass.

"I'm still not convinced—"

"May I take your order?" A chipper young woman approached their table, pad and pen in hand. Lance and Ethan told her what they wanted, and she left again.

Ethan poked Lance's arm. "Hey, there's Maya. Maybe we should talk to…. Oh, Maggie Lawson's with her."

Lance looked over to see Maya handing several napkins to a very tearful Maggie. They were sitting in a booth in the rear of the restaurant.

"Doesn't look like a good time to interrupt," he said, a little relieved to avoid the discussion until he had more time to think over Ethan's idea. He wouldn't mind spending time with Maya, though. Her obvious concern for her friend was typical, as far as he'd seen. She wasn't ornery like Liam.

She was a hell of a lot better looking than him, too.

"Bart seemed a little off last night," Ethan said, his gaze lingering on Maggie.

"You're telling me. He came to the Boot with me afterward. Drank way too much. I gave him a ride home, but I had to practically pry him out of the bar and fight him for his keys. He's going off the rails."

"That's a shame."

Lance knew Ethan was a devoted family man. Bart's antics these days wouldn't impress him.

"It's his dad's passing. I think he got a cold, hard look at his mortality. That can freak out anyone."

"I hear that." Ethan's gaze grew distant, and Lance remembered his friend had lost his parents in a car accident several years back. He should understand Bart if anyone did. "Guess I shouldn't judge."

"I hope he pulls himself together soon," Lance said. "He's going to make his life a lot worse if he doesn't watch out." He jutted his chin in Maggie's direction.

"Yep." After a moment, Ethan shrugged. "Guess all we can do is encourage him to make good choices. About the museum, though. Maya's idea…"

That was the problem—it was Maya's idea. And Maya was a Turner. And Turners kept making his life a living hell. Besides, the re-enactment was his thing, and he didn't like the feeling he was going to lose control of it. He'd been the de facto leader for the last couple of years. Warren headed the meetings, but when the time came to build the encampment and get everyone suited up and going in the right direction—Lance took over. He had no idea how to direct a play.

"We need to raise money, not turn our re-enactment into a circus. This is about celebrating the past, not caving in to people's need for constant... titillation."

"Did you seriously just use titillation in a sentence?" Ethan asked him.

"Yeah, I did." Lance couldn't help himself. He grinned again. "But I'm serious. Before we change everything about the re-enactment, let's see if we can skin this cat some other way. We need to give people a chance to raise money themselves."

"We don't have much time," Ethan pointed out. The waitress returned with their order, and he paused while she set their plates on the table. "And I heard from a little bird that Maya is already working on a script."

"The meeting was last night!"

"Okay, maybe she's not actually working on it yet, but I heard from a reliable source that one of her friends was going to convince her to start. Mia was supposed to go to Thorn Hill this morning," he explained. "She stopped by to chat with Autumn after the meeting, and they came up with the idea."

"What about putting it to a vote?" Lance demanded. The women couldn't ride roughshod over the rest of them. Could they?

"It'll take time for her to write that script. Next week we'll see how much money we've raised and whether we need to up the stakes on the re-enactment or not."

"But—"

"Here's the thing, Lance. Autumn wasn't at all interested in the re-enactment before, but once Mia called and told her about Maya's suggestion, she got excited about it. I think the women of the town have been waiting for a chance like this."

Lance began to wonder if this was why Ethan had called and invited him to lunch. Had Mia and Autumn asked Ethan to soften him up on the idea? He glanced over at Maya. Caught her looking at him, and squared his shoulders. He wasn't going to let a Turner take over running the re-enactment.

Even if she looked good enough to eat.

MAYA DIDN'T NOTICE Lance and Ethan until she was halfway through her salad, but when she did, it was hard to miss that they'd noticed her and Maggie.

Neither man looked happy, and she wondered if they were discussing her idea from the night before. She'd realized too late that by springing it on everyone at the meeting, she'd lost her chance to lobby members of the group one at a time. Judging by the pushback from Lance and the other men, that could be a problem.

She'd have to be stubborn if she wanted things to change. Ever since Mia had stopped by to press her to write the script, the idea had been growing on her. It had been a while since she'd done anything like it, and she itched to get started right now. Tomorrow, while she was watching the farm stand, she'd keep pen and paper handy. She could get a lot done in between customers.

As they ate, Maggie perked up a little. Food always helped, Maya thought. Once she'd had a few bites of her BLT, Maggie went into more details about what had happened.

"Ever since Bart's dad died, he's been acting like…" Her voice wobbled, and she struggled to go on. "Like everything we've got going for us isn't worth a damn."

"He's grieving," Maya reminded her.

"He keeps going on and on about how small our apartment is. How he never thought he'd be thirty-three and living in a basement. That all we do is work, play with Katie and sleep. I thought he needed to blow off some steam, so I told him to go out a few times. Hang out with the guys. Have a beer or two. He's right; we've been pinching pennies for a long time. But staying out that late on a weeknight? Acting like an ass when he gets home? Waking up Katie? That's not okay. What does he think it's like for me being home all day with a four-year-old, with my parents upstairs? I… lost it," Maggie admitted. "I yelled at him. Called him selfish. I'm sure Mom and Dad heard every word."

"Oh, Maggie." It sounded like Bart deserved it, but Maya knew Maggie must be ashamed about losing her cool. Especially with Katie and her parents listening.

Maggie lifted her hands in defeat. "I finally got Katie back to sleep, went back to bed and he was sleeping on top of it with all his clothes on—diagonally. I had to sleep on the sofa. I hate our sofa."

Maya shook her head sympathetically.

"He tried to apologize this morning. I was still so angry I told him to go to work. He left without eating any breakfast. We always eat breakfast together." Maggie's face crumpled. "We never fight like this."

"I'm sorry. It sounds really rough."

Maggie sighed. "I'm beginning to think I should go back to work."

Maya stilled. That was a big change of heart. "What about Katie?"

"I'm sure my parents will watch her. I hate asking them to do more than they're already doing, but they love spending time with her, and we'll be able to save money more quickly. They'll understand that."

"How long has it been since you worked?" That seemed like the kind of factual question that could steer them away from emotional waters.

"Four years. I quit right before Katie was born. Guess that was a mistake."

"Of course it wasn't a mistake. You've had four years at home with Katie—I'm sure you wouldn't give that up."

"No, of course not." A tear leaked from Maggie's

eye. "It's just, I wanted this last year—" She shook away the thought. "It'll be okay." She scrubbed away the wetness on her cheek. "She'll go to kindergarten next year anyway."

"Are you sure you want to do this?"

"Things can't stay the way they are if Bart is this miserable. Sometimes you have to take a leap of faith and trust it'll work out for the best."

Maya glanced at Lance and caught him looking her way again. It would be a leap of faith to let herself admit she'd like to get to know him better.

Probably a leap right off a cliff.

Even if she did get butterflies when she met his gaze.

THE FOLLOWING MORNING, Lance's stomach tightened in anticipation as he approached the turnoff to Thorn Hill. If he went straight, he'd see Maya at her farm stand. He definitely shouldn't do that, as much as he wanted to.

Behind those trusting eyes, Maya Turner was… well, a Turner. If she thought she could take over the re-enactment, she was as bad as Noah, who was always interfering in Thorn Hill these days. Next thing he knew Liam would think he could tell him how to run his ranch. Him and his organic certification idea. The first time Lance had heard of his plan from Olivia, he'd nearly laughed out loud.

No ranch in Chance Creek was certified organic. It took years to finish the process. It was… ridiculous.

But the idea had been nagging at him ever since.

Lance tapped his thumbs on the steering wheel. Liam couldn't be on to something, could he? Was he actually getting a jump on them with his crazy idea?

Hell.

Maybe he should visit Maya's farm stand. Get some information out of her. He'd buy something to cover up his real intentions. She baked a mean pie.

He wouldn't mind a pie.

Wouldn't mind seeing her again, if he was truthful. It wasn't fair she looked so damn good all the time. And was interested in history. He wasn't sure he'd ever dated a woman before who cared about the past.

Not that he was going to date Maya.

Lance sat at the crossroads a long moment, curiosity and hunger—and lust, he supposed—warring inside him. Hunger won out. And lust, although he hated to admit it. He kept driving, pulled in near the lane to the Flying W, parked and adjusted his hat. Maya shaded her eyes, recognized him and immediately began to fiddle with her wares, as if she was far too busy to give him the time of day, although he was pretty sure she was sneaking a look at him now and then.

He wondered if there was a little lust mixed into her curiosity, too.

Chuckling at the thought, he pushed open his door and climbed out. At least he had a good excuse handy to explain his presence on enemy territory. He'd ask if she'd come up with an idea to raise money—and see if she'd confirm she was already working on a script for the re-enactment. Last night, after talking to Ethan, he'd decided to take the bull by the horn, and he'd sent out an email to everyone reiterating that he expected them all to report on their fundraising efforts at the next meeting. It had galled him to have to ask Mia for the updated email list, but she'd supplied it cheerfully.

As he approached, Maya stuffed something under the table into a large cloth bag, reminding Lance he still had the piece of lace from her cap back at his ranch. He should probably return it.

"You again," Maya said as he approached. Was she working on another sewing project? He hoped she knew he hadn't destroyed the last one on purpose.

"Me, again," he agreed and found it difficult to go on. She was a distracting sight. It was hot enough to make her T-shirt cling to her curves. She'd knotted it at her waist and wore a pair of jean shorts. He couldn't see her long legs under the table, but he'd bet she'd kicked off her boots.

He could forget his errand, forget the re-enactment—and Liam's crazy plan to certify the Flying W—and simply round the table, pull her to her feet, tip her chin up with a finger and kiss her.

Would she let him?

Or would she deck him?

The image of her trying to knock his lights out made him chuckle.

"What?" Maya demanded.

"Nothing." He cleared his throat. "I'll take one of those peach pies."

"That's eight dollars and fifty cents."

"Eight-fifty?" Lance stopped, wallet in hand. That was highway robbery. "You charging me a Cooper tax or something?"

"A Cooper tax?" Maya rolled her eyes. "For heaven's sake, Lance—"

"Here I'm being a good neighbor, taking time out of my day to support your stand. When was the last time your family has done anything to—?"

"Lance, listen—"

Was she doing it to make fun of him? To let him know exactly what she thought of him? "You're as bad as Liam is."

"I'm not anything—I'm raising money for the Historical Society! Why are you being such a bear? *Cooper tax.*" Her tone said exactly what she thought of that. She shook a little cardboard box at him. Inside, change jangled together. "I got your email last night, and I've already raised twenty dollars so far for the museum by hitching up the prices on my baked goods. It's not a lot, but it's something. How much have you raised?"

Nothing. But he wasn't going to tell her that. He was doing a damn fine job of making an ass out of himself today. A minute passed in silence while Lance struggled to come up with retort. Finally, he reached into his wallet and shoved a wad of money at Maya.

"Keep the change." He grabbed his pie and stalked back to his truck, wanting to kick himself. He couldn't help replaying the incident in his head over and over as he made the short drive back to his ranch. He'd jumped to conclusions. Said some things he regretted. Acted like a right old fool. And he hadn't gotten any of the information he set out to get.

When would he learn to think first before he acted?

That wasn't the only thing bugging him, though. When he'd sent the email telling everyone to start raising money, it hadn't occurred to him how pressured that might make some of them feel. If Maya wanted to use her farm stand to collect donations, he'd have expected her to put out a tin with a sign asking for them. It made him uneasy that she'd raised prices on her baked goods when he was darn sure she and her family depended on her income from the stand. If people thought she was overcharging them, they'd take their business elsewhere and not come back. Thinking over it, he realized she'd placed no signage to explain the increase in her prices. No one would understand they were making a donation to the museum fund.

He should have said something.

It was too late now.

IT TOOK A while for Maya to calm down enough to pull out her notebook and get to work. Lance was so damn handsome she always forgot how frustrating he could be.

Cooper tax.

She'd scrambled to hide the pages of writing she'd produced so far this morning when Lance arrived. It would take a lot of work to get the script into shape, but she'd gotten a start.

She couldn't believe his reaction to the price of her pie. He'd been the one to send the email around demanding that all of them start raising funds on their own for the museum. Now he thought she was charging him more because he was a Cooper? As if she'd ever stoop to something so low. It bothered her he thought she would prey on him just because of the difficulties between their families.

She wouldn't let him get to her, she promised herself. Even now she was more upset about the state of the society and the museum rather than anything he'd done. She'd only just found a group of people who shared a common interest with her, and LeRoy Devlin was shutting the whole darn thing down.

Lance's orneriness was icing on the cake.

At least he was gone now, and she doubted he'd be back.

She settled in for a long afternoon.

Two days later she was back at the farm stand working on her script again when she spotted Lance's truck pulling in and parking. Her heart rose before she reminded herself he'd ripped her cap—and complained about the price of her pies. She certainly wasn't attracted to him, no matter what her body might think.

She stashed the pages away in her purse, set it under the table, pushed her hair back from her eyes and stifled a groan. She'd spent the morning sweating, despite the shade of the canopy. Her produce was wilting, her baked goods going limp in their plastic wrap. She'd had barely any customers so far. Who wanted to get out of their air-conditioned trucks to stop and shop in the baking sun?

At least she was making good progress with the script. She'd showed some of it to Mia, who'd read over it and made some good suggestions. They'd decided to come up with stories of their own, rather than trying to make them about historical personages. They simply didn't have the time to do the research that would require. Maya had written several more pages of dialogue this morning.

"Go on, get out of here," she yelled at Lance when he opened his door.

To her consternation, he just grinned, waved and ignored her. He went to the back, dropped the tailgate and lugged something out of the bed of his truck.

"I mean it, Lance. I don't have the patience to deal with you today."

Lance didn't answer. He hefted the wooden object he held in his hands and closed the distance between them.

"Do you need pie? Here, take a damn pie." She scooped one up and popped it in a bag.

"Not here for pie." Lance flipped the board around so the other side was facing her.

Maya's mouth dropped open. "Home-baked pastries and handmade crafts? What's that for?"

"Just what it says. You need a sign so people know what you're selling. That way you'll raise more money."

"You made this—for me?" Lance looked so damn good in his work jeans, boots and a T-shirt that stretched over his muscular torso every time he moved. Maya swallowed when a wave of longing washed over her. She could almost feel those hands of his on her hips—that mouth brushing over hers.

She nearly groaned again.

"Not for you—for us," Lance said.

"Us?" She had no idea what he was talking about. She was too busy imagining the things she could do with him if they were alone. Why did he always bring out this side in her?

She needed a boyfriend—

One who wasn't Lance.

"The more money you raise for the society, the less I need to do, right? Not everyone speeding down that road knows what you're selling here. Now they will." He went to prop the folding sign near the road where people would be able to see, leaving her sputtering. "Besides, no one knows what I'm selling."

Heading to his truck again, he gestured at the other wooden objects in its bed. As he began to haul out pieces of furniture and decorations, Maya stood up to see them better, her lust morphing into curiosity. Since when did Lance know how to build furniture?

The pieces were each unique and finely detailed. If she wasn't mistaken, the designs were from another era, just like her sewing. Even the sign had been crafted in a painstaking way.

She was beginning to think she didn't know Lance at all. "Did you make all that yourself?" she finally asked, not knowing what else to say.

"Yeah, I made it myself. Right after we got back to Chance Creek from Idaho. Found my grandmother's workshop. I'd forgotten about all that. She wasn't a Cooper; she was a Jones. No wonder she could run rings around—" Lance set down the last chair with a thump, and Maya wondered what he'd been about to say. She didn't think she'd ever heard Lance run down his own family before. Usually he was defending them... because usually someone else was attacking them, she realized with a twist of her gut. That couldn't feel good. "I don't know if anyone will buy anything," Lance went on, "but they're just taking up space. Maybe people will stop for the furniture, notice they're hungry and buy some pie."

He wouldn't look at her. Maya wished he would. Wished she could let him know how impressed she was at the quality of his work. Her gaze dipped to his hands. They'd made this furniture. Had rubbed it smooth.

She'd like to feel those hands on her.

All over her, to be specific.

"I sell more than pie, you know." She kept it light.

"I like your pie."

Maya watched as he arranged his pieces into an eye-catching display around her stand. They belonged in an art gallery somewhere, not on the side of a dusty road.

She should probably offer her baked goods for free to entice people to check out Lance's stuff.

She held her tongue as he worked, though, suspicious about his motives. They were both raising money for the museum, so she supposed it made sense for them to join forces and run a stand together—except that he was a Cooper and she was a Turner.

Coopers and Turners didn't do anything together, no matter what images her brain was conjuring in its overheated state.

Except for Noah and Olivia, who did everything together, she reminded herself.

What would it be like to do *everything* with Lance?

Flushing with heat, she tried to clear her mind of the disturbing thoughts. Being with the cowboy might be all kinds of fun.

All kinds of wrong, too.

"Why aren't you doing this on your own property?" she said to cover her confusion.

"Because I can't sit watching it all day. I've got work to do. Your family's already stationed you out here. You can collect money for me as well as for you."

That was handy for him, wasn't it? "Aren't you worried I'll steal it?" she asked tartly.

He stopped. "You thinking about starting a life of crime?"

"No."

"Look, we've both got the same goal. Save the museum. Warren—" He broke off. "It's killing him to think it'll be shut down."

Maya nodded, relenting a little. She didn't know Warren nearly as well as Lance did, but the strain in his voice at the last meeting had made that clear. She liked that Lance seemed protective of the older man. Lance was like Olivia; underneath that thick Cooper skin, he had heart.

She wondered if he had Olivia's imagination, too. She wished she could ask him twenty questions. Get to know what was happening inside that head of his.

"So will you help me to help him?" he asked.

He was appealing when he was uncertain. His gaze searched hers, and she wondered why someone so staunchly on the Cooper side of things was reaching out to her this way. She couldn't help remember their dance at Olivia's wedding. The gentle way he'd held her. The beat of his heart when she'd rested her head against his chest. There were depths to this man. "Okay," she heard herself say.

He held her gaze a moment longer, as if he was wondering as much about her thought process as she was wondering about his.

He nodded finally and got back to work. Maya watched him, enjoying the play of his muscles as he lifted and carried the furniture and set it into place. When he was done, he shut the tailgate and came to join her under the awning, plunking himself down on her spare folding chair. She was far too aware of him, and she had no idea what to say, so she kept quiet. So did he, until they both straightened at the sound of horses' hooves clip-clopping in the distance.

"James Russell," Maya murmured.

"Who's he got with him?" Everyone in Chance Creek was familiar with the Russells, the quirky older couple who'd thrown convention to the wind some years ago and decided to carry on with their lives as if they'd traveled back in time to the early 1800s. The

Russells' barouche—an ornate open carriage—was a work of art, and Maya had always wanted to take a ride in it.

"It's Avery—from Westfield Manor." Avery was fairly new to Chance Creek, and Maya doubted she'd be familiar with the feud between the Turners and the Coopers. It probably wouldn't strike her as odd to see Lance sitting alongside her at her farm stand. Anyone else in Chance Creek would think that pigs might start flying next.

James, a stout older man in the coat and breeches of a Regency-era English gentleman, climbed down from his high perch at the front of the barouche and helped Avery down after him. When she reached solid ground, she spent a moment setting her high-waisted gown to rights. While the Russells maintained a nineteenth-century existence because it pleased them, Avery and her friends did so because they ran a Jane Austen–style bed-and-breakfast at the manor.

"Food and furniture. I love it!" Avery's gaze immediately lit on an apron Maya had been fiddling with earlier this morning, which sat folded on the table. "And old-fashioned aprons, too! How wonderful!"

"See? I told you people would like this setup." Lance shot an amused glance at Maya.

James and Avery ended up looking over every piece of furniture, then turned their attention to the food on display, James buying several pies and a basket of blackberries, while Avery picked out a lemon strudel for herself.

"I knew there was a farm stand out here but hadn't heard about the furniture and clothing. You guys should whip up a website for your woodworking and sewing. People are going to want to know about this. Especially since the inventory will change all the time, right?"

"Right. Although I'm not selling clothes. This is just a side project. I might wear it for the Fourth of July re-enactment." Maya exchanged a look with Lance. Inventory? Website? That was way over her pay grade.

"Ooh, I heard the re-enactment's getting an upgrade this year. I plan to be at the next meeting."

"Really?" Maya smiled at her. "I'm glad to hear it."

"Autumn Cruz mentioned it when I saw her earlier. She said Mia Matheson told her about it. She told me if I want to be involved, I have to figure out what I can do for a fundraiser," Avery went on. "Something about there being a real tyrant running the show this year." She smiled impishly at Lance.

"Hey, I'm not a tyrant."

"Yes, you are," Maya told him.

"If it takes a tyrant to save the museum, I'm all for it. I like museums," Avery said. "And you two should really think about that website. Let me know if you need help," she added as she handed over her money. "I'm pretty good at that kind of thing."

"Thanks, we will," Maya told her.

"I might be back for that coatrack," James said. "I'll bring Maud."

They watched the carriage rumble off.

"I'm not a tyrant," Lance reiterated.

"Yes, you are," Maya said. "All you Coopers are bossy." Olivia certainly had been when they were kids, but Maya hadn't minded.

"That's the pot calling the kettle black. Noah's over every day telling us what to do," Lance said.

Maya laughed. "Okay, I'll grant you that Noah's bossy."

They sat in companionable silence for a few minutes. "Don't suppose you know how to make a website?" Lance asked.

"I don't even know where to start. Besides, I don't need one for the farm stand," Maya said. "It might not be a bad idea for you, though."

"Maybe." Lance shook his head. "Can't remember the last time I used a computer."

"Me neither. I'm sure I could learn, but—"

"I'd rather be outside," Lance finished for her. "Right?"

"Or working with my hands." Maya grinned at him, remembered they were supposed to be enemies and decided it was much too hot—and he was way too handsome—to keep up an old feud. "Sorry about that stuff I said earlier," she told him. "I thought you'd come back to fight."

"It was a good bet," Lance said easily. "With the heat, everyone's got a short fuse lately."

"Some fuses are going to get shorter if our family catches sight of all this." She indicated the farm stand.

"Then maybe we should give them something to really get mad about."

And he leaned over and kissed her.

Chapter Five

H E SHOULDN'T HAVE done that.

Lance didn't know what had gotten into him today. All he knew was that he'd woken up with an urge to work in his woodworking studio, and after rushing through his chores, he'd given into that urge and found the sign he'd brought here taking shape under his hands without needing any guidance from his head.

He'd been surprised to find himself joining forces with Maya for their fundraiser. He had been surprised all over again when she hadn't forced him away the minute he'd pulled up and started to unload his things. He supposed he hadn't let her. But the biggest surprise came when he'd watched James Russell—a man who could afford any piece of furniture in the fanciest store in Billings or Bozeman—gaze at the coat stand he'd made with a covetous look.

James would be back for that coat stand, Maud or no Maud; he'd bet his bottom dollar on that.

Maybe his furniture wasn't as amateurish as he'd always judged it.

"What was that for?" Maya asked sharply when he pulled away from her. She scooted her chair a few inches in the opposite direction for good measure. Her color was high, and although that could be from the heat, too, he didn't think so.

Maya wasn't immune to him.

"We made a sale."

"You're going to kiss me every time someone buys a pastry?"

"If you'll let me." Lance laughed at the look she gave him, but he was prevented from saying anything else when a couple pulled up in a sky-blue pickup, raising a fine sheen of dust.

"Lance—"

"Focus on the customers." He didn't want to hear that she didn't want him kissing her again. She'd kissed him back, and she'd tasted... good.

He'd wanted to do that ever since they'd danced together. Wanted to do a lot more, actually. Maya was so sexy in those little shorts and that knotted-up top, he wished he could get her somewhere private and do a little mutual exploring.

That wasn't wise, though. He pulled himself together and shifted in his seat. While the woman came to look at Maya's baking, the man made a beeline for a rocking chair Lance was especially proud of. The design was inspired by one he'd seen in a grainy, black-and-white Civil War–era photo of one of his own ancestors. As he'd worked on the piece, he'd imagined one of his distant family members reclining in one just like it.

"This is exactly what I've been talking about," the man called out.

"Sure it is, Larry," the woman said, giving Lance a good-natured eye roll. "He has back pains," she explained, "and they're very particular. We've looked at a hundred different chairs, and none of them suit. I'm half convinced it's all in his head."

"I'm serious, Denise," Larry said. "Haven't I been saying all along that the others are too curvy? Come look at this nice straight back."

"In a minute, dear," Denise called back, looking over a selection of shortcakes.

Lance rose and went over to where Larry stood. He needed the distraction anyway. "You can try it if you like." He held the chair steady while the old man lowered himself into it carefully. Larry made a satisfied sound as he stretched out.

"It'll rock more smoothly when it's on a flat surface," Lance assured him.

"I'm not too concerned about the rock," Larry said. "The back is perfect. I feel a decade younger."

"Nobody a decade younger than you would get this excited about a chair." Denise walked over with the cake she'd purchased in hand. She gave Lance a warm smile. "Still, if it'll shut him up, I'll gladly pay double."

"That won't be necessary." Lance loaded the chair into the bed of Larry's truck. Larry followed him.

"I'm glad to see a young couple finding a way to get by in these hard times," he said earnestly. Lance opened his mouth to correct him, then closed it again. It would be awkward to explain, and he kind of liked being paired with Maya, even if the truth was far different.

"Here's your money." Denise handed him some bills.

Lance was still standing by the road as the couple drove off. He'd never earned money from his wood-working before. Better yet, it was money that would be put toward finding a new home for the museum. He couldn't say when the last time was he'd felt a lift like this. Most days were just work, work, work, trying to keep his family's ranch afloat. He needed to get back to it right now, much as he liked spending time with Maya.

"Things over at Thorn Hill must be worse than I thought," Maya said dryly. "You've been staring at that cash like you just won the lottery."

Lance put the money in his pocket, suddenly self-conscious. "Surprised something actually sold. That's all," he admitted. "I've never tried this before."

"You didn't correct them when they thought we were... together."

Was she blushing? Lance chuckled. "Maybe we ought to let people think that; they'd come to our stand in droves just for gossip's sake."

Maya's eyebrows shot up. "*Our* stand?"

"That's what the sign says: furniture *and* baked goods." He waved a hand at it.

"You've got a ranch to run."

"I can slip out here now and then. Keep you company."

Her smile nearly undid him. How had he never noticed what a fantastic smile she had?

"You think gossip would help raise our income?"

she asked.

His spirits rose. *Our* income. He liked that. "We'd find a new place for the museum in no time. Sex sells, right?" That's what Ethan had said.

"Whoa, cowboy. Who said anything about sex?" Maya demanded.

Whoops. He'd better back track a little. Although he was spending a fair amount of time these days thinking about sex with Maya. Probably too soon to let her know that.

"All I mean is, we're good together."

Maya's lips parted, making her look oh, so kissable. Lance plunked down again in the folding chair beside her.

When he leaned closer, she didn't pull away. In fact, if he wasn't mistaken, she leaned closer, too. Lance closed the gap between them—

"What is the hell is going on here?"

Lance jumped straight out of the chair and scrambled around to face Jed Turner, who was hobbling up the lane, his cane swinging. The old man stopped when he came near, took in Lance's wooden furniture and straightened his bent back in fury.

"Hawk your shoddy wares on your own land!" Jed turned on Maya. "And you. You should know better. Aiding and abetting a Cooper? Shame on you. Best count your profits twice today to see what turns up missing."

Lance decided to get out while the getting was good, before the octogenarian riled himself into a heart attack.

"I've got to get back to work anyway," he told Maya. "Look after my things, will you? I'll be by later to load what doesn't sell. Can't stay out too long or Noah might decide to steal Thorn Hill altogether."

"Can't imagine what my nephew would want with that sorry piece of dirt," Jed called after him.

Lance winked at Maya and left without another word.

"WHY DIDN'T YOU kick that Cooper off our property? Should pile up this detritus and start a bonfire—except it's too damn hot." Jed sat down heavily in the folding chair Lance had left behind, and Maya was concerned to see how red he'd gotten. It was a long walk from the house.

"Have some water and cool down." She fished a bottle out of the ice chest she had under the table and handed it to him.

"If you can't take him on single-handedly, call your brother," Jed went on. "Liam would have him out of here in a jiffy."

"Lance just came to help raise money to save the history museum." Maya gave Jed a brief summary of the state of things. "I don't get over there much these days, but I love that old place, Uncle Jed. I don't want it shut down, do you?"

"I don't give a damn about the museum. You two looked mighty cozy when I walked up—like you were about to get a whole hell of a lot cozier—"

She needed to head him off. If Jed got it in his head

he'd seen her and Lance about to kiss—which of course he had—there'd never be an end to it. Liam would lose his mind, which they didn't need, and she'd probably have to quit the Historical Society, which she didn't want to do.

The only thing Jed cared about was winning the Founder's Prize—

The Founder's Prize.

Maya had to laugh. Saved by the feud.

"You *should* care about the museum," she asserted. "We have to do more to win the prize, right? That's what you said. Fixing the library isn't enough, so I'm going to find a new home for the museum, fund it and make it the best local historical museum anyone's ever seen!"

"How are you going to do that?"

"I'm updating the annual re-enactment. Making it something that people have never seen before." She was proud of the way her script was turning out so far, after all, even if she was overstating her efforts.

"You're going to buy someplace big enough to house all that clap-trap?"

"It's not clap-trap. It's our town's history. And our family's history is all mixed up in it."

Jed hmphed. "Mixed up is the right term. This town has never appreciated everything our family has done for it. William was one of the best deputies Chance Creek ever had, and so was his father before him. I worked with Abel, you know. Where's his exhibit in that museum? Where's all the Turner history? All that's there is a bunch of trash and teeny-tiny explanation cards you can't even read. Probably better that way. Bet they'd put you right to sleep."

"That's what I'm going to change. I'm going to make the re-enactment better, and I'm going to make the museum better, too." She had a vision of collecting examples of clothing, furniture and other artifacts. Recreating pioneer homes and businesses. Sewing reproductions that would allow patrons—children and adults—to dress up and try out old-fashioned life. Expanding it all someday into a living history area like Colonial Williamsburg or—

Jed didn't look impressed. "What do you know about history, or museums—or writing, for that matter?"

Maya was stung by his immediate dismissal. "More than you think."

"Whatever. You make sure that Cooper clears his stuff out of here." He hauled himself out of his seat and turned toward the house.

When Jed was gone, Maya sighed. The quiet had never bothered her before, but after Jed's scolding and with Lance gone, the lonely stand seemed downright oppressive. No cars approached from either direction, and nothing living stirred in the fields as the sun beat down.

She was already regretting what she'd said to Jed. She wasn't running the re-enactment, and she wasn't going to get credit for saving the museum, even if she wrote a script. If Lance sold a few pieces of his beautiful furniture, he'd far out earn the money she could raise through selling baked goods. Jed would seize on her promise, though, and hold her to it.

When she spotted Stella's truck in the distance, Maya straightened, happy for the distraction. It was Stella's day off, and she'd been running errands. Maybe she would have some gossip from town.

"Were you grocery shopping?" Maya called out as Stella parked the car.

"And practicing at the range." Stella lifted a case from the passenger seat and showed Maya through the open window before hopping out. Stella went to the shooting range at least once a week to keep her skills sharp. She'd always liked target practice.

"How are sales?" Stella came over and eyed Lance's wooden furniture. "What's all this?"

Maya filled her in, bracing herself for her sister's reaction. Maybe it would have been better if Stella had driven directly up to the house.

"Lance made all of these?"

Maya could understand her skepticism. "He's selling them to raise money for the museum."

Stella picked up a carved wooden serving bowl. "Got to admit this is pretty. Who thought he had it in him?" She turned it over, looked at the little stick on price tag and frowned. "Too expensive for me." She put it down and picked up a small carved box.

"I figured we might as well work together just this once." She held her breath, hoping that would satisfy her sister.

Stella gave her a speculative look. "You really think Lance is going to all this trouble because he cares about the town's history? Or does he have something else in mind?" Her raised eyebrow made it all too clear what she meant.

"Stop being so suspicious." Maya hoped she wasn't blushing.

Stella laughed. "Comes with the territory. He's a Cooper, or did you forget that? And I saw you two dancing at the wedding."

"I saw you dancing with Steel," Maya retorted a little too quickly. "Are you two an item now?" If Stella thought she was flirting with Lance, there'd be hell to pay. She was only laughing now because she thought the idea was so outrageous. Stella was adamant in her belief that the Coopers should be kept at arm's length, despite Noah's marriage to Olivia.

"No." Stella's tone was scornful. "That was definitely a one-time thing."

"Exactly. And no, I didn't forget." She knew exactly how problematic it would be for her to develop feelings for Lance. She simply didn't know how to stop it from happening.

God help her.

He'd kissed her once. Had almost done it again.

She'd almost let him.

Wanted him to do a whole hell of a lot more than that, if she was honest. She was in trouble, Maya realized. Now that her libido had woken up, it was taking over her common sense. "Anyway, I'm working on a script for the re-enactment," she added defensively. "Maybe if I can save the museum, it could help us win the Founder's Prize." There she went again, making trouble for herself. She was going to find herself in a real fix if she didn't stop it.

"We're already fixing the library. Isn't that enough?" Stella put the box down and came to look over Maya's baked goods.

"Jed doesn't think so."

"Jed's bored and wants to start trouble. We need to stop tilting at windmills and start focusing on our cattle operation and how we're going to bring in enough money to get through the winter. Liam's organic certification idea is interesting, but it's going to take years." She waved her hand at the pastries laid out across the stand. "You should be giving all the profits to our ranch, not the museum. Maybe it's time to think about keeping your stand open seven days a week."

Was Stella kidding? "That's impossible. It takes me all day to cook for a sales day. We've got one oven, remember? And I still have to tend my garden and do chores." And have a little time left over for a life. She didn't say that out loud, though. They were all working as much as they could.

"Maybe you should close the stand and get another job. One that pays better."

"Like what?"

"Noah helped me get my job at the sheriff's department. Maybe he can get you something, too."

Maya noticed the twist of her sister's lips, and she

wondered if Noah had ever asked himself if Stella wanted to be a secretary. Stella was a crack shot. She was smart. Calm in a bad situation. Why wasn't she a deputy—or at least a parole officer, like he was?

"I'd prefer to find something on my own." She'd prefer to keep doing what she was doing. She didn't want a job in town.

"Suit yourself," Stella said. "Let me know when you're done for the day. I'll come back and help you pack up. Meanwhile, I'll get dinner started."

"Thanks."

By the time Lance came around at the end of the afternoon to pick up the remainder of his furniture, Maya was a bundle of nerves. She'd sold three more of his pieces. Which meant three more kisses, if she wasn't mistaken.

She wouldn't let him touch her, of course. She knew better. If someone saw them, she didn't know what would happen. That didn't stop her from nervously rearranging the display on her table when he pulled up, parked his truck, got out and scanned the collection of his work.

"I sold another rocking chair, a set of shelves and a—"

Lance crossed the distance between them in several long steps, cupped her chin in his hands, bent down and kissed her like a thirsty man worshipping an oasis in the desert.

"That's one," she gasped when they finally came up for air. Lance's smile curved his mouth in a way that made her bite her lip. He pulled her to her feet, tugged her close, and this time her arms twined around his neck of their own accord. She buried her fingers in his short, thick hair and pressed her body against his, wanting to feel him—all of him.

"That's two," he murmured when they pulled apart. "One more."

"Yeah. One more."

He looked both ways, as if making sure no one was coming, threaded his thumbs through the belt loops of her jean shorts and tugged her against him. She pressed her palms against his chest, feeling the thump of his heart under the cloth of his shirt. When she went up on tiptoe, he bent down to meet her, covering her mouth with his. This time their kiss went on and on, and when his hands slid down to curve around her waist, she groaned.

She was light-headed when he stepped back.

"We... shouldn't," she groaned. "Noah and Olivia have already got our families ready to explode."

"I know, but I want to," he admitted.

She nodded. She did, too.

A truck came around the curve in the road, and they sprang apart. It roared past, kicking up a cloud of dust. Lance watched it go. Shook his head.

She knew what he was thinking: this would never work. Why were they starting something they couldn't finish?

"Can I bring everything back the day after tomorrow?" he asked.

"Sure." She wanted to kick herself the minute she said the word. She should have told him no.

She didn't want to.

He looked like he would kiss her again, but with a sigh he headed for his truck.

"See you then."

Maya watched him until he was out of sight.

Chapter Six

"I HEARD YOU and Maya Turner are planning to spice things up around here."

Lance jumped when his sister Olivia appeared at his elbow the following morning, pushing a cart laden with books. To his surprise, Tory was trailing her, carrying several more books in her arms. After waking up early and getting his morning chores done, he'd driven into town to come to the library. He'd found a stack of books on the Revolution and had been sitting at one of the scarred wooden carrels in the library for nearly an hour reading, but somewhere in the last fifteen minutes he'd stopped seeing the words and started daydreaming about Maya instead.

"Me and Maya?" What had Olivia heard—or seen? Had someone caught sight of those kisses when he'd returned to pick up his furniture yesterday? He'd barely been able to get them out of his mind. His body was aching to get Maya alone—

Which somehow Olivia seemed to know.

"The re-enactment," she prompted. "You're spicing it up to make it more interesting?"

"Oh—that." The back of his neck was hot, and he

hoped his sisters didn't notice how flustered he was.

"What did you think I was talking about?" she asked curiously. She tipped back his book. "Doing research, huh? That's good."

"Yeah. I'm researching. Got to save the museum." More like he was thinking lascivious thoughts about a woman who should be his enemy.

"What do you think of the library? Looks good, doesn't it? One thing about this Founder's Prize—it's getting all of us off our butts and fixing up this town. We should have done it sooner."

"I guess." She was right; the library hadn't looked this good in his lifetime. Lance had never spent as much time here as his sister, but he knew it was worth taking care of. Like the museum, it was something people took for granted these days. Something they wouldn't miss until it was gone.

"So who's going to get credit for saving the muse-um, us or them?" Tory asked.

"What do you mean?" He was the one spearheading the campaign. Of course the Coopers would get cred-it… "Wait, you don't think Maya's going to try to take credit for—" He couldn't even finish the thought. "She wouldn't do that."

Olivia looked thoughtful. "I heard it was her idea to extend the re-enactment with stories about the people taking part in the battle, right? Maybe Tory's right—maybe she is hoping to get credit for saving the muse-um."

"Even if she does write a script—and we decide to

use it—that doesn't make it a Turner thing."

"I never thought of the re-enactment as a Cooper thing, either," Olivia said. "I don't think anyone does. It's a group effort."

"It's been *my* effort these past two years. I'm the one doing all the hard work."

Olivia shrugged. "I've got to get back to work. I guess you'll have to ask her. See you at home later."

"See you." He was too busy picking apart Maya's motives to notice that Tory had stayed. Was Maya really trying to make this a Turner project? Steal it right out from under his nose?

No. She couldn't—

"I can't believe you all are still so caught up in this turf war after so many years," Tory said. "Don't you think it's time to let it go?"

"You know the family history," he said.

"I know all our feuding never made anything better."

"Maybe not," he had to admit. He didn't want to feud with Maya, anyway, but that didn't mean he wanted her to take credit for the re-enactment.

He was the one who would save the day. People didn't want to see plays. They wanted to see men fight. They liked the sound of the shots fired, the smoke of the battlefield, the sharp smell of gunpowder. Which meant the way to get more people to come was to make the battle bigger. Fresher. More exciting.

More dangerous.

He was going to choose a new battle to re-enact. A

specific one, rather than the general assault and retreat they'd always done before.

"I say if you like Maya, go for it," Tory went on.

Lance nearly dropped the book. "I don't—"

"None of my business. None of anyone's business. Remember that." She walked off before he could come up with an answer, leaving him sputtering his denials.

He couldn't go for it.

Could he?

No. Absolutely not. He had to focus. Pick a battle. Get this done.

He forced himself to open the book again and start reading. It was hard to concentrate at first, but he refused to let himself think about Maya, and after some time, he got sucked in.

The particular battle the author was describing wasn't one he was familiar with, and Lance was beginning to wonder if that was all for the better.

He looked back to the start of the section.

"The Battle of Cowpens?" Lance had to smile. The name alone might draw people in; folks around these parts were plenty familiar with cattle—and cattle enclosures, for that matter. Didn't they all spend half their time mending fences?

Since no one in the audience would have ever heard about this battle—except maybe Warren—they wouldn't know how things would turn out, either. It was by no means a minor skirmish. The Colonial forces, who by all rights should have lost, claimed an unlikely victory through grit and ingenuity.

It felt like a perfect encapsulation of the whole Revolution.

Twenty minutes later, Lance's excitement was wearing off. Choosing a less famous battle had seemed like a good idea, but he soon realized it would make nailing down its details a lot more difficult. There weren't enough maps in this book. He'd covered several sheets of paper with a bunch of x's and o's, like a football play diagram, trying to draw out the events the author was describing. Soon he needed to get home. He was neglecting his chores.

"Hi, Lance. What are you reading?"

He looked up to find Mia Matheson next to his table. She bent over and read the title. "*The Revolutionary War*, huh? Guess I should have figured."

Was she a spy for Maya? She'd been championing the idea of adding scenes to the re-enactment, and she was the one urging Maya to start writing a script. "Just gathering ideas."

"We need more people, less battles, if you ask me."

Lance grunted. "That's a matter of opinion."

"Have you talked this over with Maya?"

"Why should I talk about it with Maya?" Was his neck turning red again? Did everyone think they were an item?

"Maybe you shouldn't take things too far until we have a vote about what the re-enactment is going to look like."

He shoved his chair back. "I've been involved with the re-enactment a lot longer than you have."

Mia crossed her arms. "There are a lot more people involved this year, and I think we all should get a say."

"I think you should—" Lance bit off the rest of the words he meant to say. He was overreacting, and he knew it. He didn't want to fight with her.

She must have realized she was pushing him too hard. She took a deep breath, and he could almost hear her counting to ten.

"What's all this?" She pointed to a page where he'd been making lists of named participants in the battle. He was having a hard time getting the information from different sources to agree.

"Casualties. One book lists 124 of them. One of the others says it was only 121. I'm trying to figure out who's right."

"When were these written, anyway?" She picked up one of the books, opened it and checked the copyright. "1954? You've got to be kidding!" She rolled her eyes, pulled out her phone and tapped away at it. A moment later she thrust it into his face. "There were 122 casualties at the Battle of Cowpens. 110 of those were British forces. Only twelve died on our side. So much for getting your facts right. And the Battle of Cowpens is a horrible name. People will think we're bullfighting."

"They will not," Lance started, then realized she was smiling. Was she goading him on purpose?

"Just teasing you, Lance," Mia said sweetly, "but you need to join the twenty-first century." She pointed to the sheet of paper full of x's and o's. "Look." She tapped at her phone again. "See?"

Lance knew enough about technology to recognize a major company's map program. There was a satellite view of the battlefield as it looked today. Overlaid on top of it were outlines of buildings and the positions of the British and Colonial forces as they'd stood in the late 1700s.

"Hannah's Cowpens," Mia read out loud. "That was the name of the field where they fought. Interesting. I'd be glad to help with the research, you know." She pulled out a chair and sat down beside him. "I'm already helping Maya."

Great. "I don't need help," he growled.

"Sure you do," a male voice cut in. "You're a Cooper. Can you even read those books?"

Hell. It was Liam approaching, wearing an old T-shirt and faded jeans stained with paint. He must have been working on the library renovations. Any goodwill Lance had been feeling about what the Turners were doing for the place evaporated.

"To hell with you, Turner. Fixing up this library was Olivia's idea, remember?"

Liam cocked his head. "So? I know Olivia *Turner* can read. I was asking about Coopers."

Lance took a deep breath, knowing Liam always loved a chance to throw down. It was just like him to get in that dig about Olivia taking Noah's last name. Lance decided he needed some air. Standing up abruptly, he gathered his books and made for the front counter.

"Hey, wait," Mia called after him, jumping up to

follow.

"Gotta go. See you at the meeting next week."

"Call me if I can help!"

He left as soon as Marta, the librarian, had checked him out. Before he even made it to the street, however, someone else called out his name, distracting him from the doubts that had begun to crowd his mind. Mia wouldn't be the only one with her phone handy at the re-enactment, ready and able to fact-check his battle at every turn. What if he got something wrong?

Had he bitten off way more than he could chew?

"Lance, hold up!"

Now who wanted a piece of him? Lance turned around, ready to confront Liam if he'd followed him out of the library, looking for a fight, but it was Bart.

"Hey, I've been looking for you. I need your help."

WHEN MAYA SPOTTED Maggie's truck pulling in near the farm stand the following morning, her heart lifted at the thought of some company to pass the time, but it sank again a moment later when Maggie parked, stumbled out of the vehicle and rushed toward her, tears streaming down her face.

"He didn't come home last night."

Maya hastened to make change for the Wilsons, who had been loading up on vegetables and berry tarts. She could see a small blonde head in the back seat of the truck Maggie had just vacated—her daughter, Katie, peeping out at them.

"Who didn't?" she asked as soon as she'd seen the

Wilsons on their way, although she knew very well who Maggie must mean.

"Bart. He called at the end of the afternoon yesterday. Said he had something to do after work. And then he never came home." Maggie scraped the palm of her hand over her cheek, but new tears fell as fast as she wiped them away. "I was up all night. He's never done anything like this before. He finally called me again this morning. Said he got caught up with something. More like with *someone!*"

Maggie's voice slid up, and Maya knew she had to calm her down.

"Take a deep breath. People do all kinds of crazy things when they're grieving. I'm sure he wasn't with someone else." Maya wasn't really sure of any such thing. Staying out all night wasn't normal behavior for a man like Bart Lawson.

She tugged forward the other folding chair. "Sit down. I'll go get Katie."

Maggie's head swiveled toward the truck, and her mouth fell open. "Oh, my God. I forgot she was even there. What kind of a mother am I?"

"You're a very stressed one. Just sit and breathe, okay? I've got this." Maya hurried to the truck and lifted Katie from her seat. The little girl smiled at her broadly, oblivious to the drama being played out around her. "You want a cookie?" Maya asked her as she carried her to the farm stand. "I've got some fresh baked chocolate chip ones."

Katie nodded vigorously, and Maya handed her one,

holding the little girl on her lap when she took her seat again.

"I'm sorry," Maggie said, wiping more tears away. "I keep dumping all of this on you. I'm too embarrassed to tell anyone. Not that you're not someone. It's just—"

"I understand. I really do," Maya said. She hadn't wanted to tell anyone she knew when her mother had left home, but she'd still been dying for someone to talk to.

"Who do you think it is?" Maggie pushed. "How long has it been going on?"

Maya passed Maggie a cookie, too, for lack of a better idea of what to do. "Don't jump to conclusions. Maybe there's a good explanation for what happened."

Maggie buried her face in her daughter's hair. "I don't know what I'll do if he's cheating on me. I want my marriage back—the way it used to be."

"I know. So call him. Demand an explanation."

She didn't know what else Maggie could do.

"What do you need help with?" Lance asked with some trepidation. Bart wasn't himself these days, and right now he looked pretty bad. His hair was standing on end; he looked like he'd slept in the clothes he was wearing. He didn't smell too good, either.

"Can you keep a secret?"

"From who? Your wife?" Lance didn't like the sound of that.

"It's a good secret," Bart promised. "It's going to solve all my problems. I just need time—and some tools. You've got those, don't you? With all that furniture you build."

"What's going on?" Lance demanded.

"I got my inheritance. That house Maggie and I want so bad? I've got it. Well, almost," he backtracked. "It's not quite a house, but I can make it one."

Was he drunk?

Lance didn't think so, but Bart wasn't making much sense.

"How much money did you inherit?" he asked.

"Not money—a building. A warehouse on Stonewall Street. I didn't even know Dad still owned it. He bought it decades ago. It's paid in full. He even made some rent off it for a while, but the last couple of years it's sat empty. It's perfect!"

"Perfect for what?" Stonewall Street was dead in the middle of Chance Creek's industrial center, such as it was. There were a number of empty buildings on that side of town. The ones that were occupied housed car repair shops, manufacturing shops and the like.

"For a house! I'll just take it down to the studs, rearrange a few things, add some walls—" He waved his hands like he was performing a magic spell.

Lance chose his words carefully. Bart's enthusiasm was running away with him. "I'm not sure it'll be that easy—"

"I didn't say anything about easy. I don't care how hard it is—it's the answer to all our problems. We need a place of our own, and now we've got one. We've got savings—I can buy the materials. But tools are expensive. Can you help me out?"

"Of course I'll help, but—"

"Good. We'll start tonight. I've got to get back to work before I get fired. That wouldn't be good, would it?" He started to hurry away.

No, it wouldn't be good, but Lance wasn't sure operating power tools was a good thing for Bart to do tonight, either. He looked short on sleep, among other things.

"I'm not sure I can make it tonight."

Bart stopped. Turned a pleading look his way. "My marriage isn't going to last another few years in that basement."

Bart certainly looked desperate enough, and his words tugged at Lance in a way he didn't like to acknowledge.

His own parents' separation had been messy, and Lance still didn't see eye to eye with his mother, even if she'd had damn good reasons to leave his father. Dale had been breaking the law from the moment they walked down the aisle. It was a miracle she stayed with him as long as she did.

Still, their divorce had hurt everyone in the family. If Lance ever got married, he would never—

He quashed that train of thought, not wanting to examine the reason why Maya's face came to mind.

"Yeah, I'll help tonight. Got to get home and get my own chores done first, though."

"Of course. See you later. I'll text you the address."

Twenty minutes later Lance pulled in and parked in front of Maya's stand, telling himself he'd only stay a moment. He'd dropped off a load of furniture earlier on his way into town. He still had lots of work to do at home—and then at Bart's warehouse, apparently.

He was glad to see the only other patrons pulling back onto the highway. He'd get Maya alone—at least for a few minutes.

"Some of my furniture is missing," he called out as he came to join her. "Did it sell, or did Jed come and haul it off to a bonfire?

Maya laughed. "It sold! Look." She showed him a jar of money, and Lance's chest swelled with pride.

"I don't know why I never thought about doing this before. Wonder if I could make a business of it?"

"Careful what you wish for," Maya said wryly. "I used to love this stand. Now on top of insisting I sell more baked goods, Stella wants me to keep it open seven days a week. Suddenly it feels like a job I can't wait to quit." She shrugged. "On the bright side, at least I'll raise more money for the museum this way."

Lance almost brought up his research at the library but held back, remembering what Tory had said. If Maya meant to take credit for saving the museum, he had to watch out, but this close to her, he found it hard to remember she was capable of hurting his family. She was far more comfortable around him than she used to be, almost as if they were friends. He found himself wishing they could be on the same side.

Was this how Olivia and Noah had ended up to-gether?

It bore thinking about.

Meanwhile, working together with Maya on selling their wares benefitted both of them, he reasoned—and the museum, too, and if his furniture raised money, she couldn't take credit for that, even if she was manning the stand when it happened.

"I brought something for us to work on. Be right back." He got up, went to his truck and returned with an ancient laptop he'd dug out of his father's office this morning.

"What's that for?"

"I hate to admit it, but Avery's right; everyone has a website these days. Maybe we should have one, too."

MAYA HAD TO admit she was grateful for Lance's company. She'd finally caved and told Stella she'd run the stand daily for the foreseeable future, which meant she'd never have time again to see or talk to anyone who didn't stop by.

The company was one thing, the activity quite another. She was hopeless with a computer, and somehow Lance was even worse. He hadn't given a thought to the fact they would have to connect to the internet to build a website and seemed surprised to learn that neither of their ranches' Wi-Fi reached the highway. It took twenty minutes of figuring out how to connect the laptop to her phone's data service before they could even begin making the site.

"There," Maya said after they had located a free service that would allow them to build a simple page. "This one says 'storefront.' Let's try that."

Lance clicked and brought up a series of options that neither of them understood. After fumbling their way through the settings and customization options, they were finally shown a preview of their site—and Maya realized her mistake.

"This isn't a page to advertise a store," Lance said, putting it together. "This *is* a store."

Maya nodded, feeling stupid. "I don't want to sell pies on the internet. I just want to tell people where to find them." She glanced at Lance. "Maybe people would order your furniture, though?"

Lance shook his head. "I have no idea how to sell things online. I need a break." He slammed the lid of the laptop shut.

Maya rubbed her eyes, which were strained from trying to make out the screen through the glare of the sun. "I guess you'll be going," she said, hoping he wouldn't. "Doesn't look like we're going to get much business today. It's going to be excruciating sitting until closing time, especially when I know all I'm going to do tonight is more baking."

"You need a little excitement?"

"Yep. The legal kind," she cautioned, and then wished she hadn't when his face fell. She hadn't meant to make a slight against his family. "I mean, I can't get drunk or anything. I've got a lot of work ahead of me tonight."

"I don't have any alcohol on hand, anyway. But I've got something that might do the trick." He grinned suddenly, a boyish grin that made Maya feel downright girlish.

"What is it?"

"Hold on."

He went back to his truck and returned brandishing an impressively authentic-looking carved wooden replica sword and shield.

"Where did you get those?" Maya sat up, setting down the water bottle she'd just taken a drink from. "Did you make them, too?"

Lance nodded. "I didn't bother putting them out because I don't think anyone would have a use for them."

"They look great, though," Maya said honestly. "Maybe someone would want one to hang on the wall? Or for their kids. Would they break if they were played with?"

"I guess we'd better see." Lance grinned again. "Take these. I'll be right back."

He retrieved a sword and shield of his own from the truck, and Maya followed him out into the field by the stand. There was still no sign of any customers, and she was grateful for the chance to stretch her legs.

Lance gripped his shield and held up his sword. He should have looked ridiculous, but with his strong features and muscular frame, he looked enough like an ancient warrior her heart gave an extra beat or two. The whole thing was kind of hot, actually, which made her roll her eyes at herself. She slid on her shield and lifted her sword, then shrieked when Lance lunged suddenly and gave her shield a light tap with his sword.

"No fair—I wasn't ready."

"You ready now?"

He lunged again before she finished nodding, tapped her shield and pulled back again. "Got to move faster than that, or you won't last long."

"Oh, yeah?" She lunged for him but only met air when Lance sidestepped her blow. She tried again and again, but he easily outmaneuvered her. "What's that?" She stood stock-still, pointing her sword at the road. Lance turned, and she whacked his shield as hard as she could.

"Hey!"

"That'll teach you!"

This time when Lance lunged, she managed to block him. Soon they were pacing back and forth across the grass, trading soft blows, as Lance pointed out various tactics and types of thrusts. He knew a lot about this stuff, and Maya was having a much better time than she'd expected.

"This is how you disarm your opponent." Lance did a fancy swish of his sword, and suddenly hers was flying through the air away from her. "Submit, fair damsel," he declared.

"Never." She spun on her heel and ran.

"Hey, that's not how it works." Lance ran after her, tossing away the wooden implements.

She shrieked when he caught her in a flying tackle, but he rolled so he landed under her, breaking her fall. She laughed, then stilled, suddenly very conscious of his body beneath hers.

Lance stilled, too, watching her with an expression she couldn't read. He was so handsome, Maya thought. She'd grown up next to him without realizing he was turning into a fascinating man.

Now that was all too clear, and in another minute, she might lose her head. Disentangling herself, she stood up and helped him to his feet. The silence felt unbearably awkward as Lance brushed himself off, and Maya cast about for something to say. "That was fun," she managed finally. "I guess I can see why people like this stuff."

"Maybe we should re-enact the Revolutionary War with swords."

"We could do an ancient battle," she suggested.

Lance considered that but shook his head. "Doesn't go with the Fourth of July theme. Maybe we can do that another time." He was silent a moment. "I decided—I mean, I think... I think for the re-enactment we need to do a bigger battle than we've ever done before. Something more complicated that shows tactics and allows us to fire more weapons. You're right," he conceded. "We've let things get stale."

Maya was surprised he'd admitted it. "A bigger battle wouldn't hurt, but I still think we should tell the stories of the people who are fighting, too."

"That's what Mia said."

"Mia?" Maya drew herself up. "What were you doing with Mia?" Heck, did she sound as jealous as she felt? Maya hoped not.

"Just met up with her at the library."

"Oh." Maya got a hold of her emotions. "Why can't we do both? You could work on the battle. I could work on the stories. Tell me what battle you're fighting, and I'll research the men who took part in it and then see if I can figure out anything about their families. If I can't, I'll make something up."

Lance looked away, and she thought she heard him sigh.

"I don't think we can decide this on our own," he said finally. "We have to wait until the next meeting. Put it to a vote. Meanwhile, how about we go cool off?"

She noticed he hadn't said if he'd vote for her idea. He hadn't said he wouldn't, either. She supposed he was right; they couldn't make decisions unilaterally.

She would have liked his support, though.

Couldn't they ever get past the animosity between their families?

"Last one there owes the other a drink." Lance took off running, leaving her gaping at him. That wasn't fair—

"If you leave your weapons on Turner ground, they become Turner property," she shouted after him. He stopped abruptly, looking back at his discarded shield and sword in surprise. Maya laughed as she raced past him.

When she reached the stand, Maya was so exhausted from the heat she didn't bother with her chair; she simply collapsed on a small patch of grass near her stand and watched Lance hurtling toward her, both sets of swords and shields in his hands.

He got there moments after she did. Breathing hard, his forehead damp with sweat, he dropped the replica weapons.

Then he took off his shirt and tossed it aside, too.

Maya swallowed. Lance's body was as beautifully sculpted as any of his woodworking, and like his weapons, she could almost believe it was made of metal. His skin practically shone as the brutal sun reflected off a sheen of sweat, and with every breath, his muscles contracted together like a hammer striking an anvil.

"Here." Lance circled around the stand, rummaged in the cooler and poured them each a glass of lemonade. "Fair and square." His tone said her tactics were anything but, though his smile told her he didn't mind.

Maya downed the lemonade quickly, but her throat went dry all over again when she watched Lance take his own drink. The way his Adam's apple bobbed with each swallow was hypnotic.

When he was finished, Lance wiped his mouth and set his glass on the stand. He took Maya's glass and set it aside, too, then offered her his hand. Maya's legs rebelled at the thought of standing up again so soon, but the allure of his touch won out. She took his hand.

Lance pulled her up, and when she stumbled against him, he caught and held her. His hard muscles pressed against her curves.

She looked up into his eyes. *A body like iron,* she thought, *and eyes like cooled metal. They picked the wrong child to name Steel.*

But Lance's brother was the furthest thing from her mind when his mouth found hers.

She must have lost a year, Maya thought, when they

broke apart and her mind started to function again. This felt like the most natural thing in the world, when a matter of days ago, she had seen Lance as a nuisance at best, perhaps even vaguely threatening.

This should have felt wrong.

She'd never felt so right.

"Hell," Lance said and jerked away from her.

Maya blinked. Had he come to his senses? Realized this was insanity? Was it insanity? If so, did she want to be sane?

"Someone's coming." Lance caught up his shirt and struggled to get it over his head, ducking down behind the farm stand to hide what he was doing.

It should have been funny. Instead it left Maya feeling cold.

Lance hurried toward his truck as another vehicle pulled into the parking area. He turned back when his hand gripped the door handle.

"I'll pick up my stuff later and bring it back tomorrow. You said you're open daily now, right?"

"That's right. Yeah, see you tomorrow," she echoed and watched him head out.

She told herself she was being silly as she composed herself to meet the approaching customer. Of course Lance was right to want to hide that they were kissing. It was as much for her benefit as for his own. People would talk. Their families would be angry.

She plastered a smile on her face as her customer approached. "Hey, Mike. Back for another pie?"

Chapter Seven

RIDING IN A wide circle around the herd in Thorn Hill's west pasture late that afternoon, Lance brought his horse to a halt when he saw Steel leaning against the fence at the other end of the field. Even from this distance, Lance could tell his brother's intense gaze was fixed on him. Lance wondered if something was wrong.

Steel came and went from the ranch on his own timetable, helping out with chores, but he was rarely around when Lance needed an extra pair of hands. For that he had to turn to the men who worked for pay part-time on the ranch. Men who were filling in their dance card with the odd hour here and there while working full-time on other spreads.

Lance started toward Steel at a slow trot. It wouldn't be healthy for his horse to exert itself in this kind of heat.

He hadn't completed his inspection by the time he'd spotted Steel, but Lance had to admit he'd been wasting time anyway. Earlier, Noah had come to inform him he'd already done one, and all was well. Lance had ridden out at once to inspect the herd for himself, not trusting that Noah had done a thorough job of it. That was what he told himself, anyway. The truth was, whatever else Noah might be, he was not sloppy. If anything, his problem was that he was *too* thorough.

The only reason Lance was out here now was because it bothered him Noah was far more into running the spread than he was. This was his home. His legacy. He'd been too distracted lately by the museum and his desire to save it.

He was spending too much time being resentful that he didn't get to go to school, and even more time wishing he could be with Maya. Now he was playing a futile game of catch up. While he was out here gawking at cattle Noah had already confirmed were fine, Noah was probably taking care of something else his family had missed.

How had it come to this? And why couldn't Steel pull more of his own weight?

"Where the hell were you while Noah was taking over our cattle operation?" Lance demanded when Steel was within earshot. At least he wasn't the only idiot in the pasture now. Cold comfort, but he'd take what he could get.

"I did my chores this morning. Did you?"

"I do my share of work around here every day, but you're never around, you know that? I can't do everything myself," Lance said. "Noah's taking up the slack, and that's messed up."

"Things are… busy," Steel admitted.

"What things?"

When Steel looked away, Lance cursed. "Are you going to be like Dad? Screwing around to the point you lose everything?"

An expression crossed Steel's face and was gone before Lance could interpret it. "I'm doing what has to be done."

As mysterious as always. Lance was sick of it. "You think you're some kind of rebel hero, don't you? Skirting the law, getting away with whatever you're trying to get away with. Just like Dad, you're only happy if you're getting away with something."

"You don't know what you're talking about, so watch it."

"Oh yeah? What don't I know?"

"Things." Steel turned on his heel. "Came to see if you needed help right now, but doesn't look like it."

"Hold up. That's not fair. Are you talking about Dad? Saying there's something I don't know?"

Steel stopped in his tracks. "You think he's the bad guy," he said without turning around. "It eats at you. Makes you feel small. Maybe he wasn't as bad as you think."

Something twisted in Lance's chest—some ancient longing for family pride he'd thought had been obliterated with his father's jail sentence. "You're going to have to explain that."

Steel shook his head and started walking again. "Not yet. Just... hang on, okay? Let it lie. Don't poke at it. Just... hang on."

He was gone before Lance could formulate another

question, and he found his throat thick with emotion. If only he could believe Dale had some good in him—

But he was far too old to believe in fairy tales.

MAYA HAD JUST taken a pie out of the oven when Noah and Stella came into the kitchen, followed closely by Carl and Camila Whitfield—and Olivia. Until their marriage, Carl had lived in a cabin at Thorn Hill, and Camila had occupied a similar one at the Flying W. They'd gotten sucked into the Turner–Cooper feud but had refused to let it stop them from being together.

Now they owned a beautiful ranch, and much to everyone's chagrin, they socialized with both families. Maya couldn't fault Carl or Camila for that, but it certainly made things awkward sometimes. Like right now.

Stella fussed around near the kitchen sink, running water and cleaning a dish or two that Maya had dirtied. Noah put an arm around Olivia. Only Carl and Camila seemed oblivious to the undercurrents running through the kitchen.

"Maya, there you are," Camila said.

Maya stifled the urge to respond with a *where else would I be?* It wasn't Camila's fault she had to cook all night, every night now. The family needed money, and she didn't want to look for work in town.

"Good to see you," she said instead. It was true; she missed Camila's cheerful personality and fun sense of humor on the ranch. While she'd lived here, she'd been a wonderful antidote to her family's staidness.

"I'm hoping you'll come to Laurel Heights tonight. We're having a movie night. Everyone's invited."

"Everyone?" Did she mean all the Turners, or Coopers, too?

"Everyone," Carl said firmly. "We're heading home right now, and we're putting on a big spread. We're celebrating. We've got a big announcement."

"And we know you all are working way too hard, so all you have to do is show up, stuff your faces and loll around on couches being entertained. We haven't had the chance to use our movie room yet. Please, please, please say you'll come?"

"I have to cook—"

"Nope. No excuses. I'll whip up a huge batch of cookies while I'm getting ready at home, and you can have them to sell tomorrow. Come on—we never get to hang out together anymore," Camila begged.

Maya looked to Noah and Stella. They were the ones pushing her to up her income after all.

"I think Camila's right; we need to relax now and then," Stella said. "We'll be there in an hour. All of us," she added.

"Awesome!" Camila took Carl's arm. "Let's go—I've got to bake those cookies."

Stella and Noah walked them to the front door, but Olivia hung back in the kitchen with Maya. "Smells good in here."

"Help yourself to anything you want." She wished she didn't feel so stiff around Olivia these days.

Olivia grabbed a plate from the cupboard and lifted

a mini tart off a baking sheet. She found a fork in one of the drawers and lifted a bite to her mouth. "Mmm, that's so yummy. You always did know how to cook."

"Thanks. Mom taught me before she... left." Too late she remembered she was referring to a time when both their families had fallen apart.

What she'd done to Olivia's family—inadvertently or not—was... horrible. Maybe Olivia's father would still be alive today if she hadn't interfered. Then there was Olivia's mother. Would she have stuck with Dale if he hadn't been caught?

Was it time to make amends?

She took a deep breath.

"Olivia—"

Noah walked back in. "Will you be ready to leave in about forty-five minutes, Maya? I told Jed we'd give him a lift to town on the way." He moved to slide his arm around his wife again. Noah and Olivia's easy affection for each other always made Maya feel a little bereft. She thought of Lance—and just as quickly pushed him out of her mind again.

"I... guess." She glanced around the kitchen. She had several recipes on the go. "I'll have to hurry, though."

Olivia hesitated, as if waiting for her to continue, but Maya couldn't talk about the past with Noah in the room. "I guess we'd better leave you to it."

"I'll see you later" was all Maya could think of to say.

Olivia slipped out of the room. Noah didn't follow

her right away. "I think she wants to patch things up, you know. If you'd just give her a chance."

Maya wasn't sure how much Noah knew about what had happened between them, so she simply nodded. "I've really got to get to it." She indicated the bowls and cookie sheets on the counter.

"Okay. Just... try, Maya. For me?"

He left before she could answer.

"WE'RE HEADING TO Laurel Heights in twenty minutes, so hurry up," Steel said when Lance walked in through the back door. "Dinner and movies with Carl and Camila at their spread."

"Wish someone had told me that earlier. Told Bart I would help him tonight." He wasn't much in the mood for socializing. Wasn't much in the mood for anything. It had been a long afternoon catching up on work he should have done earlier, and there was a lot more he should be doing still.

"You need to show up for at least an hour."

"But—"

"Tell Bart you'll be there as soon as you can."

"Fine," Lance growled. He needed to eat anyway, and the food at Laurel Heights would be good. Camila was an amazing cook.

Carl had thrown himself into remaking his brand-new ranch into a showcase of sustainable practices. Plus, he was trying to figure out how to use passive systems to allow him to grow fruit and vegetables normally only found south of the border. Camila co-owned Fila's

Familia with Fila Matheson, and the restaurant show-cased many of Camila's Mexican recipes. Her cousin Juana had recently joined the enterprise, and the food they served had gotten that much more authentic. Carl was doing his best to fill in the gaps for the supplies they couldn't source locally. In his heart Lance knew it was a cool project, but he couldn't help resenting the fact that the Whitfields had so much money to play with, while his family scraped by without a penny to put toward renovations, let alone innovative practices.

"Twenty minutes," Steel said. "Get going. We're dropping Virginia in town on the way. Book club night."

Lance showered and changed as quickly as he could and met the others at the front door at the agreed upon time. In fresh clothes, the dust of his long day washed down the drain, his mood picked up, especially because it had occurred to him that Carl had probably invited the Turners along with his family. Maya would be there.

Sure enough, when they reached Laurel Heights, there were several of the Turner trucks parked in front of the large house.

Envy plucked at his heart again as they walked up to the front door. This was a hell of a house. A hell of a spread.

"Must be nice, huh?" Steel muttered under his breath.

"Yep."

"We wouldn't know what to do with money like this if we ever earned it," Tory said as they all waited on the front porch for Carl or Camila to open the door.

"I could think of a thing or two," Lance said. He'd go back to school. Become a teacher. Run the museum. Hire a bunch of men to do the grunt work at the ranch. He'd still keep a hand in the operation, but he wouldn't need to do all of it himself.

"Maybe you need to play more cards. Heard you win a lot." His sister shot him an arch look.

"I win fair and square." And he hadn't played in months. Lance couldn't claim he'd never cheated in the past, but it had been years since he'd taken anyone's pocket money, and it had never gone further than that.

He wasn't his father.

Everyone just thought he was.

"Then you really must have turned over a new leaf. All I remember from when we were kids is you getting in trouble. Fighting Liam every chance you got."

"Ever think that maybe it was Liam fighting me?" Lance countered.

"Keep it down," Steel said as the door swung open and Carl came out to greet them, but Lance was aware of Tory's considering gaze resting on him.

None of his siblings had any idea about his history with Liam. They hadn't been there to see the way Liam had assumed the mantle of quarterback and captain of the football team, without ever once considering someone else might deserve the position. Had no idea how Lance had ended up covering for him for years—

"Come on in," Carl said. "Glad to see you all. There's beer in the fridge. Some wine, too, Tory, if you'd prefer it. Snacks in the living room. Go make yourselves at home. We'll eat out on the deck first, because it's such a fine night, then get to the movie-watching."

"Sounds good," Steel said heartily.

As they moved through the Whitfields' beautiful house, past the enormous, state-of-the-art kitchen, Lance wondered if Carl was aware of how much envy flowed his way. What did that feel like?

Was it uncomfortable?

"Where's Juana?" Steel asked Camila.

"She's minding the restaurant with Fila tonight. It's my day off."

"And here you are cooking," Tory exclaimed. "Let me help."

"Back for more." Stella Turner appeared with an empty tray and set it on the counter near the stove. "Oh—hi," she added flatly when she caught sight of Lance's family. "How are you all?"

When no one answered right away, Lance caught Camila rolling her eyes at her husband.

"We're… fine," he said hastily. "We're all fine."

"Tory, I didn't know you were staying in town so long." Stella joined Camila behind the counter, and they both got to work spooning cookie dough onto the tray. Tory, who'd been moving to help Camila, paused uncertainly.

"Why would you?" Tory bit her lip. "I mean…"

"You mean you don't chat with Stella very much," Camila said tartly, opening the oven and taking another tray of food from the oven. Bacon-wrapped scallops, if Lance wasn't mistaken. Those looked good. "But maybe you should start, seeing that you're about the same age and you grew up next door to each other."

Another awkward pause followed until Tory said, "I'm… figuring out my next move."

Lance and Steel both turned to look at her.

"What does that mean?" Steel asked.

"What happened to your massage business?" Lance added.

"This isn't the time." She waved a hand to indicate their hosts. "We can talk about it later."

"Talk about what later?"

Lance straightened when Liam joined them. He leaned against the large kitchen island. "What did I miss? You moving back to Chance Creek, Tory?"

"Tory's moving back?" Olivia bounced into view, and Lance wondered where she'd come from. Maybe one of the Whitfields' posh bathrooms. A couple of them were bigger than the kitchen at Thorn Hill.

"I… didn't say that."

Lance wasn't used to seeing his sister so flustered. What was going on with her?

"You just said you gave up your massage business," Liam put in.

"No, I didn't. Lance was the one talking about massage."

"You aren't going back to Seattle?" Lance pressed.

"I… don't live in Seattle."

Lance met Steel's gaze and saw his brother was as

confused as he was.

"Where do you live?" Steel demanded.

Tory raked a hand through her dark hair. "We're going to do this now? Right here? Fine." She faced them down. "I moved to Bozeman when I graduated."

Lance didn't follow. "Graduated from what?"

"From the University of Washington. I got my dual degree in political science and economics last year. I want to go to law school next, but first I needed to pay off my debts, so I moved to Bozeman, where the cost of living is cheaper, got a couple of jobs and made as much money as I could."

Lance knew he had to be gaping at her. "You graduated from college?" Raw anger spiked through him. He'd wanted to go to college, and he'd been stuck all this time working the damn ranch. Now she was back because—his mind raced to complete the thought—she wanted to live here for free?

Tory nodded. "I've already been accepted at Montana State. I just need to figure out how—"

Olivia squealed and raced to pull Tory into an embrace. "You're going to stay here? Long term? I'm so glad—and you'll be a fantastic lawyer!"

Tory was still looking at Lance, though. She knew, didn't she? Knew what he'd had to do to keep their family afloat. She'd been old enough when they moved to Idaho to be aware that he'd given up his scholarship to come with them, and that he'd had to go to work right away to help pay the family's expenses when their mother left. Tory hadn't helped when she came of age;

she'd lit out for Seattle as soon as she could.

He'd stayed. Helped until Olivia was older, then had come back here to work the ranch.

And all the while Tory had been fancy free. She'd certainly made the most of it, hadn't she?

Lance fought for composure, knowing he should be happy for her.

He wasn't, though.

He was furious.

"You don't look like you want me to stay here," Tory said. For the first time she looked unsure of herself.

"I… it's not about what I want," Lance ground out, because he'd always been raised to believe family was the most important thing. "You're a Cooper. Thorn Hill will always be your home."

Just like it would always be his jail.

When the silence was about to grow uncomfortable, Steel shifted. "Someone mentioned drinks and snacks. I could use some of those."

Carl immediately moved to the refrigerator and began to hand out bottles of beer. Olivia poured glasses of wine. Stella popped the tray of cookies into the oven, and the rest of them followed their hosts to the living room when everyone had their beverages. Lance did his best to act like nothing was out of the ordinary—like his sister hadn't just sucker-punched him with the information that she'd accomplished everything he'd wanted to but couldn't.

The Coopers migrated toward the large windows overlooking the ranch. The Turners clustered near the empty fireplace.

When Tory approached him, Lance stiffened. It was all he could do to keep himself from striding away.

"I always figured you'd find a way to go to school, too," she began softly.

"Right." He wasn't having that. They might not talk a lot, but she must have known he hadn't been attending classes.

"What's that supposed to mean?"

"It means you, Mom and Dad made damn sure I didn't get the chance."

"YOU'D THINK SOONER or later Carl and Camila would give up," Maya murmured to her sister as they stood near the television.

Stella smiled and took a sip of her wine. "They're both pretty stubborn. It might take a while before they realize we're never going to be one big, happy family."

"Can you imagine living in a place like this?" Laurel Heights was like a showhouse. Everything new—and clean—and... perfect.

"Our house is just fine, thank you very much."

"It's fine, but it's not palatial." You could get lost in a house like this, even if you lived with your extended family.

"Can you imagine cleaning a place like this?" Stella countered.

Maya made a face. "No," she admitted. "But it's making me wish I had more time to do things right. I feel like my room's a mess, the house is a mess, my garden's a mess."

"I know what you mean. I just can't keep up." Stella sighed. "And Cab offered me more hours at the sheriff's office today. I think I should take them."

"Yeah." But that meant Stella would have even less time for domestic duties, which would leave more for the rest of them. "Wonder what's going on over there." She nodded toward Lance and Tory, who were having what looked like a heated discussion, although they were talking quietly.

"Lance didn't seem too happy to find out Tory went to school. Do you think he wishes he was able to?"

Taken aback by Stella's question, Maya studied him. "Maybe. He likes history. And Ethan Cruz told me Warren wanted him to take over running the museum. That probably requires a degree."

"You used to want to go to college."

Maya turned to her sister, surprised. "We can't afford that."

"The rest of us shouldn't be holding you back. Maya—" Stella paused, as if gathering her thoughts. "I'm sorry. I feel like I'm always snapping at you these days. That's not how it used to be, and I don't like it."

Maya felt a rush of love for her sister. "I know. We're all pushed to the breaking point. I don't know how to change that. I don't blame anyone for not being able to go to school, though."

"We'll figure it out. Someday. I promise," Stella said. "As soon as we get some rain," she added. "If it ever rains again."

The room went quiet, as if Stella's remark had carried.

"Anyone seen a forecast today?" Steel asked.

Three or four phones instantly came out of pockets. Maya was the first to say, "No rain in sight for the next fourteen days."

Liam whistled. "Never seen a summer start like this before."

"Bet there's going to be a few ranches up for sale before the season is out," Steel said.

"Not either of ours," Noah said firmly. "The Turners and Coopers have weathered hard times before. This won't do us in."

"That's right." Lance said, then must have realized he'd just agreed with a Turner. "I mean... aw, hell... it is right."

Tory laughed, then covered her mouth with a hand. "Sorry. Been away too long, I guess. I forgot how damn tense things get when our families are within spitting distance." She looked glad of the distraction after the conversation she'd been having with Lance.

"No one better spit in my living room," Camila called from the kitchen.

Lance guffawed, and the mood in the room lightened.

"No one's spitting," Olivia called back.

"Yet," Liam added, finishing his drink.

"Good, because dinner is served," Carl announced.

In the bustle to find seats at the Whitfields' long glass table outside on the patio, Maya found herself next to Lance and couldn't help wondering if he'd contrived it somehow or if fate had played a hand.

He helped pull out her chair, and she sat down self-consciously, finding both Olivia's and Stella's gazes on her when she'd settled in. Tory was watching them, too.

She refused to be rattled and busied herself putting her napkin in her lap and taking a sip of wine. Soon Camila and Carl were passing around huge platters of food. There were burgers, steaks and fried chicken. Three kinds of salad and several side dishes.

"Where does she get the energy?" she remarked.

"Wish someone at my house cooked like this," Lance said. "Everyone's too busy."

"Stella cooks when she can, but we're rushed all the time." When everyone was served, Maya took a bite of her burger and sighed with appreciation. "Yummy."

"You said a mouthful. Get it—a mouthful?"

She nearly choked. Since when did Lance make bad puns?

"I get it," she managed when she'd swallowed her bite. This time when she glanced up, both Olivia and Stella looked thoroughly bemused, and she realized she and Lance had been talking like old friends—

Which they kind of were these days.

Friends who kissed now and then.

"What about that announcement of yours?" Steel called out to Camila. Their host and hostess sat at the ends of the table. Steel sat on one side of Carl, Lance on the other. At the far end, Camila waved a hand, as if to say her husband would field that question.

Carl perked up. "You all have probably guessed by now, but I appreciate you letting us say it first. Camila is expecting. The baby's due in March."

"Congratulations!"

"That's wonderful!"

The well wishes came from all directions, and Maya quickly lifted her glass to the couple and called out her own words of happiness, but the truth was the news had made her even more envious of the Whitfields. Shame pierced her for her selfish reaction.

Camila had everything. A husband. A home. A prosperous ranch. A thriving business. She'd worked hard for all of it, and Maya didn't wish her ill. The opposite—she wanted Camila to have every bit of good luck she could get.

Now she would have a baby, too. A perfect family. The Whitfields' star was ascending, while the Turners' was crashing to earth.

The drought wasn't ending. Their once-prosperous ranch was sinking into neglect and debt. They were all working as hard as they could and getting nowhere. Despite what Stella had said, the chances of her getting to go to college were probably nil.

How was that fair?

As far as husbands and children went, the only man paying her any attention—the only man she wanted paying her attention—was her family's sworn enemy, and while they had weathered Noah's marriage to Olivia Cooper, it was partially because—as old-fashioned and sexist as it was—a man kept his family's name. Noah was still a Turner. He might sleep on Cooper ground, but he was still one of theirs. If she married Lance—

Was she even considering marrying Lance?

They'd barely kissed—

Lance bent forward, and underneath the table his fingers brushed hers, sending a shock through her veins that made her suck in a breath. She covered it by lifting a bite of salad to her mouth, not daring to look his way.

When his fingers tangled with hers, she tried to tug them away. She couldn't do this. Not with her whole family—and his—surrounding them. Not when she was feeling so conflicted already. Lance squeezed her hand and let go, and instantly Maya felt bereft.

What was wrong with her?

Why, of all the men in Chance Creek, did it have to be Lance churning up these feeling inside her? She caught Olivia watching her, smiling sympathetically.

Maya brought both her hands above the table and kept them there, manners be damned. If Olivia thought she knew what was going on in her head, she didn't.

Hell, she probably did, didn't she?

Maya took another bite of Camila's delicious dinner, but this time she didn't taste a thing.

Chapter Eight

"MAYBE WE SHOULD forget about re-enactments and just do a Turner–Cooper battle. That was awkward as hell last night," Lance said when he joined Maya at her farm stand the next afternoon.

"Tell me about it. Carl and Camila are saints for trying, but getting our families on the same side is about as hopeless as trying to stop an avalanche in its tracks."

"If an avalanche was heading at me right now, I'd let it come." He plucked at his T-shirt, which was stuck fast to his skin. He was sweating hard, and probably stunk, too, but there was nothing for it right now. He was stealing a few minutes from his work and needed to get back to it pretty quickly.

"Snow sounds pretty good, but five or six months from now we'll be daydreaming about summer again," Maya pointed out.

"You're right." He filched a pack of her cookies and opened the wrapping, folding one in half and popping it into his mouth.

"You going to pay for that?"

"Yup." He finished chewing and swallowed. "The

next Historical Society meeting is tonight," he went on. "Do you think anyone else has raised any money?"

"I don't know. Hey—is that new?" She pointed at an obelisk-style plant holder, with four platforms for houseplants to sit on. "I like that."

"Thanks. Banged it together the other morning. It really needs a second coat of stain, but I couldn't resist bringing it." He yawned. "Man, I need sleep." He'd been up until past midnight working with Bart after leaving the Whitfields'. Bart had been aggravated by how long he'd had to wait for him. It had been all Lance could do to keep his temper.

"I didn't sleep well last night either," she confessed.

Lance wondered what had kept her awake. Had she been thinking of him? Even after he'd gotten home, it had taken a long time to nod off. He'd been thinking of her. In fact, his thoughts had turned X-rated and left him so restless it was a wonder he'd slept at all.

Lance bent toward her and snagged a kiss while the getting was good. He couldn't seem to keep away from her these days.

"Lance—we really shouldn't—"

"Know what we should do? Watering hole."

"Go for a swim? But—the stand—"

"Put out a container for money, and use the honor system. Folks around here aren't going to cheat you."

"What if they cheat you? A chair costs a lot more than a pie."

"They won't cheat me either. All the prices are clear-ly marked. We'll be back in an hour. Come on, Maya—

live a little."

She struggled with her conscience and then lifted her shoulders. "Why not? Should I go back and grab a suit?"

"Nope." He tugged her up and over to her truck. "Let's just get the hell out of here before anyone catches us. We can't be away long."

Fifteen minutes later, he led her through the bushes to a section of Chance Creek that few people knew about. It wasn't one of the larger bends in the waterway that formed natural beaches and gave easy access for swimming, but it was private, and that was what really mattered.

Chance Creek was bigger than Pittance Creek, which ran between their ranches. Still, with the summer so dry, the current was sluggish, barely deep enough in most places to swim. Lance had discovered this deeper pool when he was a teenager, and he was happy to see no one was there when they arrived.

He pulled his T-shirt up and over his head, kicked off his boots and shimmied out of his jeans. "Come on, slowpoke," he admonished Maya.

"Are you keeping those briefs on, or were you planning to skinny—"

Lance peeled off his boxer briefs and tossed them aside, letting Maya get a good look before he turned, lunged for the creek and splashed in. He ducked under the ice-cold water and came up hollering. "Get in here, Turner!"

This was one of those do or die moments, he realized. By stripping off his skivvies, he'd issued her a challenge. If she accepted it, she was agreeing to play with fire. She was agreeing to be with him.

If she chose to stay on dry land—with her clothes on—he'd know it wasn't meant to be.

Lance took a few strokes, watching her.

Maya still hesitated.

"It's just a dip in the river," Lance lied.

It was a lot more than that. He knew it, and she knew it.

He'd probably gone too far.

And yet—

Maya started stripping down. Lance's heart gave a funny extra beat when she stood for a moment in her bra and panties, then stripped them off, too. Hell, she was a glorious sight. A moment later she followed him in.

Every fiber in his body hummed with the desire to touch her. He caught her to him when she swam close. The water in this little back eddy was deep, but he could stand with it to his shoulders. The pool itself was less than ten feet wide. Maya bobbed near him and met him eagerly when he pulled her in. He sucked in a breath when her breasts bumped his chest.

God, she was beautiful. He couldn't quite believe his luck—couldn't believe it would last, either. So much had been going so wrong for so long, he was afraid something could go so right. When her legs wrapped around his waist and her arms around his neck and she met his mouth with her own, he thought he'd died and gone to heaven.

"This was a good idea," she said when they ended the kiss. "A good idea but a really bad idea, too."

"Why is it bad?" He slid a hand to cup her bottom, holding her tight against his hardness. She had to know how much he wanted her. Seemed like she wanted him pretty badly, too.

"Because it feels so good."

"Yeah, it does." Lance kissed her again, ducked his head to take one of her nipples into his mouth, and he was lost, all thought of restraint disappearing like mist before a strong sun. Maya didn't stop his explorations of his body, and pretty soon Lance was aching with need, finding it hard to hold back.

"I want you," he murmured into her hair. "Say I can have you, Maya."

"You can have me."

He nearly groaned out loud in thankfulness. But where—

"Like this. Right now."

"Here in the creek?"

"Yes. Hurry." She sounded ready to growl. If she was ready, so was he.

"Protection?"

"I'm good. Just get going. I've been thinking about you for days."

"I've been thinking about you, too. Hell, Maya." He shifted her in his arms, nudged against her, then groaned as he pushed inside. Maya was hot and slick, tight around him. He crushed her in his arms, needing to feel every part of her against his skin. He wanted to touch all of her at once. Wanted to kiss her everywhere.

Judging by Maya's reactions, she was feeling the same way. She urged him on, pressing her hips to his, tightening her hold on his neck, moving with him, crooning in his ear.

Lance increased his pace, straining to hold her steady as he moved inside of her. He was immersed in the sensation—oblivious to anything else, captivated by Maya's every touch.

When she came, moaning in his ear, bucking against him and clinging to him like she'd never let go, she pulled him into an orgasm that had him calling out his release.

When it was over, they broke apart and floated in the water, both of them breathing hard. Maya's eyes, just above the water line, watched him as if she was afraid their encounter might have changed his mind about her.

Nothing could be further from the truth. He wanted her more than ever. He wanted her—

He caught her hand again. Pulled her close. "I don't know why we work, but we do."

"We work because inside we're the same. We want the same things."

Lance searched her gaze with his own. "What do you mean?" Somehow this conversation seemed more intimate than what they'd just done. Real and raw—the last thing he'd thought to find with the girl who'd grown up right next door.

"I mean we care about our history. We want to preserve it. We want to share it with other people. I've never met anyone like you before."

Had she been as lonely as he'd been? Lance had never put it that way before in his thoughts, but it was true. He'd felt like no one had ever truly understood him. But Maya did.

"You're amazing, you know that?" he said huskily.

He wrapped his arms around her, and when she shivered, he picked her up and carried her out of the water, setting her down on a blanket he'd snagged from the back of his truck. He caught hold of her hand and squeezed it, wanting her to know this was way more to him than a dip in the creek. She leaned back, letting the sun warm her wet skin. She looked like a goddess—like a statue carved by some ancient artist. Suddenly Lance couldn't stand the idea they wouldn't always be together.

"I mean it, Maya. You're something special."

She turned toward him. "So are you."

Was that enough when everything else was stacked again them being together?

Lance wished he knew.

WHEN THEY WERE dressed and heading back to the farm stand, Maya wondered if she'd made a mistake. Being with Lance had been an earth-shattering revelation. She'd never done it in a creek, and if the truth was told, she'd never done it with a man so confident in his own body and hers. Lance was so natural in his skin.

He'd greeted her nakedness with pure pleasure, and he'd touched her as if he already knew every inch of her body.

She wanted him to know it. Wanted him to know her mind, too.

Thought maybe he already did.

Which was the problem. How could they be together long-term?

She wanted long-term.

"What if we let the audience pick sides?" Lance said suddenly, drawing her from her thoughts. She watched the road unfold before them, trying to focus on his words.

"Audience? What do you mean?"

"Sorry. Thinking about the re-enactment. Whenever I get into a fight at the Dancing Boot—which doesn't happen except when Liam's around," he hurried to add, "people always pick sides and jump in. What if we let the audience pick sides before the re-enactment? They wouldn't be able to jump in, but they could cheer on their side."

"Won't everyone want to be on the Colonies' side?"

"Usually, but we could explain what we're doing and that it would be more fun if people picked a team."

"But we all know how the battle ends." She decided she was relieved Lance was talking about something other than their impossible relationship. Time enough to figure that out later. "People won't pick a losing team, will they?"

"They might. We could get some flags or patches or

something. Team Colonies or Team Redcoats. That kind of thing."

"I like that idea."

"I like you." Lance cleared his throat. "I mean…" His voice warmed. "Well, it's true. I do like you."

Maya sighed. Back to the impossible. "We're playing with fire, you know," she said.

"I always liked playing with fire."

She hadn't thought she did. She'd kept a straight and narrow course over the years. No one had ever doubted she was a good girl.

A good girl who'd caused the dissolution of her best friend's family. What would Lance say if he knew it was her fault his dad went to jail? Her fault his mom abandoned him?

She'd been so self-absorbed back then she hadn't stopped to think before she'd acted. Her own mother had just left, after all. Made Liam drive her to town and then kept right on going. Maya would never forget that awful day. Waiting for Mary to come home. All of them sure she'd come back—

Until it was clear she wouldn't.

Liam had blamed it on the Coopers. He'd told her Enid Cooper had driven their mother away.

She'd taken it as gospel truth. Shattered by her mother's desertion, she'd told the sheriff what she'd seen in the Coopers' barn. Deer hides curing out of season.

Next thing she'd known, Dale had gone to jail.

Back then, she'd been too young to understand that

the Coopers had nothing to do with her mom's desertion. Mary wasn't cut out for ranching life. Had always wanted something more.

Had reached her breaking point.

The truth was the Coopers couldn't make the Turners stop liking each other. The worst they could do is shine a light on problems that were already there.

Maya studied Lance, trying to piece it all together.

"What are you thinking?" he asked, cupping her chin in his hand.

"Nothing." She couldn't tell him what was running through her head.

Lance pulled in near the vegetable stand and parked the truck. When he kissed her again, she wondered if she was making the biggest mistake of her life.

"THERE YOU ARE," Lance said when Maya finally arrived for the Historical Society meeting later that night. "Been waiting for you." His whole body came on alert, eager to get close to her again. The wasn't the time for that, though.

"Here I am." She glanced into the meeting room, where other attendees were taking their seats. "Not as many people as last time."

"The first meeting is always the biggest. People lose interest when they realize how much work it's going to be. By the end it's always the same people who show up and follow through. I was worried you might not come."

"Why wouldn't I?"

He hesitated. Pitched his voice lower. "I was a little afraid you'd change your mind after we—"

Maya met his gaze. "I haven't changed my mind, but I don't know what we're going to do, either. If Liam finds out—"

"Fortunately, Liam's not into history." Unless it was Turner history.

"True enough."

"So how do you want to handle this?"

She didn't pretend not to understand him. "I'm not ready for Liam—and the rest of my family—to know about us."

It was the answer he expected, but it hit him like a blow. Ego, he figured. He knew she was right. Steel would have a lot of choice things to say if he knew about them, and he couldn't imagine how Virginia would react. "We'd better sit apart then."

"I guess so." But she lingered next to him. "I wish—"

"I know." He definitely knew. If there was a way to get her alone right now, he would. He was aching to touch her.

"Let's get started, folks," Warren Hill said.

Maya slipped past Lance into the room, brushing his arm with her fingertips as she did so, and went to sit by Mia. Lance found a seat next to Bart, his whole body pulsing with need.

"I shouldn't even be here. I've got too much to do at the house," Bart complained.

"Warehouse," Lance corrected him testily. It was far

from resembling a home, no matter what Bart thought.

"What's up with Maya?" Bart asked him, ignoring the barb.

"We were just talking about fundraising." He wasn't going to admit what was really going on.

Bart squirmed down a little in his seat, and Lance didn't bother to ask him how much he'd raised.

"What does Maggie think about the warehouse?" he asked, just to ruffle Bart's feathers.

"I told you I'm keeping it a secret until it's done."

"I'm not sure that's the best course of action." Lance had two sisters, and in his experience women had definite opinions about where they lived. "Don't you want her input?"

Bart gave a stiff shake of his head. "She's not even talking to me. She's pissed I keep staying out so late. I told her she has to trust me."

"How'd that go over?"

"It'll all be worth it when I show her our new place."

Warren brought the meeting to order, and Lance made a mental note to take the matter up later. It could take months to get the warehouse in shape. He wasn't sure Bart would still be married by then.

"The Fourth of July is coming right up," Warren began. "We need to settle things about the re-enactment."

"What about the fundraising we've all been doing?" Lance called out. It irritated him that Bart had blown it off, and he wanted to know if everyone else had, too.

"Should we each stand up and see what we've raised?" Maya called out from the other side of the room.

A rush of gratitude coursed through Lance. He was starting to feel like he was the only one outside Warren who saw just how dire their situation was, but Maya had his back.

"I've raised nearly twenty-five dollars putting out a donation cup in my business," Mia said.

"I've raised thirty-one dollars and twenty-five cents from our B and B guests," Autumn Cruz said.

"I made seventy-five dollars," Rick Crandall said. "Did three dump runs for people with my truck, and I'm donating all the proceeds."

"That's great," Lance said, although inside he was reeling with disappointment. The numbers were tiny. "I got about two-hundred and fifty selling furniture." A murmur ran around the room.

"About sixty-five for me," Maya put in. "I'm charging extra for my baked goods at my farm stand."

By the time they'd heard from everyone, Lance estimated they'd raised nearly eight hundred dollars all told. That wasn't nearly enough.

"That's a good start." Warren tried to be hearty, but his voice was strained, and Lance knew why. Looking around at the animated faces of the participants, he hated to be the one to bring them back to reality.

"How much do we need?" Bart asked, doing the job for him. At least he was paying attention for the moment, Lance thought.

"I have some numbers," a female voice rang out.

Lance craned his neck to see who'd said that and was surprised to see Megan Lawrence stand up. He remembered she'd gotten her real estate license straight out of school and was working hard to grow her sales as an agent in town.

When no one stopped her, she went on. "As you know, I'm a real estate agent, and I can tell you right now that it's most likely impossible for us to raise enough money to purchase a building for a permanent home for the museum before our contract with LeRoy is up. The only thing we can do is find a commercial rental to house the collections. We'll need two months' rent to move in, and we'll have to carry an insurance policy that will protect the owner of the building since it will be open to the public. We need money to renovate the building and create new exhibits. I think with a lot of volunteer help, and maybe some donations in building supplies, we can get this done for a fairly reasonable number." She named a sum that made Lance wince. She was right; it was reasonable but a far, far cry from the amount they'd earned.

Someone whistled. Everyone deflated.

"We're going to need to do a lot more fundraising," Mia said, echoing everyone's thoughts.

"Like I said, we've made a good start." Warren spoke up after too long a pause. "I'm proud to see everyone pitching in."

"But we need a lot more pitching in," Lance said, unable to contain himself. "No slackers." He sent a significant look Bart's way.

"We'll keep at it," Sean said. "As we go, people will figure out what works and what doesn't."

It sounded logical, but Lance had seen this happen enough times to know the opposite was true: enthusiasm was highest at the beginning of a project. If they didn't build momentum right away, they would start small and only get smaller.

"Fundraising on our own isn't working," he asserted. "We need to try something else." Maya had backed him up. Maybe it was time for him to return the favor.

Sean shrugged. "Like what?"

"Maya came up with a suggestion last week, and I've got a suggestion, too. I think we can make this reenactment the best damn bit of local entertainment anyone's ever seen."

"Go on," Warren said.

Lance nodded his thanks. "Like Maya said, we'll make the re-enactment like a cable television historical drama. We'll hype up the story ahead of time until people are salivating at the mouth to see what happens." He talked about getting people to pick a side to support. "We'll introduce characters on both sides of the fight and get people hooked into their stories by acting out several scenes. Then we'll execute a real battle—the Battle of Cowpens, one of the most important fights in the war. When that's done, we'll show what happened in the characters' lives afterward. We'll raise our rates, get our vendors to give us a cut of their earnings, ask for volunteers to cover all the costs—"

"Wait—last week you were against all that," Mark said.

"Last week I was wrong," Lance told him. "So I changed my mind."

"We've only got a few weeks until the re-enactment," Warren cautioned. "Where are we supposed to get this... story?"

"I'm almost done with a script," Maya spoke up.

"I've already got the battle all mapped out," Lance said. He went on to describe all the plans he and Maya had talked about.

"Sounds like you've got a new partner to help you run this thing," Warren said to Lance. "The last few years you've shouldered too much of the responsibility for the re-enactment. Having help should make it a lot easier. You okay with that, Maya?"

"Of course," she said eagerly.

Lance was caught off guard by Warren's suggestion. A partner? Maya? But—

This was supposed to be his thing. He remembered Virginia's warnings. They needed to secure the Founder's Prize. Win the Ridley property. This was supposed to be his contribution.

"I'm not sure—"

"I'd love to help, too," Storm Hall called out, cutting him off. "Avery, we could partner up and get the word out about the re-enactment. We'll write copy, hit all the social media outlets and get posters made up—"

"Riley and I could partner up getting all the props and supplies we need," Mia said. "We could make banners and pennants for each side."

"Sean and I will partner together to make sure everyone's got their replica weapons in working order," Mark said.

Suddenly people were chatting all around the room. Partnering up and volunteering for the various jobs. Lance knew he should be grateful for their enthusiasm, but instead panic was building in his gut. Now this definitely wasn't a Cooper affair anymore. By the time the meeting broke and he caught up with Maya in the parking lot, it was far too late to do anything about it. Warren had set their next meeting in three days, at which time the script was supposed to be ready and people were going to be assigned parts. The whole thing had gotten out of hand.

Virginia was going to be furious.

"Guess we're really on the hook now," Maya said happily. She seemed in high spirits. He wished he felt the same. What was he supposed to say? He couldn't tell her he'd meant to keep control of the re-enactment. That would be churlish. He leaned against her truck, at a loss. "Thanks for backing me up in there," he finally said. At least the re-enactment should be a good one.

"Thanks for backing me up." Maya plucked at her blouse. Even the nights were hot lately. On any other occasion, Lance would have been perfectly happy to stand there in the parking lot, beneath the stars, chatting until morning. Maybe stealing another kiss or two. Or a whole lot more.

But when he saw a figure moving toward them, he

was almost relieved. Virginia had put him in charge of winning the Founder's Prize, and he'd blown it big time tonight.

He stepped back, straightened his shirt and tried to assume a casual stance. "I'll be in touch," he said loudly. "Looking forward to seeing that script."

"Lance, I thought I'd missed you," Bart said. "Oh, hey, Maya. Good meeting, huh?"

"Yes, I think we made a good start." She took a step or two back from Lance, increasing the distance between them.

Bart had already lost interest in her. "Lance, let's go do that thing."

"What thing?" Maya asked.

"Guy stuff," Bart said. "Don't you worry about it."

"But—"

Bart took Lance's arm and dragged him away. Lance thought Maya might follow.

"Isn't Maggie expecting you home, Bart?" she called after them. "She said you've been staying out pretty late this past week."

"I'll be home when I'm home. Come on," he added to Lance.

Lance looked back helplessly and shrugged as Maya shook her head. He wondered what Maggie had been saying to her.

"I really think you should tell Maggie what you're up to," he told Bart when they were far enough away for Maya not to overhear.

"Not until I have the walls up inside the warehouse.

She needs to be able to visualize what it'll look like when it's our home."

Lance wasn't sure walls would be enough. "I can't help you forever. I've got my own chores to do."

"MAGGIE?" MAYA SAID when she answered the door a half hour after getting home. She was tired, but she still needed to spend a few hours baking before she could get to bed. When someone had knocked at the front door, she couldn't think who it would be at this hour. Now Maggie was standing on her front porch, looking so woebegone, she waved her right in. "What's wrong?" she asked when Maggie was seated at the kitchen table with a glass of lemonade.

"It's gone. All our savings."

"What do you mean?"

"Bart emptied our bank account. He's been staying out until all hours, going to work in the morning and doing it all over again. I went to take money out for groceries tonight and checked the balance on our savings account. It's at zero."

A chill ran down Maya's spine. That didn't sound good. "I saw him a half hour ago at the re-enactment meeting."

Maggie shut her eyes. "I was afraid he'd left town."

"I don't think so." Maya remembered what he'd said. "He grabbed Lance when the meeting was over. Said they had to go do something."

"What?"

"He didn't say. It seemed like a secret. Maybe it's a

surprise."

"What kind of a surprise costs all our money? We've worked so hard to save it."

"Don't panic. There's got to be an explanation." She couldn't think what it could be, though. She hoped Bart hadn't decided to splurge on a new truck or a vacation or something that would set them back on their plans. Getting a place of their own was obviously a big priority for Maggie—and for him, given everything he'd been saying.

"I've been looking for work, but I haven't found anything yet. If Bart leaves me—"

"He won't leave you." Maya hoped she was right. What was the man thinking? Lance would never act this way—

As if she would know anything about how Lance would act.

"I've got to go. Mom's putting Katie to bed, and I said I'd be home soon. I had to tell someone, but I couldn't admit to my parents what he did. Maya, what if it's all really gone? What are we going to do?"

Maya didn't know what to tell her. "I'll call Lance. I'll ask him to have Bart call you."

Maggie nodded numbly.

"I'm sure it's all going to work out," Maya said as she left. She wished she could do more. When she called Lance, he didn't answer. She left a message. Told him to have Bart call home.

And quickly slipped the phone back in her pocket when Stella walked in the front door.

"Was that Maggie?" she asked as she carried a bag of groceries into the kitchen. "Lord, what a mess."

"I'll clean up before bed." Maya wished she could go to sleep now. The day had been too long.

"I'll help. I know you're working hard."

"You're working hard, too."

How much more of this could they all take?

Chapter Nine

"THIS IS QUITE the order," Heather Hall said almost a week later, scanning the list that Lance had brought with him to the hardware store she owned in town. "I think we have most of this. I'll help you find what you're looking for." Leading him down the aisles, Heather chuckled. "I hope this isn't to start rebuilding the Ridley ranch already. Last time I saw Virginia, she told me that in her mind it already belongs to you Coopers."

"Nah, we're saving that project for next year," Lance said easily, but he tensed a little at the reminder of the ongoing contest. A problem for another time, he decided. "I'm doing some work for the re-enactment," he told Heather.

"The Fourth of July event? I thought you would already have everything you need. You've put it on so many times before."

Lance grinned. "Things are going to be a little different this year."

The preparation was already a lot different than he was used to. Maya had brought the rough draft of her script to the last meeting, and everyone had been pleasantly surprised by it. Even the old timers admitted it was good. With everyone now on the same page, tryouts for the speaking roles were in a few days.

While people were deferring to Maya about the script, they were coming to him with questions about the battle. He realized he must have done a good job the last couple of years if the other society members respected his opinion so much. Several of the men had called him up to ask for his advice on fundraising outside of the re-enactment, too, and he'd been happy to talk to them.

He'd volunteered to help build sets, knowing he'd enjoy the work far more than helping Bart with his warehouse. Bart was acting like a bull in a china shop these days, far too short on sleep to be safe around power tools, which meant Lance was doing his ranch chores, helping with the sets and then working late into the night rather than leaving Bart alone. The last time he asked about Maggie, the man nearly took his head off.

Maggie wasn't too pleased with his ongoing absences, but Bart refused to tell her what he was doing. Lance had a feeling the whole thing was going to backfire on him, but who was he to hand out advice? His surreptitious flirtation with Maya—which was all it was these days since they had no time to spend with each other—was probably going to lead to disaster, too.

"Different how?" Heather asked when they stopped to examine different types of wooden planks.

"I probably shouldn't say too much," Lance said. "You'll hear about it soon enough."

Heather smiled. "I think I already have. Is this what Storm was talking about, making it have more of a story? She's been talking about the re-enactment non-stop since she joined the publicity team. She's been designing posters and social media announcements."

Lance nodded, remembering that both women lived at Crescent Hall. "Something like that. It's going to be big, and you won't want to miss it."

"I'm excited already."

He wasn't sure if she was just humoring him or if she meant it, but talking about it made him excited, too. Lance hadn't felt this energized in a long time. He'd never felt so much a part of his community, either. His life was turning around, and he couldn't help thinking it was all thanks to Maya.

"YOU LOOK FANTASTIC in that dress. You definitely need to be one of the actresses in the re-enactment," Alice said, stepping back to look Maya over from head to foot.

Maya, clothed in a Revolutionary War–era gown, posed in front of one of the full-length mirrors in Alice's sewing workshop on the second floor of her carriage house at Two Willows. She'd come to help Alice comb through her costumes for the ones that would be suitable for the re-enactment. Many people in the Historical Society had their own that they'd bought or made over the years, but she wanted to get more people involved, and Maya knew that providing ready-made costumes to them would help.

Stella was manning her farm stand for an hour. When Alice had suggested she try on one of the gowns, she couldn't resist. She'd made Alice try one on, too.

"You look great, too. Maybe you should get involved," Maya said.

"Maybe. I've always been the one to dress up the actors, not be one myself."

"But—"

"Knock, knock—anyone home?" a man called up the stairs.

Was that Lance? Maya stiffened, suddenly self-conscious, although her old-fashioned outfit was quite modest. Its skirt reached the ground, and the fitted top had long sleeves and buttoned up to her neck. With an apron tied around her waist, she was almost matronly.

"Come on up," Alice called out.

A moment later Lance bounded into the dressing room. "Cass told me you'd be up here—" He broke off. "Maya, what are you doing here?"

"She's helping me pull together a bunch of costumes to bring to your next meeting." Alice turned to face him and pulled Maya in beside her. "Which do you like better?"

"I, uh… they're both nice." But Lance kept his gaze on Maya, and Maya began to feel her cheeks heat. She thought she caught Alice smiling.

"Did you need something?" Maya asked Lance.

"Just here to pick up a few things Alice has for our stage sets."

"I'll go grab them." Alice moved to the far side of

the room. Lance came closer to Maya. "Been thinking about you," he murmured and snatched a kiss.

Maya's breath caught. She'd tried to convince herself that she was making too much out of the fact they'd been together, but whenever Lance was near, she found it hard to keep things in perspective.

"Been thinking about you, too," she admitted. In the past few days, she'd almost convinced herself she should break things off before someone got hurt, but now that he was here with her, all she could think of was how they could be together again.

"Love that dress. How can something so un-sexy be so sexy?" he murmured.

Maya laughed. "I'm not sure. I wonder if your uniform will be like that, too?"

"You better believe it." He tugged her a little closer. "God, I want to be with you," he whispered into her hair, his mouth near her ear, his breath warm on her skin. "I've been thinking about you all the time."

"I know."

Alice appeared again and moved to another part of the room, gathering things as she went. Maya sighed and stepped away from Lance, searching for something else to talk about.

"Have you seen Bart lately?" she ventured.

Lance's expression was hard to read. "Here and there," he said. Alice disappeared into a corner behind some racks.

Maya moved closer to Lance again. "Maggie's distraught. Did you know he cleaned out their savings account?" She bit her lip. "Shoot, I shouldn't have said that."

Lance's surprise seemed so genuine she knew he hadn't been in on that. "Cleaned out their account? Hell."

"He didn't mention that?"

"No." He ran a hand through his hair. "Look, I can't tell you details, but maybe you could get a message to Maggie. Tell her he's trying. He might not get it exactly right, but he's really trying."

"What's that supposed to mean?"

"I wish I could tell you." Lance shoved his hands in his pockets. "I'll say one thing. I'm going to give him what-for when I see him again."

"Don't tell him I told you anything," she rushed to say. "Maggie would hate me for that."

He shook his head. "Those two are hopeless. I mean, if people like that can't get it right, who can? Maybe all this love stuff is just impossible."

"Is that what you really think?"

Lance glanced up. Held her gaze. "No. I think it must be hard. Lots of people screw it up. That doesn't mean it can't be done right, though. I want... well, when I get married, I want it to be forever."

"Me, too," she said softly. It was time to turn the conversation to something less personal, though. Alice would be back any second. She bustled over to the next table and picked up a length of cloth, the full skirt of her old-fashioned dress swishing around her ankles. She couldn't help but smile at the feel of it, and when she looked over her shoulder, Lance was smiling, too. "What?" she asked him.

"There's something right about you in that old-fashioned getup."

"Well, I like old-fashioned pastimes. I guess I like old-fashioned clothes, too. Sometimes, at least. I can't imagine digging a garden in this."

"Guess I'd have to dig it for you." He pitched his voice low and moved closer.

"Back off, young man," Alice barked, and they both jumped. Alice laughed long and hard at them. "Figured if you two were going to get all nostalgic for the old days, you'd better get a taste of what they were really like. You'd better believe the two of you would have a chaperone like me getting in the way."

"There's nothing to get in the way of," Maya said quickly.

"Unfortunately." Lance must have realized what he'd betrayed. He shot a glance at Alice. "I mean, unfortunately, I've got to get going."

"Here are the boxes."

"Thanks." Lance moved to take them from her.

"I didn't know you two were friends," Alice said.

"Lance has been selling furniture at my farm stand," she explained quickly to Alice, hoping she wasn't blushing and giving herself away. "People stop to buy my pies and end up taking home a rocking chair."

"Anything to help raise money," Lance added.

"That sounds nice. I'll stop by sometime."

"You should wear that getup while you man the

farm stand," Lance said to Maya. "I bet it would pull in the customers like crazy. And it would be advertising for the new and improved re-enactment."

"That's a great idea," Alice said. "You can take the costume home with you."

"It would be awfully hot to wear something like this all day out in the sun. I think I'll save dressing up for the re-enactment. See you later, Lance." She wished Alice was somewhere else so he could kiss her again.

"See you."

Maya had a feeling he wished they were alone, too.

LANCE ENTERED THORN Hill's stables later than he'd meant to that evening, cursing himself for getting so far behind when he still had hours of work to do. When he glanced around, however, he saw the stalls had already been mucked out, the saddles had been polished and all the gear neatly put away.

In fact, he hardly recognized the place. Lance had to admit he wasn't the neatest man, especially when it came to ranching. His father, for all his propensity to cross the line with the law, had been particular about the way he ran his ranch. He would have had something to say about Lance's practices.

Lance rubbed a hand over his jaw as he took in the way the tools stored nearby had been cleaned and oiled.

Noah was making him look bad. Again.

Outside, he looked around the ranch and realized Noah had been busy. One of the nearby fence posts, which had been leaning for months, was straight now.

The cattle looked well-tended. Everything was ship-shape.

What was Noah's plan? Was he trying to call out the slovenly way they were running the ranch? Was he trying to take over Thorn Hill while Steel was off doing whatever it was he did when he was away, and he was busy with Historical Society business?

Speaking of Steel.

Lance watched his brother descend the back steps and cross the lawn to join him.

"What's wrong?" Steel called out as Tory opened the back door and followed him. "Why are you standing here like that? Aren't there chores to do?"

"Noah beat me to them."

Steel was nodding along before he finished. "Yeah, he did a bunch of mine, too." He smiled lopsidedly. "On the one hand, he's getting things done, and we could use some help. On the other, I don't like Turners messing around in my business."

Lance stilled, suddenly uneasy. Was there something in particular Steel was worried Noah might discover? They'd grown up with the need to keep quiet, and Lance remembered this anxious, low-in-the-gut feeling all too well. Whatever Steel was involved in, Lance hoped his brother was smart enough to keep it far away from Thorn Hill.

He would have to sort that out later, though. When Tory wasn't standing nearby.

"I think you should let Noah have at it," she said. "We can take the profit and let him do the work."

"No can do," Steel said firmly. "This is our ranch."

"How about we give him a taste of his own medicine?" Lance asked.

Steel narrowed his eyes. "How?"

"Let's sneak over to the Flying W and see how Noah likes it when somebody messes with his ranch."

Tory held up her hands and took a step back. "I'm staying out of this."

"You stay out of everything, don't you?" Steel asked bluntly. "One of these days you're going to have to decide if you're one of us or not."

"Whatever." Tory headed back toward the house.

Both men watched her go. "I can't figure her out," Steel said.

"I can't, either."

"She wants to be a lawyer."

"I know."

What would their father have thought about that?

ASIDE FROM HER brief trip to Two Willows, Maya had spent all day at the farm stand, and now she was facing another night of baking. It was hot, she was tired—and hungry—and all she really wanted to do was go to bed, so when Mary called just before dinnertime, she could barely find the energy to pick up.

"I'm just about to eat, Mom."

"I know. I meant to call you earlier, but I had such a full day with Liz."

Maya rolled her eyes. Had her mother really called her just to remind her she loved her new daughter more?

"I told Liz about your re-enactment," Mary went on. "She thought the idea was really fun and wondered if she could get the community here to put one together. We spent the whole day going around to different museums, looking for inspiration."

"You might want to let her know it's a lot more work than she thinks," Maya said tiredly.

"Liz is so smart, though. I'm sure she's up for the challenge."

She heard the front door crash open, and Liam rushed into the kitchen. "Someone's on our property."

"I'll have to call you back, Mom."

"But—"

Maya hung up. "Who is it?" she asked Liam, following him through the house to the study, where he knelt down to work the combination lock of the family's gun safe.

"I don't know. I was working on the organic certification paperwork and saw the stable door hanging open." Liam got the safe open and pulled out a rifle. "Someone's out there."

"You sure it's not Noah?"

"Noah's in town with Olivia."

He stood and moved to shut the safe again, but Maya caught the door before he could. "You're not going back out there alone." She pulled a second rifle out of the safe before shutting it tightly. Then she followed Liam back to the kitchen, where they kept the ammo in a drawer.

"You remember how to use one of these?" Liam loaded his weapon, then passed the box of ammo to Maya.

"Of course I do." She'd grown up around firearms and knew as well as her brothers how to operate and maintain them. She wasn't sure how effective she would be right now, though. This was just what she needed at the end of a long day, when she had another long day ahead of her tomorrow.

As they left the house, she found herself more afraid than she'd usually be. There'd been all that trouble at Two Willows recently, and those murders in Silver Falls. Usually Chance Creek was a quiet town, but it didn't seem as quiet these days.

Of course, it was probably a couple of local kids just trying to make trouble. At worst, maybe a vagrant looking for a place to sleep for the night. Still, it put into stark perspective how thin she was stretching herself these days. With so much going on, there wasn't any time in her life for something to go wrong.

Before she and Liam made it to the bottom of the stairs in front of the porch, a truck pulled around the house and parked. Already on alert, Maya tensed at the sight of it, but it was just Noah and Olivia coming home.

They climbed out of the vehicle and quickly came to meet them, both of them visibly startled at the sight of their weapons. "Going hunting?" Noah joked, but his stance told Maya he was ready to join in if there was trouble.

"There's someone out in the stables," Liam said.

Noah immediately sobered. "Wait in the house with Maya," he ordered Olivia, reaching out to take Maya's rifle.

Maya pulled it away from him. "Go get your own rifle. This is my home, too, remember?" More than likely he had a sidearm on him anyway.

For a moment it looked like Noah would argue, but Liam was already heading off across the field. Maya followed, and Noah and Olivia fell in behind her.

At least she could use this incident for inspiration, Maya thought grimly as they approached the stable. Defending home and family, that's what their new story for the re-enactment was all about.

When they were close, she heard a thump and a quiet curse. She heard someone else say something and a scraping sound. One of the horses made a soft noise, but the animals weren't panicked, which meant whoever was in there knew their way around horses.

Liam stopped a few yards from the building and leveled his rifle at the entrance. "Whoever's in there, come out where I can see you. Slowly."

Another muffled curse came from inside.

"Don't make me come in there," Liam called. Maya positioned herself beside him, her weapon at the ready.

"Settle down. We're coming out," a man's voice responded.

Maya knew that voice. She lowered her weapon.

"Lance?" she asked a moment before he stepped out with a pitchfork in his hand. Steel stepped out beside him carrying a shovel.

Beside her, Liam scowled. "Coopers! I should have known. What the hell are you doing in there—trying to steal our horses?"

"We're not stealing anything," Lance said.

Maya looked from the pitchfork to the shovel. Both showed signs of being used. "Are you... mucking out our stables?"

Both Cooper men looked mighty sheepish. "Yeah," Lance muttered finally.

"We're teaching your brother a lesson," Steel added. He pointed to Noah. "Stop interfering at Thorn Hill."

"That's right," Lance said. "You meddle at our ranch, and we'll meddle at yours." He waved his pitchfork at Noah.

"Isn't that the way it should be?" Olivia spoke up. "Both our families helping each other? We're all related now."

Lance recoiled. "What the hell side are you on?" he demanded of his sister.

"Both sides—that's the whole point." She marched forward to face him. "It's time to stop all this bickering. Noah is your brother-in-law whether you like it or not, so stop being such a big baby."

"Watch it," Steel said. "Just because you married Noah doesn't mean everything that's ours is his. He needs to stay on his land."

"And you need to stay on yours," Liam blustered. "Don't think you're going to get away with this, Cooper. You can't come in here and..."

"And what?" Noah demanded, stepping forward. "Clean our stables? What the hell is wrong with you, Liam? They can muck out our stables any old time they want to. Olivia's right; we should be on the same side now."

"We aren't on the same side. Never have been, never will be," Liam stated.

"Hell, Liam, get back to the house and put that thing away." Noah waved at Liam's rifle. "Steel, Lance—thanks for your help. I appreciate it." He moved forward and shook Steel's hand before Steel could react. He shook Lance's, too. "How about we sit down together over coffee soon. Make some plans and see if we can find some efficiencies—"

"The only efficient thing to do is get rid of every Cooper around! To hell with this." Liam turned on his heel and strode back toward the house.

"Any other chores you two want to do on our ranch?" Maya asked, knowing that Liam would be impossible for days.

"No," Steel said shortly.

"Then I guess we should all say good-night," Noah said. He sounded tired.

"Night, Maya," Lance said, earning a look from his brother.

"Night, Lance. Night, Steel," she said evenly.

Time to bake some pies.

Chapter Ten

WHEN LANCE DROVE up to Maya's farm stand the next morning, he hesitated a minute before getting out of his truck. He hadn't been this embarrassed about anything since the time he'd fumbled a football at the three-yard line.

In the light of day, retaliatory stall-mucking seemed like a damn foolish thing to do, and he wondered how Steel was coping. His older brother had slipped out long before daybreak. When Lance had made it to the barn, he could see Steel had made sure to do his morning chores. So had Lance. If Noah came by, he wouldn't find anything to do.

"I hope you saved me a pie," he said to Maya as he pulled a couple of new nightstands from the bed of his truck. Pretending last evening hadn't even happened seemed like the best course. He'd returned to the Flying W and then gone into town to help Bart, as usual. He'd given his friend a lecture about the need to come clean with his wife. Bart hadn't listened any more than he ever did, even when Lance threatened to pack up his tools and leave.

Should he just tell Maya what was going on and let

her tell Maggie? Would that save a lot of heartbreak or just make it all worse?

He wasn't sure.

Maya gave him a wry look. "I did. I was afraid if I let you down, you would break into my kitchen and bake me two pies to get back at me."

"Go on, get your digs while you can. Your brother is an interfering old fart." Lance found he didn't mind her teasing, though. He deserved it for being an ass.

"Tell me about it." A smile quirked her lips. "But Liam could have shot you. You need to be careful."

"Won't happen again," he promised.

"Too bad. I wouldn't mind seeing some cooperation between our families." When he didn't answer, she sighed, boxed up a pie and slid it his way. "Here. On me."

"Thanks." He couldn't help but smile when she looked at him like that. Then he shook his head. "I know I'm being stubborn, but me and Liam—we've got a past."

"Want to tell me about it?"

"Ancient history." He waved it off. He didn't need to revisit high school, even if Liam couldn't seem to let it go.

Maya didn't press it. "At least out here, on our own, we can just be ourselves," she said.

"Sometimes I think you understand me better than my family does." He took her hand. Kissed her palm.

"You mean that?"

"Guess that's why you're my girlfriend. We're compatible."

"AM I YOUR girlfriend?" Maya asked, still tingling from his kiss.

"Aren't you?"

Maya wasn't sure how to answer that. She wanted to say yes. It felt like she'd be lying if she said no. Judging by how she felt in that moment, and how they'd been acting these past weeks, the label fit.

Before she could say so, however, all her worries and doubts rushed to the forefront of her thoughts. Could she be his girlfriend if nobody was allowed to know she was his girlfriend? Would they even be able to keep things hidden if they kept going like this?

What would happen if they couldn't?

Noah and Olivia had survived going public, even if their relationship still caused drama around both families' ranches on a daily basis. Maya knew things would be different with her and Lance, though.

For one thing, Lance wasn't Noah. The incident the night before had thrown that into stark perspective. Even with all that was going on between them, Lance couldn't resist making trouble, trying to get back at Noah over an imagined slight. Noah, on the other hand, kept working tirelessly to bring the families together, as if he could repair the split between them through sheer will.

Not likely.

Maya had to admit she didn't want Lance to be Noah, anyway. Noah was too even-tempered. Lance had spirit. She was attracted to that. She liked that he stood up for himself. She had to admit she kind of liked his bad boy streak, too.

It would be chaos if they brought their relationship into the open, however. Lance couldn't coexist with her family even if he wanted to. He and Liam were sworn enemies in a way that Noah and Steel never had been. Jed would have a heart attack if he knew they were together. Stella would get all distant again. Who knew what Virginia Cooper would do.

The silence stretched out awkwardly, and Lance saved her from having to answer. "I want to see you tonight," he told her. "Alone. Somewhere private."

Maya knew it wasn't a good idea. Still, she heard herself say, "I'll see if I can get away," knowing she would need more time to make a decision. "I'll text you."

Lance hung around a little longer, clearly unwilling to leave. "Guess I'd better not leave the cattle alone for too long," he said finally.

Casting about for something to keep him there, Maya asked a question she'd been wondering about.

"Did you always know you wanted to be a rancher?" She thought Liam had. She couldn't imagine her brother doing anything else. Lance seemed kind of restless these days, though.

Lance chuckled but not in a humorous way. "I'll let you in on a little secret. I've never wanted to be a rancher."

"Really? What do you want to be?" She hadn't expected that answer at all.

"Seems stupid to say it when it's got no chance of coming true."

"Tell me." Suddenly she needed to know. She liked feeling close to Lance, which meant she needed to know his secret aspirations.

"A history teacher. Thought I'd have my degree by now. Thought I'd work part-time at the museum, too. Warren always said he'd pass down the job to me."

"I had no idea."

"What about you? Have you always wanted to run a farm stand?" He shifted his hand in hers, his fingers tracing her palm.

It was her turn to laugh. "I've never wanted to run a farm stand."

"What do you want to do?"

"You'll make fun of me," she told him.

"Bet I won't."

"I want to turn the museum into a full-on living history place like Colonial Williamsburg. I want people to be able to dress up and try handicrafts and live for a day like our forefathers did. I want to set up houses and gather costumes and re-create a whole town."

"You dream big," Lance said approvingly.

"I do. It'll never happen—not here."

"Maybe not," he said, "but it sounds like the two of us could run the museum together handily."

"I wanted to go to college, too." She leaned against his shoulder. "I guess we have that in common."

"Maybe we'll get a chance someday." He kissed her

temple.

"Maybe."

"I really have to go."

"I know."

Lance kissed her one more time, took his pie and drove away.

The afternoon turned busy, and a few hours later, having run out of most of her baked goods—and vegetables, too—Maya decided to close up early. She'd spent the whole time thinking about Lance's proposition—and their conversation about what they wanted from life.

As she packed away a number of zucchinis, she arrived at a measure of clarity that had previously evaded her. She had been telling herself she couldn't have a future with Lance because her family wouldn't accept it, but her family had never fully accepted her for herself anyway. They hadn't backed her desire to attend school, rarely asked her what she wanted from life. Made fun of her hobbies.

She'd been so wrapped up in trying to please them, she hadn't even considered what would happen if she walked away with Lance.

The thought of it made her breath catch. The last few weeks had been more exciting than anything that had happened in a long time. The brief moments she spent with Lance made her feel alive like nothing else did.

It had been so long since she'd had anything to look forward to. Why was it so wrong to want to be with

Lance?

He'd put aside his dreams for his family's sake, too.

Didn't they deserve to have a little fun?

She returned to her work with renewed vigor, suddenly determined to finish quickly. After she had loaded everything into her truck but before making the short commute down the driveway, she pulled out her phone and texted Lance.

Camila's old cabin? she sent.

Hell, yeah, he texted back.

WHEN LANCE ARRIVED at the cottage, he found he'd beaten Maya there. It was unlocked, so he slipped in and set two glasses on the kitchen counter along with a bottle of wine he'd bought in town.

Bart hadn't been pleased to lose his help at the warehouse, but as far as Lance was concerned, Maya came first. He still wasn't sure how his simple life had become so complicated, but he liked Maya. Was beginning to care for her in a way that went beyond casual. He knew he should walk away from her, but he didn't see how that was possible. Not now.

Not when they were getting so close.

Was this how Olivia had felt when she and Noah started having feelings for each other? Lance had to admit he was having a hard time staying angry at his sister these days. You didn't choose who you loved; you just fell for a person. Sense had no part of it. It was as if Fate liked to laugh at people who thought they had control over their lives.

Lance stared at the bottle of wine. The two glasses.

He wished he was the kind of man who could offer something to a woman like Maya. What would she want with a dead broke cowboy? A man destined to keep doing the same damn things in the same damn town on the same damn ranch forever.

The door opened, and Maya slipped in, her eyes widening when she spotted him. "You beat me here." She'd changed into a little dress but was still wearing cowboy boots. Lance's heart warmed to see her, and he fought to clear his defeatist thoughts from his mind.

"Guess so."

She closed and locked the door behind her but leaned against it, taking him in. "What's wrong?"

Could she read him so well already?

He lifted his hands in a question. "What are we doing here?" He didn't want to stop this thing that was so good between them, but he couldn't pretend they weren't playing with fire.

"In Camila's cabin?" She grinned wickedly. "I know what I hope we're doing."

"I mean together. We can't fight our past, you know. You'll always be a Turner. I'll be a Cooper. We'll keep fighting drought and rising prices and too many chores and not enough money—" He stuck his hand in his pocket and drew out the scrap of lace he'd ripped from the cap she'd been sewing the first time he stopped to talk to her. He'd found it again this morning and was determined to return it.

Now it seemed to him to represent everything that

kept them apart. The chasm between their families he didn't think they could ever quite bridge.

He handed it back to her. "This is yours."

She took it, ran her fingers over it and nodded. "Thanks."

"I'm sure you already fixed the cap."

"I tried, but it wasn't quite right—this will help."

"I'm glad." He scratched the back of his neck. "Seems everything I touch these days goes wrong."

"Hey." She slipped the scrap of lace into her purse, set it down, crossed the floor and took both of his hands. "This isn't like you."

"You don't really know me," he pointed out.

"I think I do." She went up on tiptoe, and Lance couldn't help himself. He met her halfway, his hands going of their own accord to rest on her hips, their mouths meeting in a rough kiss. "Forget the future. Let's just be here now."

Sounded good to him.

He gave in with a groan, standing up and tugging her closer, letting his mouth range over hers. What the hell, he thought. It was only one night. They could figure out the future tomorrow.

He led her into the small bedroom, gratified to find it still contained a double bed. There weren't any sheets or blankets, but he wouldn't let a little thing like that stop them.

Maya was already undoing the buttons of her dress. He helped her slip it up and over her head, then laid it on the mattress. Adding his shirt, he reached around her back to undo the clasp of her bra. As her breasts swung free, he nearly groaned out loud. God, they looked good. They were going to feel good, too, just as soon as he—

Aah, yep. Awesome.

Maya shrugged the rest of the way out of her bra as he palmed her breasts, feeling the weight of them, caressing them until she sighed. When he crushed her to him again, those beautiful nipples of hers pressed against his chest, and Lance slid his hands down to tug at the waistband of her panties.

Maya pushed him away and shimmied them down in a matter of moments. She kicked off her boots and in one lithe movement dove onto the bed, where she propped herself up on one elbow and smiled at him.

Hell, what a sight, Lance thought as he quickly stripped down, too. A moment later he joined her, rolling her over onto her back and commencing a thorough exploration of her curves. Soon his need to join with her was reaching dire proportions.

Maya cocked her head and took a good long look at his body below the belt. "Guess I don't have to ask if you want to take this further."

"Guess not." Lance shifted to place himself between her legs. "What about you?"

"I absolutely want to take this further." She pulled him close, an invitation if there ever was one. Lance paused, savoring the anticipation for a beat before shifting his hips and pressing inside of her.

They sighed in unison, and when Lance began to

rock against her, Maya moved with him. His need built up quickly, the sweet friction they were creating together heating him up until he could barely hold on.

Maya clung to him, urging him on with her hips, her hands—her mouth. When she cried out, he picked up his speed, driving her into a climax so strong it rocked him. He followed her, thrusting hard, crying out, too, unable to hold back.

When she fell back against the mattress, he collapsed on top of her, out of breath. He couldn't give this up, he thought as soon as he could form sensible sentences in his head. Maybe she was a Turner. Maybe he was a Cooper.

But they had to be together.

"Maya, I—"

A thunderous pounding on the front door stopped them both. Maya's fingers dug into his skin.

"Who's that?"

"I don't know."

MAYA PULLED BACK as best she could, and Lance slid out of her. She pushed him off her, rolled over and scrambled to find her clothes.

"Who's in there? You're trespassing on private property!"

"It's Liam," she hissed. She exchanged a helpless look with Lance. The light of their candle must have been visible through the heavy curtains. If she didn't answer the door, he'd probably break in. "Get dressed."

He already had his jeans back on. He shoved his feet

in his boots and strode toward the living room. Maya, still doing up the buttons of her dress, followed him. She was clothed—barely—but they wouldn't fool Liam.

She grabbed Lance's arm. "Slip out the back."

"And then what? Pretend this never happened?"

"Exactly. Liam will kill you if he finds you here."

"But—"

"Lance—please. For me."

He hesitated. "Maya—"

"We'll sort this out tomorrow, okay? Just… not like this. What if he has a gun?"

Lance nodded finally. "We'll definitely sort this out tomorrow," he promised her. He stole a kiss. "What'll you tell him?"

"I'll think of something." She shoved him toward the back of the cabin as Liam pounded on the door again.

"Open up!"

"Wait." Lance backtracked, grabbed the wine and glasses, and made for the back door.

Maya waited until Lance was gone, set her dress to rights, smoothed her hair and pulled open the front door. "What the hell, Liam? Can't I have any privacy?"

"What are you doing here? Who's in here with you?"

"No one. It's just me. I'm going stir-crazy these days hanging out at the farm stand all day, and every night I have to bake until I want to scream. I just needed to be alone for a minute. Can't you understand that?"

She hoped she wasn't laying it on too thick, but to

her surprise, Liam nodded and set down his rifle, which of course he'd brought with him. "Yeah, I can understand that."

"What's wrong?" She could smell alcohol on his breath. She tugged him inside and shut the door, leading him to the faded couch, glad for the opportunity to keep him busy for a while. "Sit down. Let's talk. We never seem to do that anymore."

"Were you sleeping?"

"Trying to," she lied, "but what about you? Why aren't you in bed?"

"Can't ever seem to sleep these days."

"Something on your mind?"

He was quiet for a long time. "It's this organic certification thing. There are so many details just to get it started, and then it'll take years to get it done. What if I—?"

"Screw it up?" she finished for him.

When he flinched, she leaned closer. "Liam, you won't screw it up. You can do this."

He stared at her a long time before looking away. "Yeah. Of course."

"I think it's a brilliant idea. When our ranch is certified organic, we'll have access to a niche market, and our meat will fetch a higher price. It'll be great for our bottom line. You're going to save us once and for—"

He surged to his feet, cutting her off. "Stella's waiting in the house. I told her to stay there. Come on—she'll be worried."

"Let me grab my boots." Maya hurried to get them

on and followed Liam, not releasing the breath she was holding until they made it to the house without incident. She had the feeling Lance was still nearby, watching them, making sure she was safe. She paused at the back door, looked into the darkness but couldn't see anything.

"You coming in or what?" Liam asked.

"I'm coming."

They met Stella in the kitchen. "It was just Maya," Liam said. "She needed some time alone."

"Alone, huh?" Stella didn't look convinced.

"That's right. Alone," Maya asserted. It wasn't anyone's business who she was with.

"We need to talk about the Coopers."

Maya kept her expression neutral. Stella was fishing, and she wasn't going to bite. It was hard, though. Just minutes ago Lance had been inside her, and she didn't think she'd ever get enough of how it felt to be with him.

"We can't trust them, Maya," Stella went on. "You're getting way too friendly with Lance, working on the re-enactment with him, selling his furniture at your farm stand."

That wasn't the half of what she'd been doing with him recently, nor was it half of what she wanted to do keep doing with him. She needed Lance. Wanted him desperately. Her desire for him wasn't slaked one bit, even though they'd just made love. She wasn't about to give him up now.

In fact, she'd had enough of the rivalry between

their families. Didn't Stella realize all their bickering made their lives worse, not better?

"I remember you caught me with Olivia once when we were kids, and you said the same thing," she retorted angrily. "You forbade me to ever talk to her again because you said she was trouble. But in the end, it was me who betrayed her. Because Liam here pushed me to. He told me it was the Coopers who drove Mom away, and I believed him because I was just a kid, but you know what? From everything she's said and done since, Mom would have left us no matter what. She never wanted to be a rancher's wife. I don't know why she married Dad in the first place."

"The Coopers did drive her away," Stella argued. "Enid Cooper destroyed our family."

"Stella," Liam said warningly.

Maya shut her eyes. She didn't want to hear it anymore.

"Why shouldn't Maya know?" Stella demanded. "She isn't a kid anymore, and Dad's dead. Who are we protecting?"

Us, Maya wanted to say. They were all protecting the versions of themselves that needed to believe that Turners were morally superior to everyone else.

Trouble was, they all knew that wasn't the case.

She opened her eyes to find her brother and sister squared off with each other. "It's all Enid's fault," Stella said again. "She pursued Dad until he lost his head and had an affair with her. That's why Mom left."

Maya stiffened. An affair? Something clicked into

place. The missing piece. She should have known. Why else would Mary have chosen that moment to leave? She might never have wanted to be a rancher's wife, but she'd stuck around that long—

Stella's cheeks were flushed, her eyes unnaturally bright, and Maya had another flash of clarity. It wouldn't have been Enid pursuing William. Enid was a beautiful woman. Had her own mother already been pulling away from her dad? Had William reached out to another woman to fill the void?

"It's true. I saw them!" Stella said as if Maya had argued with her.

"Together?" Maya made herself ask.

"Not—together," Stella said. "But I heard what they said. Enough to know it's true."

"Stella," Liam said again.

Maya didn't know who to feel sorrier for. Mary. Stella—or herself.

All of them so hurt.

Who was really to blame for any of it?

"Are you sure?" she asked Stella, to say something. Anything.

"I'm sure," Stella said bitterly. "And now Noah's married to Enid's daughter. And you—" She swallowed. Looked at Liam. Shook her head and walked out of the room.

Maya found herself blinking back tears. Not because of Stella's unfinished accusation but because of her sister's obvious pain.

She was in danger of repeating her father's mistake,

Maya realized. Making a bad situation worse by looking for comfort from an enemy. William didn't end up with Enid, so whatever had been between them hadn't lasted, but their short tryst had blown up two families.

Why on earth did she think her relationship with Lance could end any better?

Chapter Eleven

H E'D MADE A mistake—a big one.

Lance sat in his truck, staring at the empty space where Maya's farm stand should be. He had a truck bed full of furniture to set out, and he'd hoped they could use the time together to discuss what they should have talked about last night, but by the looks of things, Maya wasn't going to give him a chance. When he'd walked out—at her urging—he'd let her down. Had Liam guessed who'd she'd been with? Had she realized that all this sneaking around wasn't for her?

He pulled out his cell phone and texted her. Waited a minute.

No answer came.

He tossed it aside on the passenger seat finally and turned the truck around. He had to give her time, but he wished like hell he knew what was going on.

He came home to find a stack of boxes in front of the house and realized that in all the chaos recently, he had forgotten to put their standard supply order in for the ranch. Thank God Steel had remembered it. He was surprised his brother hadn't given him hell about it already.

Lance bent to retrieve one of the boxes, eyed the packing slip taped to the front and frowned. That wasn't the brand of cattle supplements they usually used.

He set the box back down and checked the others. What the hell was going on here? Half of this was wrong.

He opened the door to the house and hollered inside, "Steel? You there?"

Chances were his brother would be long gone this time of day, but heavy steps approached, and Steel came around the corner from the living room, pocketing his phone.

"Did you sign for this delivery?" Lance asked him. "I don't think it's for us."

Steel frowned. "I thought you signed for it. I was on the phone when I got here, so I didn't look it over." He did so now and shook his head. "This isn't right."

"Olivia must have signed for it. We're going to have to send half of this back. It's all wrong, for one thing, and…" He didn't want to mention the total he'd seen on the bill. Steel must have noticed the way he was skimping on orders. They needed to make their money stretch.

Steel bent closer. "It's got our name on it. If you didn't put this order in, who did?"

"Didn't you? Oh, hell, it was Turner, wasn't it?" Now it seemed obvious, and Lance didn't know what to do about it.

Steel made a face. "Must have been. Come on, let's sort this out. Now."

Lance followed him reluctantly. Here they went again, but Noah had crossed a line this time, and they couldn't let it slide. They found him working in the doorway of the stable at the Flying W, where Lance and Steel had so recently made fools of themselves. Were they about to embarrass themselves again? Lance hoped not, except it had occurred to him they wouldn't be able to talk about the order without exposing how short of cash they were. That was the last thing he wanted Noah to know.

Noah stood up from where he'd been working, brushed himself off and turned to face them.

"Having a problem with the door?" Lance said by way of a greeting.

Steel short him a questioning look, but Lance ignored him. They needed to come at this issue sideways if they wanted to hide the financial trouble they were in.

"Yeah. It's been getting harder to open for a while now, but today I had to shove it open with my shoulder. I took it off and shaved it down on the corner, but now I can't get it to close correctly."

Steel folded his arms over his chest and shook his head as Lance moved closer to take a look. It didn't take him long to figure out the issue. "It's not the door that's the problem. The walls are shifting." He took a step back and craned his neck to study the roof. "Hell, this whole building is leaning."

"I know." Noah made a wry face. "Drives me crazy."

"You had the right idea. You just need to sand it

down more, probably." He scratched his chin. "But resizing the door is a band-aid solution. Those walls will keep shifting, and pretty soon everything will be out of alignment. Then you'll be right back in here, doing the same job." This was good. He was coming off as the expert. Noah was the petitioner.

"I was afraid of that," Noah said. "How would you fix it?"

"Honestly? It's probably a foundation issue. You're going to need a new roof soon, too."

Noah spread his hands. "We can't afford any of that right now. Unless the building is literally about to fall down, I'm just going to have to come up with some other fix."

Lance exchanged another look with Steel. So Thorn Hill wasn't the only ranch with money problems. That was good to know. It explained why Maya was working so hard.

"It's not going to fall down," Lance said finally. He'd found out the information he needed. If the Flying W was as hard up as Thorn Hill, then they were on equal footing, and it was okay to talk about the order.

"Guess I'd better get used to adjusting the door, then," Noah said.

"I could help," Lance offered in spite of himself. It felt good to be in a position to offer assistance for once.

Noah raised his eyebrows. Steel straightened. Lance went on before Steel could interfere. "You handled the order. I'll fix the door."

"About that order," Steel growled.

"It came? Good." Noah faced him. "I saw you were low on a few things, too, and couldn't get either one of you on the phone, so I went ahead and placed it for both our ranches. About half of it is for the Flying W. I'll come over with my truck and load it up. I wasn't sure about some of the brands you used, so I got my usual. If you don't like them, I'll buy the extras from you and just have more on hand for a while. You can place your own order separately. But for now, your part is—" He pulled out his phone and tapped it a few times, then named a sum they could pay handily. Relief coursed through Lance.

"I hope I saved you some money," Noah finished up.

"You did," Lance admitted. He shrugged when Steel sent him an exasperated look. "He did," he told his brother.

"Whatever. You two sort it out." Steel strode off in disgust.

Noah watched him go. "I saw some of the furniture you made at Maya's stand" was all he said, though. "I never knew you could do stuff like that."

"It's just a hobby." Lance shrugged again. "Started with fixing things around the house, then moved up to making my own pieces."

"You must have stuck with it a good long while to be able to turn out furniture like that."

Lance nodded. "More like it stuck with me." He cleared his throat, suddenly remembering to whom he was talking. "Let's get started on that door."

"Gladly."

THREE DAYS LATER Maya was still doing her best to avoid Lance while she sorted through the costumes Alice had brought to the museum. Soon the Historical Society would meet to hand out parts and try a first read-through of the script she and Mia had finalized in the last couple of days. Lance was across the room with Bart going over set pieces he'd been building. He'd looked her way more than once. She was working hard not to meet his gaze.

It had been hard to ignore Lance's texts. She felt like she was betraying him, but on the other hand, she felt like maybe she'd betrayed her mother for years, the way she'd blamed Mary for the breakup of her family. She didn't know the chain of events that had led William to take up with Enid, but no wonder her mother had left so suddenly. She must have been humiliated to find out her husband was sleeping with the woman who lived next door.

Maya had been wracking her memory, trying to come up with details of those first days and months after Mary left. When she tried to remember her father's reaction to the news, she recalled how flabbergasted he'd been. Then had come his attempts to track her mother down. His prolonged absences. What had he been doing? Searching for her himself?

As the weeks passed, he'd been home at odd hours, coming and going, his expression pinched. He'd lashed out more than once during that time, barking at any of them who got in his way. He'd blamed his temper on—

Work.

Why had he blamed it on work when his wife had just disappeared?

She tried to ask Stella about it once, but Stella wasn't talking. "He was trying to hide his affair," she snapped.

"What about Mom?"

"Mom's just as much at fault. She didn't leave only him—she left us."

Maya had given up. She didn't know what to do about any of it. All she knew was that everyone in her family was unhappy in their own way—

Except Noah, she supposed.

He seemed happy enough.

She didn't know what to do about Lance, either, knowing what she knew now. Pursuing a relationship with him would drive a wedge between her and Stella she wasn't sure anything could repair. Meanwhile, she didn't think she could bake one more pie, or she'd lose her mind. The temperatures soared into the high nineties day after day. She couldn't sleep. Didn't want to eat.

Didn't want to do anything, if it came to that.

Still, there was the re-enactment to prepare for. If everything else went sour this summer, at least they could save the museum.

Which meant she couldn't avoid seeing Lance today. So far he'd kept his distance from her, even though he'd glanced her way curiously more than once. When Maggie and Katie came in, she breathed a sigh of relief for the interruption, but it was short lived.

"Daddy! Daddy!" Katie cried and launched herself across the room into Bart's open arms.

Maggie made her way to Maya's side. "I figured this was the only way I'd get to see Bart before three a.m. Katie's missed him like crazy. Maybe she can convince him to come home."

Maya bit back a startled exclamation when she got a look at Maggie's face. The circles under her eyes were darker than they'd been the last time she'd seen her, and it looked like she'd lost ten pounds. "Are you okay?"

"No, I'm not." She blinked back tears. "I think he's going to leave me, and if he is, I wish he'd just do it. I can't stand this!"

Maya remembered what Lance had said and swallowed the guilt that clogged her throat. She should have passed on the message sooner. "I don't know what's going on with him, but Lance said something."

"What?" Maggie demanded.

"He just said to trust that things are going to turn out okay. He said Bart's trying."

"Trying what? To drive me crazy?" Maggie bit her lip when several people turned to look at her.

"Just… hang in there. I don't think Lance would have said that if he didn't mean it," Maya told her.

"I don't know what else I can do." She gazed at Katie, who had wrapped her arms around Bart's neck and was holding on for dear life. "I probably shouldn't have come. She'll never sleep tonight now."

"Of course you should have come," Maya said.

"You love the re-enactments, and you haven't been at a meeting yet." Maya remembered Maggie's tallow candle dipping setup from previous years. She always had an old-fashioned tent and a fire pit over which she hung a cauldron from a spit. Maya had more than one set of lopsided candles she'd made under Maggie's tutelage in years gone by.

"I used to love them. This year is going to be hard."

Maya reached out an squeezed her hand, taking in the way Maggie was watching her husband and daughter. It was obvious she didn't want her marriage to fail. She still loved Bart, but he was close to losing her.

She caught Lance's eye for a moment, then looked away. She wished she could go to him. Get back the closeness they'd had.

But all their families did was hurt each other.

It was all such a mess.

"I'd better go after Katie," Maggie said.

"Or you could let her spend a little more time with her dad."

"The man who cleaned out our bank account and barely ever comes home?"

"I didn't say you had to forgive him for that."

"Katie really misses him," Maggie said, rubbing the back of her neck.

"I'm sure you do, too."

Maggie didn't answer. Instead, she picked her way through the crowded room to retrieve Katie, who clung to Bart's leg.

Maya turned away as the scene grew uncomfortable.

Katie wouldn't let go, even when Bart started remonstrating with her. Finally, he had to peel her off and hand her, kicking and wailing, to Maggie.

"... have to trust me," she thought she heard Bart say as Maggie hurried from the room. Maya was certain she wouldn't be back anytime soon.

"Sometimes people make simple things so complicated," Alice said sadly, joining her.

"Sometimes things are complicated."

"That doesn't mean they aren't worth fighting for." She nodded toward the men standing near the set pieces.

Maya knew she had to mean Maggie should fight for Bart.

So why did she get the feeling Alice meant something else entirely?

"WHAT'S UP WITH you?" Lance asked Bart. The man was still slumped down in the metal chair he'd collapsed into when Maggie had hauled Katie away. "We don't have much time—I need your help."

"Katie was so upset."

"She hasn't seen you in weeks. What did you expect?" Lance had little sympathy for him.

"All I need is a few more days."

Lance blew out a frustrated breath. Bart must have a lot of faith in Maggie's imagination. The last time he'd worked on the warehouse, all he'd seen was a warren of rooms and halls marked out by the unfinished partitions Bart was framing in. Maybe someone could turn the building into a house—despite the lousy part of town it was situated in—but Lance was beginning to think Bart wasn't that person. He needed to hire an architect.

Lance doubted he could afford one, though.

"You need to go straight home and spend some time with your little girl, no matter how miserable you're set on making her mother."

"I'm not trying to make Maggie miserable. I'm trying to give her a house. Why is that so hard to understand?"

Lance didn't know how to answer that. He wasn't the most tactful person, but he had enough awareness to hesitate to tell Bart that Maggie wasn't going to like the warehouse no matter how many walls he built inside it.

"You saw the way Katie was crying. She wants her father," he reiterated.

"She'll have her father the minute I get the house right," Bart said mulishly.

Lance gave up. Some people just didn't want to be happy. If Bart was going to keep playing contractor, Maggie was probably going to give up on him and find someone else who would pay her the time of day—

He bit back a grin.

There was an idea that just might work.

"I've got to make a call," he told Bart. And just possibly kill two birds with one stone while he was at it. He missed Maya. Needed an excuse to spend some time with her again.

He went outside and took out his phone. A quick

check of the Dancing Boot's website confirmed there was live music playing the next night. He texted Maya. *URGENT—it's about Bart and Maggie. I'll call.* He was pleased when she picked up on the first ring.

"What's going on? And where are you? You were just here."

"I'm outside, and what's going on is Operation Get Bart and Maggie Back Together. Do you think you can help her find a sitter for Katie and get her to the Dancing Boot tomorrow night?"

"I doubt it. I mean, the sitter part's easy enough, but Maggie will never agree to go to a bar."

"You've got to get her there. Rain on Monday is playing. They're a great band."

"I don't think that will work."

"I'm going to get Bart there," Lance pushed on, determined to allay her doubts. "And you're going to get Maggie to dance with some other guy."

There was a long pause. Then a chuckle. "That's devious."

"Bart is a man who can only hold one thought in his head at a time. You aren't going to believe this, but the reason he's staying out all night is he's trying to make Maggie happy."

"You've got to be kidding me."

Lance couldn't blame her for her reaction. He could imagine her shaking her head over the costumes she was sorting inside. He paced in a circle in the parking lot. "I know. I can't tell you any more than that, but what I can say is that I can't push him out of that one track no matter how hard I try. It's going to take something big to do that."

"Like thinking he's losing Maggie to someone else."

"That's right." Would his ploy work? If he got Maya to the Dancing Boot, surely the music and relaxed atmosphere would make it easier to talk to her. It was killing him not to know what had happened after he left the other night. He wouldn't bring that up now, though.

"I'm on it. And Lance—thanks. For caring about them. Not many guys would work so hard to fix someone else's problems."

Lance turned to make sure no one could overhear his part of the conversation. "Love's worth fighting for." He hoped she knew he wasn't only talking about Bart and Maggie. "Don't you think so?"

She didn't answer, and the moment stretched out. "The meeting is about to start," she said finally. "Better get back in here."

"You'll get Maggie to the Dancing Boot tomorrow night?" he asked. He wasn't ready to admit defeat yet.

"We'll be there. I promise."

"I CAN'T BELIEVE I let you talk me into this," Maggie said the following night as she surveyed herself in Maya's bedroom mirror. Under supreme duress from Maya, she'd put on a sexy little red dress and cowboy boots, and had styled her hair and put on makeup, too. She finally looked like the Maggie Maya used to know.

"We're both in a slump. We're working too hard, stressing too hard, and we're not having any fun. We need to get out on the town and clear our heads," Maya said for what had to be the hundredth time. She was beginning to think it would be a miracle if she actually got Maggie to the Dancing Boot.

"You think going to a bar is the way to clear your head?"

As far as Maya was concerned, seeing Maggie's tiny, wry smile meant they were already on their way.

She had pulled on her go-to outfit for their night out: a deceptively simple blue dress with shoulder straps that had a tendency to slide down. Thigh high, it exposed her long legs, made longer by her high heels. She pulled her hair into a messy updo whose charm lay in the fact it might slide down at any moment. She hadn't worn the outfit in ages and was happy to see it still fit just fine.

"We'll have a great time," she told Maggie, but she wasn't sure who she was trying to convince. At the very least, she'd enjoy being out and hearing the music at the Dancing Boot, even if she didn't do more than people watch and drink a beer. Lance would be there, which would be… hard, if she was truthful. If only she could dance the night away with him. Go home with him after. Spend the night—

She checked her phone. It was a little early to head to the bar, but she was afraid if they hung out too long, Maggie would lose her nerve and want to head home.

Afraid she'd lose her own nerve about seeing Lance and keeping her distance. She thought about him all the time. Closed her eyes at night and relived making love to him. Something had to give.

"We'd better get going," she said just as Stella poked her head in the door.

"Hi Maggie, it's good to see you. Where are you two heading off to tonight?"

"The Dancing Boot. Rain on Monday is playing," Maya told her and had an inspiration. "Want to come?" If Stella was along, there'd be two of them to strong-arm Maggie into the club.

She could tell Stella's first response was to say no, but then she shrugged. "Why not? I haven't had any fun in ages. Give me a minute to change?"

"We'll help you pick out an outfit." She had to keep Maggie invested in the evening, and she thought it was working already. Maggie seemed interested to see what Stella had to wear.

Maybe this would work after all.

Chapter Twelve

"WHERE ARE YOU off to in such a hurry?" Tory asked Lance when she and Steel met up with him in the front hall.

"Dragging Bart to the Dancing Boot to see Rain on Monday. I've got a plan to fix things up between him and his wife." He filled them in on the details.

"We're going to the Dancing Boot, too," Tory said.

"Looks like a family outing," Steel added with grin.

Lance was surprised Steel had managed to convince Tory to go. She'd been mostly hanging around the ranch since she arrived, lying low, as if she didn't want to see the town she'd left behind. She still wouldn't confirm or deny her decision to stay at the ranch during the school year. Lance had a feeling she was looking for a job, but jobs were hard to find in Chance Creek. He wondered if she'd consider putting her shingle out to do massage, but he could see her predicament. Renting an office space in town would eat heavily into her profit margin. She didn't really have a space to do it at the ranch, which might be preferable.

He decided to ask her another time. Steel drove them all into town, stopping on the way to pick up Bart at his warehouse. Lance hadn't given him any head's up about the plan. He intended to kidnap the man and throw him in the back of the truck if that's what it took.

When he, Steel and Tory all turned up in the warehouse, Bart blinked at them like an owl that had just woken up.

"Hey," he said finally. "You aren't supposed to tell anyone—"

"Steel and Tory know how to keep a secret," Lance said.

"What are you building in here?" Tory asked, turning around in a slow circle to take in the space. The large main room was bisected by a wall with a space left for a doorway. Lance knew that if you walked through that door, you'd find a maze of other rooms laid out behind it. None of the walls had been sheet rocked yet, so it was hard to really get a sense of how it would look when it was done, but Lance still wasn't convinced Bart had the layout right.

Tory didn't wait for an invitation. She leaned in through the doorway, then kept going into the hall behind it. A minute later she was back. "Is it going to be an office building?"

Lance, standing behind Bart, made slicing motions across his neck at her. He didn't want Tory riling up Bart.

"It's going to be a house! It's a surprise for Maggie," Bart said.

"A… house?" Tory blinked, and Lance realized they were one step away from disaster.

"Did you all come to help?" Bart asked.

Steel took his arm. "Yes. After we all go have a drink." He firmly propelled Bart toward the front door.

"But—"

"After the drink," Steel said again.

For once Steel's reputation came in handy. Bart looked like he wanted to protest, but he also looked afraid to try. He meekly got into Steel's truck when they made it outside.

"Just one drink," Bart sputtered as Steel fired up the engine.

"Whatever you say, man."

Lance was having a hard time hiding a smile. He had the feeling Tory was giggling quietly. For the first time in ages, he felt on the same page as his siblings, and it was... nice.

When Steel drove into the lot outside of the Dancing Boot and pulled into an empty space, Lance spotted Maya across the parking lot with Maggie. Good. The plan was working.

But then he spotted Stella with her—and there was Liam loping across the parking lot to join them. By the looks of things, Maya hadn't known he was coming. She stiffened and scanned the vehicles parked nearby, as if afraid he and Bart might be close.

They were close enough. If they all walked in together, the night would end in a fight before it even began.

Unsure what to do, he cleared his throat. Steel caught the signal, swept the parking lot with his gaze, caught sight of the Turners and stiffened. "Wait a minute," he said as Bart reached for the door handle. "I don't like this parking spot." He quickly backed out of the space, made his way out of the parking lot and parked down the street.

"But this is farther away," Bart protested.

"Don't want anyone to scratch my ride," Steel said firmly.

Lance bit back a guffaw. Steel's ride was as scratched as they came. Still, he'd bet Bart wasn't going to question him.

"Know what you mean," Bart said seriously, proving him right.

By the time they made it to the Dancing Boot's front door, the Turners were nowhere in sight. Cab Johnson was standing near the entrance, though, his wife Rose on his arm. Cab caught sight of them as they approached, and Lance swore he saw the sheriff sigh. He straightened when they got close and crossed his arms over his chest.

"Hey, Cab," Lance said as cheerfully as he could.

"Hey, yourself."

"How are you tonight?" Tory asked.

"Just fine. Tonight's my night off, and I intend to spend it having a good time with my wife. I've already decided if anyone starts trouble inside, I'll make sure they spend a good long stint in custody. Got that?" His gaze shifted from Lance to Steel.

"Loud and clear," Steel drawled.

"I'm not planning to start any trouble," Tory said

sharply.

"Glad to hear it." Cab stepped aside to let them pass. Lance chuckled at his sister's affronted expression. She'd been gone from Chance Creek far too long to know he and Liam had already gotten into it a few times at the Boot. Tonight, Cab's presence would work in his favor, though, so he was happy the sheriff was here. He planned to get up to mischief but not the kind you could arrest him for.

"Have you all been making trouble that Cab has to sort out?" Tory asked him as they entered the club.

"Now and then, maybe," Lance said. Steel gave him a look, but he ignored it. When he got inside, he noticed the Turners had found a table near the back of the bar. Tory yanked on his sleeve and pointed to another free one in the corner near the front. He followed her to claim it, keeping an eye on Maya as best he could across the crowded establishment. Bart came, too, and took a seat. He still hadn't realized his wife was here. The band had been warming up, but they broke into their first song, and immediately the noise level rose significantly.

"I'll get us a pitcher of beer," Steel said and headed for the bar. He ran into the waitress halfway there and stood talking to her, nodding toward the table and coming back when he was done. "That was easy enough."

The waitress returned a few minutes later and set out a pitcher and mugs. Lance tried to enjoy the music. Tory slipped away after a while and went to speak to some people near the dance floor. Steel sipped his beer, scanning the crowd as if watching for trouble.

"Hey." Lance turned to find Bart staring at Maggie. "What's she doing here?"

"Looks like she's here with Maya. Probably needed some time off."

"Time off what? Where's Katie?" Bart glanced around as if his daughter might be there, too.

"At home with Maggie's parents, I guess," Lance said.

"But… Maggie's supposed to be taking care of her. Why's she at a club?"

"Why are you at a club?"

"You made me come here. Otherwise I'd be working on my house."

"Right—you'd be at the warehouse, while Maggie would be spending the night at home with your daughter—again. Maybe she got sick of being alone all the time and wanted to spend time with friends."

"But—" Bart watched, as flummoxed as if his wife had grown wings and started flying. "She doesn't mind staying home. She says we should save money."

"You emptied your savings account and didn't tell her why, right?" Lance challenged him. "Maybe she figures saving isn't what it's cut out to be. Maybe she's ready to have some fun instead."

"Wait—who the hell is that?" Bart half stood. Lance yanked him down into his seat again. He figured it was a good idea to let this play out a little.

A man had come to stand next to the Turners' table, his hands on his hips. Judging by the smiles on the

Turners' faces, he'd told some kind of funny story or joke. Even Maggie was laughing. Dressed up, a little makeup on, she made a far different picture from the woebegone woman she'd been lately.

The man leaned toward her. Asked her something. Maggie's eyes widened, but Maya gave her a little push. He couldn't hear their voices, but he could guess what they were saying.

"Did that guy just ask my wife to dance?" Bart said incredulously.

"Don't fly off the handle—"

"I'll kill him!"

"Bart!" Lance watched Maggie stand up, looking about as uncomfortable as she could. Maya got up, too, and all three of them moved to the dance floor.

Too bad Maggie and the stranger weren't slow dancing, Lance thought. The guy must be some friend of the Turners. He was dancing with both women. Lance wondered if Maya had set it up beforehand or if things had just worked out.

"He's harmless," Lance said to Bart, but he didn't like the way the man was looking at Maya. That little dress she was wearing was practically falling off her. The stranger didn't seem to mind one bit.

"I swear to God," Bart started.

"Sit down and shut up." Steel put a hand on Bart's shoulder and shoved him down again.

Bart stayed there this time, but his eyes were wide with shock.

"You've been an ass to your wife, right? Stayed out

late for weeks, didn't answer her questions, stole her money, acted like you knew better than she did," Steel told him. "Seems to me you're getting exactly what you deserve. You sit there, watch her dance with another man, and when the song is done, you go ask her to dance with you. And then you make up with her. Got it?"

Bart nodded, and Lance bit back a chuckle. Leave it to Steel to set things straight.

The song seemed to go on forever, and the stranger spent more time than Lance would have liked focused on Maya. Finally, the song ended. Bart was on his feet again before the last chords died away. He strode across the room, pushing his way through the bystanders, and took Maggie's hand.

"Having fun?" Maya asked, appearing suddenly by Lance's side. He'd been so busy watching Bart, he hadn't noticed her coming his way.

Lance shrugged. Fun? Not really. It had been torture watching someone else get to be close to her. "The music is good." He could say that much.

"It is good."

"I saw you dancing. That guy a friend of yours?"

Maya nodded. "Noah knows him from the Sheriff's Department. Did it work?"

"Did what work?"

"Maggie dancing with him, silly. Did it get Bart off his ass and ready to apologize like you thought it would?"

Steel smiled. He was nursing his beer, his eyes on

the crowd, but he was obviously listening. Lance bit back a curse. He'd been getting so hot around the collar about the way that guy was ogling Maya he'd forgotten it was his idea to start with to make Bart jealous.

"Guess so. He went off like a shot the minute the song was over."

"Mission accomplished, then."

Not exactly, Lance thought. He wanted to dance with her. He wanted a hell of a lot more than that, feud or no feud.

"How about you and me give it a go?" he asked after a moment. After all, Cab was here. Liam couldn't kill him with the sheriff present.

Steel straightened. Maya hesitated, and he thought she'd say no. Probably for the best.

"Oh, why the hell not?" she said. "You don't mind, do you, Steel?" she challenged his brother.

Steel opened his mouth, shut it again. Shrugged. "I don't mind," he said.

Lance had a feeling his brother had given up on anything making sense. He knew how that felt. He took Maya's hand and led her to the dance floor before anything could happen to stop them.

Maya put up no resistance as he slid his hands to the small of her back and guided her against his chest. She felt so good pressed up against him he would have let out a groan if they weren't in public. As it was, he had to keep from burying his face in her hair and breathing her in. Maya didn't say anything, just rested against him and swayed in time to the beat with him. He liked the feel of his hands on her hips. He couldn't help himself. He inched his fingers lower, knowing he was playing a dangerous game but still unable to stop himself. He thought Maya might pull away. Instead, she shifted closer. Lance swallowed, aware of a stirring down south that would make his thoughts all too clear to the woman in his arms.

"God, Maya," he said into her ear. He felt rather than heard her quick intake of breath. "I wish…" He trailed off. What did he wish? That things were simpler? That their families were just… families? That there never had been a feud between them at all?

Feeling he was being watched, he glanced back at his table to see Steel trying to catch his eye. His brother cocked his head. Lance turned in the direction he indicated.

"Uh oh."

"What?" Maya tipped her head back.

"Nothing," he said quickly. "Just wish the song could go on forever."

"Me, too," she said dreamily and settled in again.

That wasn't the problem, though. The problem was staring at him, face rigid with hatred. Liam was watching him. Stella, too. She looked grim, Liam furious.

He didn't care. Maya was worth it.

He admitted to himself he was in far over his head. He'd never wanted another woman as much as he wanted her, no matter what had happened in the past. His hands, as if they had a mind of their own, slipped lower, and he pulled her even tighter against his body.

This was a night to throw caution to the wind—

"Lance."

"I want you." He moved one hand up to cradle the back of her head and bent down, intent on kissing her until she melted in his arms, but Maya pulled away.

"Our families—"

"Why should they decide if we get to be happy?"

Maya bit her lip. "There's something you don't know—"

When Liam jumped up from his seat and started across the room, Lance stiffened and readied himself for trouble, but Liam veered in a different direction, stalking toward the table where Tory had rejoined Steel.

Maya frowned and followed his gaze. She sucked in a breath. "Shit, what's he up to?"

Lance let go of her and stepped back, ready to rush to his siblings' aid, but another swaying couple moved in front of him and blocked his view. When he side-stepped to make out what was happening, he nearly tripped when he saw Liam on the dance floor—

Holding Tory's hand.

"What the hell?" Lance exclaimed loudly enough that the band slowed for a second before regaining the beat.

Liam pulled Tory into his arms, swung her around and smirked at Lance over her shoulder. Behind him, Steel had gotten to his feet and was watching both couples, an expression on his face Lance couldn't interpret.

Tory had a dazed look that seemed to say she had

no idea how she'd gotten there—or how to get away, but then she shrugged, rested her palms on Liam's shoulders and let him guide her around the room.

"Goddamn it." But Lance knew he was beat. He couldn't go for Liam any more than Liam could come for him. Not with Cab Johnson watching them from his seat, an exasperated smile twitching his lips. When Cab lifted his beer and saluted Lance with it, Lance moved back to Maya's side and took her in his arms again. What else could he do?

"I guess if we can dance, Liam can dance with Tory," Maya said.

"It's different," Lance contradicted her. "I care about you. Liam is just doing this to mess with me."

Maya eyed him. "How do you know that?"

"Because he's—" Lance broke off.

"Because he's a Turner? Was that what you were going to say?" Maya rolled her eyes. "I'm a Turner, too, remember?"

"Because he's *Liam* Turner," Lance corrected her, "and Liam Turner hates me."

"Why is that?"

Automatically, Lance began to sway again, his gaze still on Liam. Maya moved with him, but she was stiff in his arms, and he knew he was losing ground with her.

"He's always hated me," Lance said.

"Always?" she challenged.

"Since high school."

"Since the semifinals, senior year, you mean."

Lance stumbled. "What do you know about that?"

"Only what everyone knows. You told Coach Andrews he was drunk. Got him kicked off the football team. Took his position."

"I told Andrews he was drunk? Hell, everyone knew he was drunk. It was my job to—" He bit back the rest of his sentence. He was a lot of things, but he wasn't a snitch.

"What?" she prompted when he didn't go on. "What was your job?"

"Ask Liam."

"Lance."

Lance shook his head. "Ask Liam," he said again.

"He's not a bad guy," she said after half a minute during which they swayed together in silence. "He works hard. Always has. Practically runs the whole ranch these days now that Noah's splitting his time between his parole officer work and helping at Thorn Hill."

"I know."

"Football was his thing. He knew he wasn't going anywhere else. He wasn't interested in college. He was going to be a rancher—"

"I know."

"You took his position—"

"Jesus." Lance dropped his hands to his sides and stared down at her. "Are you kidding me? I kept him in that position for years."

"What are you talking about?"

Emotions warred within him. Liam had screwed up a lot of things for him over the years, but Lance followed the unwritten code of small-town life. Gossip flowed rampant here, everyone in everyone else's business, but some secrets were kept by unanimous decision. Liam's problem with alcohol was one of those secrets. Coach Andrews had kept it; the whole football team had kept it. Was she trying to tell him Liam's own family wasn't in on the cover-up?

William sure had been.

"What, Lance? Tell me!" Maya demanded. "I've been willing to overlook what you did to my brother all this time, so if you've got something to say—say it!"

Willing to overlook what *he'd* done?

That was too much.

"Liam drank," Lance blurted out. "Before every single game. It was my job to cover for him. To catch the damn ball no matter where he threw it!"

"You're lying."

"No, I'm not."

Lance saw the questions building up in Maya's mind and wished he didn't have to answer them. Liam had been a decent quarterback—when he was sober, but he was never sober when it mattered.

"Catch the damn ball, Cooper," he remembered Coach Andrews ordering him more than once, starting as far back as sophomore year. "I don't care where Turner throws it; just get your ass there."

"How the hell can I catch it if he can't throw it?" Lance had complained.

"Figure it out."

And so it went. It was senior year before Lance finally confronted his coach. Told him Liam was drinking before every game.

"I've never seen him drink," Andrews said stolidly.

That was the way things operated in Chance Creek. The Turners were gods. The Coopers mere mortals. No one would have covered for Lance if he'd been drinking.

"How long?" Maya asked, interrupting his memories. "How long did you cover for him?"

"Years," he said firmly. Now that the truth was out, he wasn't going to candy-coat it. "You're right. It came to a head during the semifinals our senior year. He hid a bottle among his stuff, was taking swigs from it every time he returned to the bench in between plays."

Maya shook her head as if denying it, but Lance remembered it clearly. He had been sure they would lose that game.

"Liam bungled a play, held on to the ball too long—got dogpiled by the other team. When I got to the bench, I told Coach Andrews he had to do something, or those guys would kill him."

"Coach Andrews knew?" Maya looked stunned.

"Of course he knew. Everyone knew—everyone on the team, at least. I thought Andrews would can me right then and there for finally saying it out loud, but Liam could hardly keep his feet under him when he walked off the field. I saw Andrews make up his mind. If he kept covering and Liam ended up in the hospital, it could be the end of his career."

Maya stared at him. He knew she was going over it

all her in mind. Trying to figure out who was the liar—
him or Liam.

Liam was her brother. That's where her loyalty lay.

"Andrews made you quarterback," she said slowly.

"He didn't have a choice. He didn't want to cross
your father, believe me, so he would have kept the
status quo if it had been at all possible. Liam was pissed.
He said your dad would have Andrews's head."

Maya frowned. "Coach Andrews wouldn't take that
kind of talk."

"He didn't. He told Liam his deal with your dad
didn't include this."

"Deal? What deal?"

Lance let her work it out for herself. The other couples on the dance floor kept swaying around them. He
wished they were somewhere else. Just the two of
them—

"You think Dad pressured Coach Andrews to make
Liam quarterback?" Maya asked.

"Maybe not to make him quarterback but to keep
him there long past when anyone else would get thrown
out."

"But he did get thrown out, and you led the team to
win the finals."

"I made Liam hate my guts," Lance countered.

Her shoulders lowered. "Dad was so pissed. I remember him yelling at Liam. But you never said a word
about it. I never heard any rumors—"

"Your dad was a deputy. Mine was a criminal. I
couldn't open my mouth if I wanted any kind of future

here." Might as well be honest. It was all out in the open now.

Of course, he'd had to leave town anyway in the end.

"Maya—" He needed her to know it was all in the past. That if Liam would stop hounding him, he'd let it go.

"Oh, my God," Maya said, her eyes widening. She was looking over Lance's shoulder.

Lance spun to see what was wrong. Stopped short.

Steel was dancing with—

"Stella!" Maya shrieked.

Lance couldn't believe it. Steel wasn't just dancing with Stella, he had her pulled in close, molded against his body, and was moving her around the floor like they were lovers who knew every inch of each other's bodies.

Maya turned on Lance. "Stella would never say yes to him. Did he force her—?"

Lance snorted. "She doesn't look like she's being forced."

Stella's gaze was pinned to Steel's face, and she was clinging to him, as if afraid she'd collapse if she let go.

"I'm serious! She'd never—"

"They're just dancing." They'd done so once before at Noah and Olivia's wedding, although not like this, he had to admit.

Maya whacked his arm. "You're not taking this seriously! Your brother's a—"

"A what? A criminal?" Lance looked down. "He's never been charged with a crime in his life."

"But everyone says—"

"What do they say?"

She looked at him helplessly. "None of us should be dancing with each other. All our families do is fight. All they'll ever do is fight."

"What about Noah and Olivia?"

"The exception that proves the rule." She looked close to tears. What was bothering her so much about Steel and Stella? He thought it was kind of... funny.

"We don't have to buy into this whole feud thing." He stepped closer to her, wanting to feel her in his arms again. There were no more secrets between them now. Surely they could find a way to get past all this.

"Lance." He saw regret in her eyes. Then determination. "There's something I need to tell you."

She'd said that before. "I'm listening." He held her there, letting the noise of the bar, the band and the swaying couples all spill around them.

"I know why my mom left. I think it's why your mom left, too. Your mother and my father—they were—*together.*"

It was as if the room slipped sideways. Like he'd lost his balance. He couldn't have heard her right. Lance kept swaying, but the music went funny in his mind.

"Lance? Did you hear me? Enid and my dad had an affair."

"My mom and your dad?" Lance dropped his arms and stepped back. "That doesn't make any sense." Or did it? His mom had hated the way Dale skirted the law. Had William Turner seemed more to her liking?

"Stella and Liam both say it's true."

Liam knew?

"No. I don't buy it."

Maya swallowed. "It doesn't matter if you do or don't, because there's something else. Something much worse."

He wanted to stop her. Whatever she was going to say would change everything. He knew it.

"Maya—"

She held up a hand. "Hear me out. I—I'm the reason the sheriff found out about the hides in your barn. I'm the reason Dale went to jail. I saw them one day when I was hanging out with Olivia—and then Mom left town—I didn't know why back then. Liam told me your family was to blame. He said you all had driven her away. I was eleven. I was stupid. I knew it wasn't hunting season. I went and told the sheriff—"

"Olivia was the one who told the sheriff," Lance protested. He'd learned that recently and had forgiven her for falling for a trap Cab Johnson's father had laid for her.

"The sheriff questioned Olivia because I told him about the poaching. He knew what to ask her—where to look. Lance, I'm sorry—"

Lance opened his mouth, but no words came. He reached a hand out to her, then drew it back just as quickly. "You... put my dad in jail?"

Dale had died there.

Maya's eyes beseeched him to understand, but he couldn't understand. When Dale was caught, Lance's whole world had turned upside down. First his father was gone, then his mother rushed them off to Idaho, then she ran away, and with her went all hope of him attending college. All hope of having a future.

Maya was the reason he'd lost his parents. The reason he'd never escape the endless toil and struggle of wresting a livelihood from his family's hot, dusty Montana ranch.

She must have read his thoughts. Tears gathered in her eyes, and she turned and fled the Dancing Boot, leaving Lance shaken to his core.

How many secrets could two families have?

"I'M REALLY SORRY I ran out on you last night," Maya said to Maggie again as she cradled her phone to her ear. She was washing up after a crack-of-dawn baking session, up to her elbows in sudsy water, her head aching and her eyes stinging after all the tears she'd cried the night before. She had to watch the clock. She always got an early-morning rush at the farm stand from people who were heading into town for work. She wished she could hide in her room all day. Sleep.

Forget the look in Lance's eyes when she'd told him what she'd done.

"That's okay. I had… fun." Maggie's voice was far more chipper on the other end of the line than it had been in ages. Maya was glad someone had enjoyed their night.

She wished she could turn back time and never go to the Dancing Boot in the first place.

Maya dried her hands and repositioned the phone. "I saw Bart ask you to dance. What happened next?"

"I said yes. I wasn't sure if I should, given the circumstances, but I did. It was… nice." She sighed. "He said he was sorry. Said he should have talked to me about the way he was feeling when his father died, but he just… couldn't."

"What about staying out all night? What about the money?"

That sounded far more cynical than she meant it to. She wasn't feeling very romantic today.

"You'll never believe what he was up to."

She sounded almost… amused. Maya couldn't imagine why that would be. "What?"

"He was trying to surprise me… with a house!"

It took Maya a moment to process that. "A… house?"

Maggie laughed, and Maya realized things really were better with her. She hadn't heard such a light tone in her voice in ages. "By the time the will was read, Bart had already realized he'd screwed up. He didn't handle his father's death well at all. He was drinking too much, staying out, being dumb. His dad had a lot of bills, and most of his assets, including his home, needed to be sold to cover them. Bart hadn't expected anything to be left. But there was. A commercial property at the edge of town. His father invested in it ages ago but hadn't had a tenant for a couple of years. It's just a big barn of a building surrounded by a lot of asphalt, but Bart thought it had promise. He took all our cash to renovate it—to make a house out of it for me and Katie."

"Oh, Maggie—that's so sweet!"

"Not really," Maggie said. "Maya—it's awful!"

Maya braced herself for tears at Maggie's tone, but they didn't come.

"I mean, I can't fault him for his impulse," Maggie went on, "although I told him it was a darn good thing I stopped him before he ordered the materials for the inside of the house, because his taste in finishings is—" She snorted. "But even if I pick out the tile and appliances and everything—oh, Maya, it's truly the ugliest property you've ever seen. He started putting up walls inside to make rooms, and he laid it out all wrong. And I don't want to live over on that end of town with the car lots and pawn shops—"

"Did you tell him that?" Maya asked gingerly.

"Of course not. It's a house—sort of. We always wanted a house."

"What are you going to do?"

"Let him renovate it. Do my best to make it a home however it turns out. Build my daughter a pretend yard on a sea of concrete."

"She'll be able to ride her bike on it, at least." Maya pulled a tray of tarts out of the oven and set them to cool.

"Yep." Maggie didn't sound impressed.

"Maybe it can be your starter home," Maya told her. "Live there a few years and then trade up."

"That's exactly what I've been telling myself. It's only temporary, right? And I did catch him before he painted it lavender."

"He wasn't going to—"

"Oh, yes, he was. Katie's favorite color!"

"Oh, Maggie." Maya had to laugh. At least Maggie and her husband were reconciled. That was what really mattered, wasn't it? "But you two—you're okay?"

"We're okay," Maggie confirmed. "You should have seen the look on his face as he was showing me everything. He'd worked so hard. He was trying—" Maggie half laughed, half sobbed. "Maya, I don't know how I'm going to stand that place, but at least I know my husband loves me."

"Lance has been helping. Maybe... maybe he could get some of us to come in and help, too. Maybe we can convince Bart to get the layout right, at least?"

"Maybe. I don't know. Enough about me. Did something happen with Lance last night? Things looked pretty hot and heavy there for a minute," Maggie asked.

Maya returned to her sink full of dishes, rinsed a plate and put it in the rack to dry. "For a minute. But that's over now."

"Why is it over?"

"Because of our family history. And because of something I did. It hasn't been the easiest twenty-four hours over here, either. Can you keep a secret?" She felt the need to tell someone about what she'd done. She'd kept it all bottled up for so long.

"Actually, I'm pretty good at that."

Maya filled her in on some of the details of what she'd told Lance the night before and found that Maggie was a sympathetic listener.

"You were a little girl back then," she said when Maya got to the part about turning Dale in. "Dale was a grownup. He's the one who decided to poach. He put himself in the position to get caught. You can't take the blame for that."

"I was old enough to know not to snitch on a neighbor. Especially when that neighbor was my best friend's father."

"You were doing what you thought was right."

"I was getting back at the Coopers, and I hurt Lance's family. Mine, too, in the end."

"So what are you going to do about it now?" Maggie asked. "You can't go back in time to fix any of that. Staying away from Lance now won't change the past, either. All you can do is start where you are."

"That's exactly what I'm doing. I'm backing away before anything worse happens."

Maya heard a noise behind her and turned to see Liam, dusty and sweaty from his early morning chores, leaned in the doorway watching her. Stella trailed in behind him. Time to pay the piper for her transgressions at the Dancing Boot, Maya figured. "Gotta go," she told Maggie and ended the call quickly.

"What the hell do you think you were you doing last night?" Liam demanded the moment she slipped her phone into her pocket.

"What were you doing?" Maya countered. "I saw you with Tory, Liam. You looked like you were having a good time. And you," she said to Stella. "Dancing with

Steel? What was that about?"

"You're the one who started it," Stella countered. "Cozying up to Lance like that. Liam was getting back at him for hitting on you. I was, too."

"By dancing with Steel?"

Stella turned abruptly and pulled open the refrigerator door. She rooted around inside it but took nothing out.

Maya turned to Liam. "How about you? Was Tory good and chastened after you waltzed with her?"

Liam reddened. "Just letting Lance know what it feels like when a lowlife hits on your sister."

"So you're a lowlife now?"

"That's not what I meant," he growled.

It would have been humorous if she wasn't so angry. She was sick and tired of the squabbling between their families and of having to always explain her actions. For once she'd like to do what she wanted, when she wanted—and with whom—without her family offering their two cents.

"You need to stop dancing with him," Liam told her. "Stop talking to him. Stop encouraging him. Did you forget about the Founder's Prize?"

"Did you?"

"Tory Cooper has nothing to do with the prize. She's only back in Chance Creek to go to school. Lance is the one we have to worry about," Liam said. "He hates our family. Always has."

Maya remembered what Lance had said the night before. If Lance was right, Liam had been lying to her for years.

"You always said he stole your position on the football team."

"Yeah? What of it?"

"You said he told the coach you were drinking when you weren't. But he said everyone knew you were drinking."

Stella shut the refrigerator door. "Lance is a Cooper. What do you expect him to say?"

"He said he was just doing his job. That Coach Andrews expected him to make Liam look good no matter how drunk he was on the field."

Stella turned to Liam, frowning. "Did you drink during games?

"I don't know what you're talking about." He had the same stubborn look on his face he'd always had when he'd gotten in trouble with their parents. Stella exchanged a troubled glance with Maya.

"Were you drinking the day you got kicked off the team?" Maya pressed.

"Everyone drank in high school," Liam snarled.

"When they were about to play one of the most important games of their lives?" Maya challenged him.

Stella watched them, but she didn't interrupt.

"Fine," Liam said. "You want the truth? I was drunk. So what? I drank at every game. And I still always won. Never screwed up a game for my team. You know that. Everyone knows that. Lance Cooper is an interfering ass, and I don't want him anywhere near my sister, you got that?"

"No, I don't got that." Maya's hands were shaking. Liam *had* been lying. She remembered the way their team had won the championship finals that year, but she also remembered the rumors that swirled around Lance's switch to playing quarterback in the second to last game. People had talked about him pushing Liam out. They'd hinted maybe Dale had threatened Coach Andrews. Everyone knew he was a criminal, after all. Lance had lived with those rumors all this time. "I'm not going to stay away from Lance," Maya said. "I'm going to help him save the museum. It's the least we can do after everything else we've done."

"You're going to help him win the Founder's Prize, you mean." Liam stepped forward when Maya struggled to answer. "You think Lance would be so gung-ho about that stupid re-enactment for any other reason? The Coopers want to tie up the competition for the prize, and you're playing right into his game."

"I'm doing just as much for the re-enactment as he is," she pointed out. Who was Liam to point fingers? What else had he lied about?

"I haven't heard anyone in town talk about Maya Turner's Revolutionary War re-enactment, but I've heard plenty of people mention Lance when they talk about it. It's his thing, not yours."

"Liam's right," Stella said. "Lance has got you working your ass off to make the re-enactment a success. When you raise all that money to move the history museum, he's going to take credit for it."

They were both missing the point. Their family had

run Lance down for years over stealing Liam's thunder. Liam had let everyone think he'd been blameless in it all.

"Lance isn't running the re-enactment to win a prize. He's doing it because he loves that museum."

"The history museum?" Liam's eyebrows shot up. "Su-ure." He drew out the word sarcastically. "I remember going to that place in grade school. It was a laugh a minute."

"Are you sure you remember it, or were you drunk then, too?"

She regretted her words the minute she said them. Liam stepped back, the light going out of his face. He shook his head. "You don't know what the hell you're talking about."

The flatness of his tone scared Maya. He sounded pushed to his limit. Like maybe there was something else she didn't know.

Was Liam in some kind of trouble?

"We should sabotage the re-enactment," Stella said, distracting her.

"Sabotage it?" Maya couldn't believe what she was hearing, but then Stella always came to Liam's defense, as if she were his mother, not his sister. She'd had to play mother to all of them when Mary left, Maya supposed, but this was going too far. "We can't sabotage the re-enactment. Warren Hill doesn't deserve his life's work to be ruined like that. He's the one with the most to lose here, or did you forget that?"

Stella's lips thinned, but Maya's arrow had hit its mark.

"What do we do then?" she demanded. "We can't let the Coopers win. We're hanging on by a thread here, or have you forgotten that?"

"We... help," Maya said. "More than we're doing already. That's what Turners do, right? Help their community?"

"I'm not helping with that damn thing," Liam said.

Stella was thinking. "Yes, you are. Maya's right; the way to stop Lance from claiming the Coopers are saving the museum is for us to save it instead. We have to take over the re-enactment. All of us have to join in. Together we can do far more than he's doing."

Maya's heart sank. When Stella got an idea, you couldn't shake her, and she didn't see what she could do to stop her siblings from taking part.

She couldn't wait until Fourth of July was over and she could forget about the whole damn thing. This wasn't the way she wanted it to go at all. She'd had such a good time writing the script and participating in planning the re-enactment. Getting closer to Lance had been amazing while it lasted. Now they were going to use it to get revenge on the Coopers?

"When's the next meeting?" Stella pressed. "We'll all have to go."

"Thursday. It's at... Thorn Hill."

LANCE COULDN'T WAIT until the re-enactment was over. Ever since Maya had run out of the Dancing Boot, time had crawled, and he was beginning to think he was stuck in some kind of infernal loop.

He spent his days hot, cranky, wishing for a storm to clear the air—

His nights wishing for a way to stop thinking of Maya—

And the past.

Today the entire Historical Society was coming to Thorn Hill. Parts would be assigned, scripts handed out, and they'd run through the action several times, reading from them. As if that wasn't enough, Enid had called twice. He needed to talk to her. To confront her—

And then what? Did it matter if she'd had an affair with William? Dale was dead. So was William. Couldn't the past stay buried?

Should he tell her it was Maya who'd gotten Dale thrown in prison, or should that stay buried, too? The more he thought about it, the more he suspected he'd overreacted when Maya had confessed to him. She'd been, what—eleven at the time? A child. How many times had Dale crossed the line over the years? Hadn't it been inevitable that sooner or later he'd be caught?

One thing confused him. No one had ever come out and told him what Dale was imprisoned for. Theirs was a household of denial—the less you talked about a thing, the more you could pretend it wasn't happening. Had his father been jailed for *poaching*?

Was that even possible?

Fined, sure. But jailed?

He could only assume Maya had been misled. Cab's father must have known far more about Dale's transgressions than he let on to her. Investigating Dale's poaching would have been excuse to get on Thorn Hill property with a search warrant. Once he had that warrant and had questioned Olivia, he must have known where to look for proof of other crimes. What was it that had finally brought down Dale?

He didn't have time to wonder about it now. He had to get all these cans of pop chilled and find some serving bowls for the chips he'd bought. Hungry actors were cranky actors. Better safe than sorry.

Bad enough he hadn't even mentioned to his aunt Virginia yet the rehearsal was happening here today. The museum was great for meetings, but it lacked the space they needed for this kind of rehearsal, and the town square, where they would hold the real deal, was too public. In prior years, the Historical Society had practiced in a field at the elementary school, but this year the soccer league was using it, and Lance had volunteered Thorn Hill's big front lawn.

When trucks began to pull up in front of the house, Virginia stood up from her seat in front of the television in the living room. Lance headed for the front door to welcome his guests, and she followed him.

"What's all this?"

"Rehearsal. For the re-enactment."

"Humph. You'd better tell all those people to stay off the grass."

"We're going to practice out there on the grass." And why not? No one had cared for the yard for years, except for taking a few passes over it with a riding mower each year before the summer sun dried it into a brittle stubble.

"They'll compact the soil."

Steel, walking through the room to the kitchen, raised an eyebrow but didn't comment. He kept going, and Lance knew they wouldn't see him again today. Earlier he'd said he had something to take care of this afternoon. What it was, he wouldn't say. He sure as heck wouldn't be caught dead at a re-enactment rehearsal, though.

"That soil's so compact you could bounce a bowling ball off it." Tory joined them in the front hall, craning her neck to look at the new arrivals through the screen door. "Maybe you should take up flower gardening, Virginia."

"Maybe I should," Virginia said tartly. "No one else in this family seems to have a homely touch."

Olivia, just entering the room, made a U-turn and walked back out.

"I see you, Olivia," Virginia hollered after her. "Don't think I don't. You're not one to fuss around the house, either, are you? That cabin of yours is plain as day."

"I'm too busy for fussing," Olivia said, coming back. "But I'll drive you to the store so you can buy some flats of annuals if you like."

"Humph. Like putting lipstick on a pig," Virginia said. "This house needs an overhaul top to bottom."

Lance couldn't fault her there. Judging by the looks on his siblings' faces, all of them agreed.

"I'd better get out there." He escaped gratefully

outdoors and began to divide people into teams, Redcoats and Colonials. For now, he made the Redcoats tie red strips of cloth around their arms. Later they'd practice with uniforms. Maya arrived with Mia and Avery. They had printed copies of the script, and they began handing them out. Avery gave him one, and he noticed one of the character's names had been written on top of it.

He was too busy watching Maya to pay it much attention. She kept her distance. That was fine; he didn't have much to say to her, either, despite his body coming to attention the moment she stepped out of her truck.

When most people had arrived, he called out, "Not everyone is here yet, but let's get started anyway. We have a lot to do. Maya, how about you handle the stragglers as they come? The rest of us will try out one of the scenes."

Maya pressed her lips together in a tight line and nodded. What was she disgruntled about? He hadn't sent her father to jail—inadvertently or not.

"We've gone ahead and tentatively assigned roles to people," Avery called out, coming to stand beside him. "You can see the name of your role written on top of your script. Ella, Rod and Gary, you're in the first scene together. Come on up, and let's try running through your lines."

"Good idea," Lance said. "Why don't you three stand over here. The rest of us will take a couple of steps back."

When they'd all done so, Avery stepped forward

again. "This scene takes place in South Carolina, where Louise Hicks is discussing the war with her husband and grown son. Louise's son is trying to convince his parents they're going to have to choose sides, while they're hoping the fight won't come to them. He's for independence. His father is vehemently against it. Louise, of course, feels caught between them. Ready?"

The three actors nodded. Lance had to admit Avery had done a good job setting up the scene. He remembered hearing that she'd studied acting at school and had even made a movie or two.

"Ella, take it away," Avery said.

"Donald. Rufus. Time for dinner," Ella said in her part as Louise. "What news did you hear in town today?"

"A lot of ruckus about the trouble getting closer," Rod said woodenly. "Some men think there'll be fighting even here."

"Don't you think they're right?" Gary belted out so loudly they all jumped.

"Woah; hold up." Lance strode in among them. "Ella, you nailed it." As she should, he thought. After all, she'd been a movie star up until a few years back. "Rod, you need to put more oomph into the part. Talk like it's happening to you. And Gary, take it down a notch, all right? Try again, folks."

Avery rustled the pages of her script in her hand. "Right. Let's try it again."

"Donald. Rufus. Time for dinner," Ella started over.

This time when it came Rod's part, he belted the

line like a town crier. "A lot of ruckus—"

"Hold up!" Lance stopped them again. "That's too loud."

"Lance," Avery said. "We're just getting started. Let's let people get into it."

"You told me—" Rod began.

Lance interrupted him. "I said say it with feeling. That's not the same as shouting. Try again."

Ella exchanged a look with Avery. "Donald. Rufus," she said a third time and continued on with her lines.

"A lot of ruckus up north," Rod whispered when it was his turn.

Lance balled his fists, but the look on Ella's face said if he interrupted again she was going to lose her cool. Avery was rustling her script again. Lance let the group carry on a few more minutes until Ella said, "Rufus, don't speak to your father that way!"

Gary didn't answer. Neither did Rod. Everyone waited.

"Whose line is that?" Lance finally asked.

"It's Gary's." Avery waved her script at the man.

"Whoops. Sorry." Gary flipped through the pages of his script, a flush working its way up his neck. "Guess I lost my place." All around them, the other participants fidgeted. This was painful.

"You're going to have to memorize those lines, you know," Lance said.

"This is the first time I've done this," Gary protested.

Ella bit her lip. Was she trying not to laugh? Lance

didn't think this was particularly funny. Neither did Avery, by the looks of things.

"Memorizing your lines will help you really understand the part," Ella told Gary placatingly, as if realizing things were coming to a boil. "You want to feel like you are Donald Hicks. Like you know trouble is coming. Like you want everything in your life to stay the same even as your son wants it all to change."

Ella was making a lot of sense, but with every word she said, Gary's features hardened.

"It's not my fault I'm not some fancy Hollywood actor," he started. A low buzz of conversations started all around them. People were already losing focus.

Someone was pulling in late, too. The truck was familiar, but it wasn't until Liam, Stella and Noah got out of it that Lance realized whose it was.

Why were they here? Had Maya asked them to come?

Speaking of Maya…

He watched her stride into the middle of the players, take Avery aside and talk to her. Then she turned and called out, "Hey, everyone, we've decided to make this more efficient. Each scene features a separate group of characters. Break up into your groups, and read over your lines. Avery and Ella will come around and help you out. Gary, you're doing a fantastic job. Remember, this is only the first day. You'll get the hang of it."

Just like that, she'd taken control of the situation. Ella came up to consult with her and Avery. Alice did, too, carrying a costume.

What was happening? He was supposed to lead these rehearsals. He'd always led the battle practices in the past. Lance stepped quickly through the small crowd and took Maya's arm. "Can we talk a minute?"

"I'm kind of busy—"

"Doing *my* job." Avery, Ella and Alice were all watching them, so he tugged Maya farther away. "Why is your family here? What's going on?"

"They want to help, just like everyone else. And I'm doing your job because you were about to set off a mutiny. You can't yell at people like that. We're all volunteers!"

"I'm not yelling. Gary was saying his lines all wrong—"

"Honey catches more flies than vinegar, which is why we're going to let Avery and Ella take charge of this part. Both of them are real actresses. Let them lead the others."

"This is my re-enactment—"

"It's everyone's re-enactment."

Looking around at the small groups reading from their scripts, Ella and Avery making their way between them, he had to admit she was right. He wasn't going to get any credit for this.

He never got any credit for anything.

MAYA'S STOMACH WAS twisted in knots, her hands shaking. She hadn't realized how it would look to Lance when she'd stepped in and headed off the disaster she saw coming. Gary had been turning purple in a combination of embarrassment and rage. Someone had needed to stroke his ego—not annihilate him in front of everyone.

Still, now she'd gone and done exactly what Stella had wanted her to do—taken away the one means Lance had to claim success at saving the museum for his family. Which wasn't fair. From the sounds of things, he'd pretty much single-handedly gotten the thing off the ground these past few years. "Not everyone can get a bunch of men with replica guns headed in the same direction" was the way one old-timer had put it to her recently. "Lance is a natural-born leader."

Now she'd sidelined him while Ella and Avery were running things.

"You really hate me, don't you?" he growled and walked away.

"I don't hate you!" Far from it. He was already gone, though, and she couldn't run after him without everyone present hearing what they said. She'd have to track him down later. Get him to understand.

She'd never wanted to hurt him. She simply kept doing so by mistake.

Why were relationships so impossible?

She spotted Maggie and Bart a few yards away, standing close together, bent over a script. They looked happier than she had seen either of them in a long time. Maggie had told her she'd convinced Bart to slow things down on the renovation so they could take time to figure out how to make the commercial structure a true home. She was determined to make the best of a bad situation and had started drawing up new plans, hoping to figure out a way to make the big building comfortable.

Maybe love wasn't a hopeless proposition, but it seemed like it was.

"Shouldn't you be practicing your scene?" Stella asked, startling Maya. She hadn't seen her sister approach.

"I guess." She looked at the front door, through which Lance was disappearing into the house. He was giving up on something he loved. She'd proven to him she was a Turner through and through. Bound and determined to ruin things for his family.

Stella followed her gaze and sighed. "It had to be done. We couldn't let him claim the re-enactment for the Cooper side."

"I just stole Lance's dream like you told me to, the same way I busted up his family years ago because Liam said they'd busted up ours. I never even stopped to ask what he meant back then. Just assumed because he was a Turner he had to be right. Now I've done it again."

"Maya—"

"No. Don't say anything, because I'm not listening to you or Liam anymore. You aren't right. You never have been. We Turners aren't any better than the Coopers. You know what? I think we're worse."

"Maya—"

"I love him!" She lowered her voice when several people turned their way. "I love Lance. I know it doesn't make any sense. I know it makes you angry and will make Liam hate my guts. I know we don't need any more drama in our lives, but that doesn't change anything. I love him. And now I've driven him away for good."

Chapter Thirteen

HARD AT WORK in his shop early the next morning, eager to get all memory of the re-enactment rehearsal out of his mind, Lance was surprised when a shadow crossed his door, and he looked up to see Stella Turner. He was still burning from Maya's betrayal. Bad enough she'd ever made him think she liked him. That she'd stolen his heart and made love to him like she meant it. That she'd nearly convinced him they weren't on opposite sides. The fact she'd deliberately undermined his standing at the re-enactment was the last straw.

"What are you doing here?" He set down the rasp he'd been using to smooth a piece of wood and waited. Stella Turner might look innocent, but she was as much an enemy as the rest of the Turner clan.

She didn't give a rat's ass about Chance Creek's history, or the museum, but she'd shown up out of nowhere yesterday and bustled around to help everyone with their tasks. Liam had, too. He knew it couldn't be a coincidence they'd arrived at the same moment Maya was handing his leadership role over to Avery and Ella.

"I was looking for you." She entered the shop.

Lance wanted to kick her right back out, but he was too well-bred to do it.

He offered her a seat in an unfinished chair instead.

Stella sat down and crossed one leg over the other. She was casually dressed, but her back was as straight as if she was wearing a crown, her expression just as regal. He thought she meant to chew him out, but instead she said, "I'm afraid, okay?"

"Of what?" Was she laying a trap for him? He didn't know what to think of her presence here.

"You. Your family. The future."

"You don't have to be afraid of us." More like the opposite, to his way of thinking. Turners took everything that wasn't nailed down.

"Your father's criminal tendencies drove your mother into my father's arms." She leaned forward to make her point. "She destroyed my family."

"Hold up there." Lance crossed his arms and leaned against the workbench. "Dale wasn't perfect, and there are plenty of things I wish he hadn't done, but if my mom slept with your dad, it was her own choice. *If* she slept with him," he emphasized. "What she'd want with a self-satisfied, smug prick like your dad I can't fathom. I notice she didn't stick around. He must not have satisfied her, if they were together."

"Don't you talk about my dad like that!"

"Then stop dragging my mother through the dirt."

Stella took a breath. Blew it out. "Maya needs someone who will give her a good life, not some petty criminal."

"I'm not a petty criminal, but you don't worry about it either way. She's obviously not interested me. If she was, she wouldn't have done what she did yesterday."

"You have no plans. How long before you get sick of being poor and decide to make a little cash on the side, the way your dad did?"

"I just said—"

"Maya wants to go to college. You can't afford to send her there anymore than we can right now."

"She doesn't want me!" Lance roared. And he didn't want her, either.

Even if he couldn't stop thinking about her.

"I've already had to accept Noah being with Oliva," Stella went on as if she hadn't heard him. "At least Noah's got ambition. He'll make something of himself. If you and Maya end up together, you'll both go no-where. How is that a good thing?"

"I'm going somewhere!" He ran a hand over his jaw. She was really something, wasn't she? "You think you're something special?" he snapped, losing his cool. "You're the one who's stalled out, far as I can tell. Working at the sheriff's office, answering phones? Any high school dropout could do your job. The Flying W is going to seed as fast as Thorn Hill is. Seems like you're no better off than me. Worse, even. But it doesn't matter, does it? Because Maya doesn't give a shit about me! None of you Turners care about anyone but yourselves!"

Stella stood up. "Maya shouldn't give a shit about you, because you're going to break her heart, one way or another."

She walked out the door. Lance went after her, but when he got outside, Stella was already halfway to her truck.

Maya *shouldn't* give a shit about him?

Did that mean she did?

MAYA WAS SITTING at her farm stand, picking out the stitches where she'd joined the replacement lace to her cap, when a large black truck arrived. She'd decided she didn't care if she had to join the two torn pieces of the original lace together to make it work. Didn't care if the repair showed. Back when she'd started the project, she'd searched high and low for the vintage material, and it was perfect. The plainer, newer lace she'd replaced it with simply wasn't right.

The door swung open, and a man's boot appeared, then a leg encased in worn jeans, and Steel Cooper stepped out. Maya's back straightened, not because she thought Steel might do her any harm—although he certainly had a dangerous reputation—but he always had a look on his face like he had just heard some bad news.

This morning he looked like he was about to deliver some bad news.

"We need to talk about Lance," he said curtly, striding over to stand before her so she had to look up to make eye contact.

"What about him?" Everything between them was over.

He thought she hated him.

She'd sure acted like she did.

"You need to end it." Steel braced his palms on the table and leaned over it, legs spread. She wondered if he'd vault it next.

"I already—"

"Look, you like Lance, I get that, but you need to be practical."

Maya had never been so close to Steel. His gaze held hers, and a muscle in his jaw flexed. Was he angry?

Or worried?

"But I—"

"Break it off. Now. Stop leading him on."

"I'm not leading him on." She wasn't doing anything. He was the one who—

Steel leaned closer. "You don't want to be with him for real. Admit it."

Maya leaned back. "What makes you say that?" Steel didn't know anything about her.

"I saw your face when I danced with your sister. You hate us. You think you're better than us. So go ahead and say it—you're playing with him. You're not in it for the long haul."

"No one's talking about the long haul." They hadn't gotten that far yet. They never would now.

"I know what you did thirteen years ago. I know Olivia was sneaking away to see you. I know you were friends. You tossed all that out the minute you thought you knew something bad about my father. You'll do the same with Lance when things get tough. And they will get tough—you know that as well as I do." Steel looked beyond her toward the horizon, as if he saw a storm that no one else knew was coming. "Lance has a heart. He doesn't need it broken by a woman like you."

"What the hell does that mean, *a woman like me*?" Maya had heard just about enough. And how did he know about her and Olivia? And what she'd done?

"A woman who has no staying power. Who runs at the first sign of trouble." Steel pushed off the table and stood tall. "A woman who'll never truly love him, simply because of his last name."

Maya fumed as she watched him walk away. Who did he think he was to tell her what she did and didn't want?

"He's the one who walked away from me," she shouted after him. "He's the one who can't forgive the past."

Neither could Steel, she realized suddenly. He was afraid all women were like his mother, wasn't he? That they'd run away when things got hard.

Steel stopped. Turned around. Walked back to her.

"You're not the victim here."

She stood up and faced him over the table. "Neither are you." She watched surprise flash over his face and pressed her advantage. "You're right; I've hurt your family, and I'm sorry for that, but you hurt Lance, too. You didn't go to Idaho when Enid took him and your sisters away. He was the one who had to support Tory and Olivia when your mom bailed on them. He's the one who has to work your ranch now while you flutter around doing who knows what."

"I don't… flutter."

"He's the one who's given up his dreams—for you." She watched her barb sink into his skin. "You're right; I hurt him. Bad. So he doesn't love me anymore. I deserve that. It doesn't mean I don't still love him, though. I'm paying for my mistakes. How about you? Are you going to pay for yours?"

He stood still as stone, until Maya began to feel afraid. Steel was man with a lot of secrets—had she misjudged the way he'd accept her criticism?

"I'm paying," he finally said. "More than you know."

She shook her head. He wasn't paying nearly as much as she was.

Maybe he could read her mind, because he stepped back. Ran a hand through his hair. Turned away as if he'd leave.

Turned back.

"He still loves you, too."

She could see it cost him to say it. He turned on his heel and strode away. Climbed into his truck, slammed the door and roared off, leaving Maya to clutch the edge of the table and fight to catch her breath.

Was Steel right? Did Lance still—

No. She couldn't let herself hope he was right.

Lance had made it perfectly clear he was over her.

LANCE USED THE tail of his shirt to wipe the sweat from his eyes and kept loading his truck with equipment for the re-enactment. Without his trysts with Maya to look forward to anymore, his days dragged. There was plenty of work to do with ranch chores, re-enactment rehearsals and his time working on new furniture to sell to raise money. Still, each day seemed longer than the last. What a mess he'd made of everything.

He'd decided he'd heard Stella wrong. Maya had been all too clear she was done with him, and her behavior in the interim hadn't indicated any change of heart. She kept her distance at rehearsals. Avery and Ella ran the acting portions of the show, and he took over when it was time to do the battle. He was having trouble feeling any enthusiasm for the endeavor this year, though.

Lance was in several scenes with some of the Mathesons, who lived at the Double-Bar-K. Maya was in a scene with Manfred Willis and his sister, Leslie. Manfred and Maya were playing newlyweds, while Leslie was a young widowed bride who'd lost her husband in one of the earliest battles in the war.

Manfred and Maya were supposed to kiss goodbye, one of the most heart-wrenching scenes in the preliminary part of the program. Ella had advised them to save the kiss for the actual production so as not to get too caught up in the awkwardness of it during practice.

"On the day of the re-enactment, you'll get so into your parts it will come naturally," she'd said.

It had better not come too naturally, Lance had thought, and then had felt worse when he realized he didn't have the right to be jealous anymore.

He reminded himself he wasn't supposed to care who Maya kissed, but the thought of her mouth—and her body—and hell, just her—was keeping him up nights and distracted all day.

He did care who she kissed. He wanted it to be him, no matter what she'd done. It was hard to keep remembering she'd made it impossible for him to take credit for saving the museum. That she'd been instrumental in putting his father in jail. At least her family wouldn't get credit for the re-enactment, either.

Avery and Storm had whipped up a website for the show, complete with an online option for buying tickets. They'd been posting all over social media, and Lance was beginning to realize that his backward little town had a strong online community. He'd never even known about the *Chance Creek Chronicles* page, where anyone could post happenings and events.

Storm and Avery had made posters, too, and evidently a bunch of the women, including Maya, had hung them up everywhere. He hadn't even been asked to be part of it.

"You okay?"

Lance turned to find Tory a few feet away. "I'm fine," he said shortly.

"Don't seem fine. You're touchy as hell these days. What happened between you and Maya?"

He was about to say nothing, but anyone could see something had happened, and why was he still keeping secrets? What had that ever gotten him?

"She's the one who put Dad in prison." He laid out

what Maya had told him without holding back. Maybe shining a light on the past could burn all the pain out of it.

When he was done, he snapped the tailgate into place and moved to the driver's side door. "I've got to go."

"Hold up." Tory was processing what he'd said. He could practically see her turning it over in her mind. She looked up at him. "You… love Maya, don't you?"

He froze, gripping the handle.

"It's obvious. At least to me. And I think—I think Maya cares for you, too."

"No, she doesn't," he said. "And it wouldn't change anything if she did."

"Come on, Lance. Maya had to have been twelve or something when all that went down with Dad."

"Eleven."

She gave him a look. "Too young to bear the responsibility for what she did. Dad was the one breaking the law. All the time," Tory added, repeating the same things he'd been thinking these past few days. "You know it. I know it. Mom knew it." She took in a deep breath. "Mom was dumb. She made a mistake marrying Dad. I bet she thought he'd settle down when they got married and had kids. He didn't. So he went to jail, and she looked for happiness somewhere else. It has nothing to do with Maya—or with you or me."

"You really believe that?"

"Seems to me we're all paying for what Mom and Dad did. Maybe we should start living our own lives, don't you think?"

"Is that why you're back?" he made himself ask.

"I told you why I'm back. School."

"Exactly, which sounds a lot like living your life. I'm… glad, you know. Missed you."

"Missed you, too, but I'm not letting this place eat me alive. I'm focusing on my future. You should do the same. You wanted more than to be a rancher."

She was right; he had. But he'd lost his chance.

When he didn't answer, she sighed. "At least don't give up on Maya. Let yourself be happy."

"Maya's the enemy," he said tiredly.

"What if she isn't? What if she is simply a woman who lives nearby?"

His body's reaction was swift and sure. If Maya was just a woman—a neighbor—someone without a century of rancor between their families—he'd go find her, now, and make her his wife.

"Forget the feud. Forget the Founder's Prize. Forget all of it before it destroys you the way it destroyed our parents," Tory advised him. "At least think about patching things up with her, will you?" She turned to go.

Think about it?

Like he could do anything else.

Chapter Fourteen

O N THE FOURTH of July, Lance stood in the predawn light looking at the town square, where the re-enactment would take place in just a few hours. Everyone had worked late into the evening the previous night to set up the food and vendor booths, build the encampment and get the sets into place for the actual performance.

He and some of the most dedicated members of the society had come back well before sunrise to finish up. They were ranchers, and used to working hard, but they were behind schedule.

He knew he ought to be panicking. Instead, he worked at his tasks methodically; his fear they might not be ready in time had become a dull ache, something he was aware of but that didn't seem to matter as much as it used to.

He couldn't stop thinking about what Tory had said a few weeks back. Was he making a mistake? Should he talk to Maya?

Was there a way to put the feud behind them?

Somehow he hadn't been able to make himself take the first step.

He hadn't been able to ask his mother about the past, either. Couldn't even make himself call her.

Some part of him was afraid there might be more skeletons to uncover in the family closet.

"Lance? Can we get your help?"

Two men were passing by lugging a load of lumber between them. He hurried to follow them. It was too late to do anything until this day was over, anyhow. He had too much to do, and so did Maya. He owed it to everyone to keep his eye on the prize.

It was hard to feel much anticipation about saving the history museum, though. He'd looked forward to finding it a new home, making new exhibits, researching the artefacts and presenting the information, but last night he'd overheard Warren talking to Bart about how well Maya and Mia had done writing the script for the performance and how he thought they should be nominated to work on the new exhibits, too.

Maya and her friends had won, which was a good reminder that the woman he still cared about, no matter how many times he tried to harden his heart against her, didn't care about him at all.

He had no idea what he'd do when this day was over. The Historical Society had been his one outlet in a life that seemed awfully flat lately. It was bad enough his family wouldn't be able to count saving the museum toward their accomplishments in town when it came to the Founder's Prize. Losing his chance to fix up the museum was... crushing.

All he'd ever be here in Chance Creek was a rancher—on a ranch that was fading away with every day that passed this long, hot summer. Maybe Tory was right. Maybe he needed to get back to school—somehow. Or simply leave—

"Think we're going to get this done on time?" Warren asked, hurrying over to him.

Who cares? he nearly said out loud before he managed to bite back the words. No matter how badly his own life was going, he wouldn't take it out on the older man. Warren had kept Chance Creek's history alive despite low pay and few resources. He didn't have a family or a ranch or anything else to sustain him, but he never whined or moaned when things went wrong.

A wave of self-disgust washed over Lance. When had he become such a quitter? When had he decided there was no hope for him at all?

"Lance, do you think we're going to be late?" Warren asked again. "People will be here in a few hours, and I don't—"

Even if nothing else in his world was going right, he could help a good friend save his life's work. And then—then he could stop being such a wimp and figure out how to go after his own dreams.

He could call up Montana State. See if a scholarship was still available to him. Talk to Lance—and Stella—and Olivia and Noah, for that matter. See if they could work something out.

His dreams had nothing to do with the feud, or the past. He didn't have to give them up because he and Maya weren't together anymore.

"Do you think we should call it off?" Warren's voice rose in panic.

"No." Lance gathered his thoughts. "No," he said louder. "We're not calling anything off. We're getting this done. We're saving the museum. Now. Today."

Warren nodded eagerly. "Good."

"And I'll tell you what—" All around him, men straightened from their tasks to see what the commotion was about. "I'll tell you what," he said again even louder. "I don't just want to save the museum, I want to build the new exhibits. I want to research every part of our collective past. I want to make it the best damn repository of history anyone's ever seen. Warren, you've done a damn good job running the place for the last thirty years, but you told me you were ready to step down. Here's your notice. I'd be proud—damn proud— if you'd consider me for the job of running it when you call it quits." To hell with what anyone else thought.

"I'm glad to hear it. I hope you mean to get that degree—"

"Hell, yeah. Soon as I can."

Someone started clapping behind him. He turned to find Maya there, and he stiffened. Was this another trick?

"You're the best person for the job of revamping the museum, Lance," she said. "I'm glad to hear you're going to go after it. Don't let anyone stop you, especially not me or my family. Tell me how I can help, because I owe you that."

Lance didn't know what to say.

Warren peered at her. "You're that girl who always came to look at the pretty dresses, aren't you? Didn't put it together before when you started coming to the meetings, but now I remember."

"I love history," she told him. "Especially period clothing."

"Maybe you should work at the museum, too. Lance will need some help."

Maya was already shaking her head. "I'm not ruining anything else for you," she told Lance. "I've made enough trouble already. I'm… sorry. I really am."

He wasn't sure what to say. He was hesitant to trust her after everything that had happened.

"I didn't mean to take over the re-enactment," she went on. "You were getting so frustrated with the actors, and I wanted to head off any trouble. I over-stepped—"

"No. You didn't," he found himself saying. "You're right; I was getting frustrated. I've organized the battles before, but I never had to get anyone to do more than die convincingly. I didn't know how to make Gary say his lines right. In another minute we would have been fighting."

"That's what I was afraid of," she admitted.

"I do tend to get into fights now and then."

"So… if you wanted, I could help you write new cards for the museum exhibits," she offered shyly. "My cursive is pretty good." A mischievous grin lit up her face, and in spite of himself, Lance found himself grinning back.

It felt so good to smile at Maya.

"I'm not really into all that clothing stuff. You could do that part—and write up all the notecards to explain what the mannequins are wearing."

Warren frowned. "We need something more up-to-date, I think. I never could read those handwritten cards…"

Lance laughed. "All right, you've convinced us."

Warren peered at Maya again. "You don't have a degree, either."

Maya shook her head. "I've never had the chance to go to school."

"Then we'll have to find you both scholarships. You could travel to Billings together for class. Split the museum hours and still find time for your other chores. I figure you'll have a passel of volunteers to help you." He gestured to the crowd. "But first we need to raise those funds, or there'll be no museum. We need to get back to work!"

Lance met Maya's gaze.

"I can back off," she assured him in a low voice. "I know you don't want to be around me."

Was she crazy? All he wanted was to be with her. "I don't want you to back off," he managed.

"I don't expect you to forgive me, but I hope some-day you can. When that happens, maybe we can be friends again?"

He wanted a lot more than Maya's friendship, but he decided they'd taken their first steps toward a future that suddenly looked a lot brighter than it had a few minutes ago. That was enough for now.

"I'd like that."

Maya's smile widened, and hope lit her eyes. Lance's heart squeezed. He wanted to kiss her. Assure her he'd never stopped loving her.

He'd never told her he loved her, though.

"Warren's right—we have to hurry," Maya said, checking the time on her phone. "I think we need reinforcements." She waved a hand at everything that was still undone.

He'd tell her later, he decided. First they'd save the museum. Lance pulled out his phone and tapped the screen.

Steel picked up right away, no trace of sleep in his voice. "What?"

"I need as many men as you can muster. Now."

"Be right over."

Thank God for Steel. You never needed to waste time with explanations. He dialed Tory next. "Hey, we're running short on time over here, and we've got a lot to do. Can you come?"

"Be right there."

"Know anyone else who could help?"

She was quiet a minute. "Yeah, I'll call a few people."

He hesitated before making one last call.

"What's wrong now?" Virginia snapped when she answered her phone.

"I need help. Lots of it. At the town square."

He hung up. No sense wasting his time. Virginia

would either pull through or she wouldn't.

"Lance," Maya said and stopped.

"Yeah?"

"I've... missed you." She turned on her heel and hustled off. Lance watched her go.

He'd missed her, too. Later on, he'd figure out what to do about it. For now, he had to get to work.

He surveyed the square, took in the state of the various projects and went to lend a hand setting up the vendor booths and picnic area. Soon he was unloading tables and chairs and carrying equipment along with a group of men. Lance found that when he picked up his pace, they did, too, and soon everyone was hurrying. He moved from project to project, urging everyone on, lifting, carrying and assembling booths, tables and anything else that needed it.

When he looked up again he realized the number of people working had grown substantially. There was Steel—and a number of his friends. Men whose activities Lance didn't want to look into too deeply.

There was Tory and a bunch of women he recognized as her old school friends. He hadn't seen her hanging out with them since she'd been home, but they'd come to help now.

And there—Lance laughed in surprise—there was Virginia, stepping primly between workers, carrying a light load of paper cups to one of the food tents. Now that he looked around, he recognized a number of denizens of the Prairie Garden—Chance Creek's retirement home. Not exactly old friends of hers. More like old minions.

"We're getting there," Warren said, appearing at his elbow. "I think we're going to be ready after all. You're good at this. Ever thought of running for office in town?"

"No," Lance said truthfully. Him—a politician? That was laughable.

"You should think about it. Maybe not yet. First get your degree, work at the museum and get some years teaching under your belt. Then become a town councilor. You'd make a good one." He slapped Lance on the back and hurried off to help Rod move a cooler of soft drinks.

Lance watched him go, a strange feeling in his chest that had been flickering there since he'd stood up and declared his desire to run the museum.

Happiness—and something else. Pride, Lance realized. People had accepted him. Praised him. Looked to him.

Maybe he had a future here after all.

"I THINK WE'RE all set," Avery said. "Has everyone checked in?"

Maya ran her pen down the list of actors and actresses with parts in the re-enactment.

"Wait—where are Manfred and Leslie?" she asked with a sinking heart. She realized she hadn't seen the Willises in a couple of hours. "They were here first thing this morning. Manfred was helping with the food tents. They never came to check in, though."

Everyone looked around, and Avery pulled out her phone. She tapped in a few numbers. "I've got everyone in my contacts," she told them.

"I should have thought of that," Maya said.

"Manfred?" Avery waited. "You're at the hospital? Are you hurt?" She waited another beat. "Okay. Yep. Okay. Don't you worry about a thing. We'll handle this." She hung up and faced them. "Cooler landed wrong on his finger. Looks like a sprain. Leslie is there with him. They're waiting for the doctor. They'd hoped to be in and out quickly enough to get back here, but it doesn't look like that will happen."

"What are we going to do?" Maya asked.

Avery picked up her script and flipped through the pages. "They're in that scene with you, Maya. It's an important one—a real attention-getter."

"Who can fill in? Who'd know the lines?" Storm asked.

Maya thought fast. "Lance could do Manfred's part," she said. "He knows all the parts. I've heard him give everyone their cues over the past few weeks."

"But he's in a later scene—"

"We'll have to do a clothing change," Avery said thoughtfully. "I can do Leslie's part," she added. "I know all the lines in the show."

Maya nodded. "That would work."

"Let's get Lance and rehearse," Avery said.

She led the way, and Maya followed, only now realizing what she'd done. Her scene with Manfred was heart-wrenching. Could she act across from Lance and get it right?

They caught up with him near the encampment.

"Everything ready?" he asked, looking up from some notes he'd jotted on a pad of paper.

"Not quite. We need you." Avery took his hand and pulled him unceremoniously to one side of the hubbub. She explained the problem and offered him a script.

"I know those lines," Lance confirmed.

"Come on, then, let's give it a try—quickly," Avery said.

In the scene, Avery played a widow who'd lost her husband during an earlier skirmish. Lance was a young soldier determined to put his life on the line. Maya was the bride he'd be leaving behind, torn between pride in his sense of duty and her love for him.

Avery stopped them before the final kiss. "Save it for the real deal," she said.

Lance made a face. Avery didn't catch it, but Maya did, and she bit back a laugh even though the thought of kissing Lance had her hot and hungry. She'd thought of little else in the time since they'd fought. Now that they'd made up—at least partly—it was all she could think of again.

In less than an hour they'd kiss for real.

She couldn't wait.

Avery made Maya run through their other scene— the later one in which Maya was waiting for Lance to finally come home again, and then Avery said, "Come on—we've got to go finish getting ready."

Maya didn't think she'd ever been so nervous as

when Warren called the proceedings to a start an hour later. The crowd in attendance was far larger than she'd hoped for, and the wide lawn where they were seated was so full hardly any grass was visible. She'd put on her costume, including the cap, which she'd finally finished. The place where she'd stitched the two torn pieces of lace together was visible to a keen eye, but Maya didn't care. The result matched her original vision, and if it was imperfect, well, so were most things in life.

Warren made the usual greetings and announcements, and when he was done, Ella, Gary and Rod took the stage. Soon the show was off and running, and in no time flat it was their turn to head onto the grassy stage. Maya's old-fashioned costume helped bring her into the scene, but the size of the audience unnerved her.

"Don't go!" Avery cried, and the scene began, with Avery beseeching her "brother" not to go off to war and Maya as his wife trying to be stoic as she said goodbye to him. Just like Ella had said so long ago, she got caught up in the story as she acted it out, and by the time Lance was at the door, ready to leave to join the Colonial forces, she was nearly in tears.

"Just say you'll come back," she said, clinging to Lance, who'd never seemed more handsome to her than in his homespun replica uniform. "I don't know what I'd do without you!"

"Who can say where the winds of war will blow me, but if it is in my power, I'll be back and never leave your side again."

Lance pulled her into a kiss, and Maya went up on

tiptoe to meet him. His mouth on hers jolted her with a longing so bare she couldn't pull away, even though she knew she had to. Her arms went around his neck, and his around her waist, and she kissed him until she grew dizzy. Only then did the cheering of the crowd penetrate her tangled thoughts.

Maya pulled away. Lance touched her cheek and hustled off the side of the stage area.

When she hurried in the other direction, she met Liam's furious gaze.

"THAT WAS SOME acting," Warren said.

"Yeah, yeah." Lance changed quickly. He had to be in uniform for the big battle scene. Warren was right, though. That kiss had been a real humdinger.

No acting needed on his part at all.

The rest of the scenes that led to the battle ran smoothly, and soon he was lining up with the rest of the men in his contingent. He was on the Redcoat side. When Steel slid into place beside him, uniform on, holding a replica musket, Lance couldn't hide his shock.

"What are you doing?"

"Helping. Just like you asked."

"I just meant we needed help setting up—"

"You're going to need a lot more than that." Steel jutted his chin at the Colonial forces mustering on the far end of the field. Liam stood front and center, calling out orders, getting his men in straight lines.

"He sounds pissed," Lance said.

"And he's been drinking."

Lance turned to Steel again.

"You just kissed his sister like you were getting ready to strip her down and take her right there. Didn't you think that would set him off?"

Hell.

"You weren't thinking at all, were you?"

"Maybe not," Lance conceded.

"Watch your back when this starts."

"Not much he can do with a fake rifle," Lance pointed out.

"Men clobbered each other's brains out with the stocks of these things during the real war," Steel countered. "Whatever you did to him, he's looking for revenge."

Lance swallowed. Steel was right. He should have had things out with Liam years ago. It had built up until the problem seemed impossible to confront.

It occurred to him he'd never asked Liam why he drank before the games. It had to be nerves. Was there something he could have done to help calm Liam down?

"Noah doesn't look happy, either," Steel muttered.

He didn't, but not in a murderous way, like Liam. More like in a hopeless way. He could see the coming danger, too. Didn't know how to stop it any more than Lance did.

"You could cut and run," Steel said.

"Are you shitting me?"

Steel chuckled. "Didn't think you'd go for that."

"Would you?"

"Probably not."

"This is going to be a disaster," Lance said. His brother grunted, not taking his eyes off the Turners.

The other actors were starting to feel it, too. At first, all the men on the field had struggled to contain their excitement for the big scene, with the Hall men brazenly breaking character to wave and wink at their women in the audience along with other men among the ranks of both sides.

People on the sidelines held up banners and signs proclaiming which army they were supporting. It should have been fun.

As the Coopers' and Turners' tension started to infect the rest of their respective sides, however, Lance gripped his replica musket more tightly. Each actor was turning in an award-winning performance: shifting anxiously, gripping their muskets with sweaty palms, watching the enemy lines with real apprehension.

The field of spectators quieted down. People stopped waving their banners. It seemed as if everyone was holding their breath.

The re-enactment had never captured the audience like this before.

"Better get this over with," Steel muttered.

Lance, playing the Redcoat general, stepped forward, preparing to give the order to charge. He gripped his musket, testing its weight, as Liam faced off with him across the field.

Maybe this would be a good thing in the end, he decided. The feud between their families had been simmering for too long.

It was time to have it out once and for all.

"OH, HELL," MIA Matheson said as the two forces stood eyeing each other across the field. "Is anyone else seeing what I'm seeing?"

Maya sure was.

"Liam looks ready to murder Lance," Avery said.

"Steel looks ready to murder everyone," Maggie said.

"Those weapons aren't real, are they?" Storm asked.

"No, but they can still do a hell of a lot of damage." Mia stepped forward, as if ready to run between the two lines, then stepped back. "What do we do?"

"What can we do?" Avery said.

"We should—"

Lance called out the command to charge. As the armies hurled themselves toward each other, a few of the men followed the script, firing harmless rounds at their foes, but the majority kept going, led by the Turners and Coopers, turning their firearms around to use them as bludgeoning weapons. With prop guns, it was the only maneuver that would let them dish out real damage.

"What do we do?" Mia screamed.

Maya looked around for help. Spotted Olivia standing at the edge of the field near Tory, her eyes wide with horror. As if she'd felt Maya tap on her shoulders, she turned and met Maya's gaze. Understanding passed between them. They had to stop this, or someone they loved would be hurt.

Maya didn't even know she was running until she reached Olivia. She caught a glimpse of Lance fighting with one of the Dawson boys. Liam had been detained by one of the Mathesons. They hadn't reached each other yet.

"How do we stop them?" Olivia cried.

"The same way we always stop battles. We're angels of peace, remember? Come on!"

A smile broke out over Olivia's face. "Angels of peace. Of course!"

She grabbed Maya's hand, and together they ran out onto the field.

"Women!" Maya shrieked as loudly as she could. She got the attention of some of the members of the crowd. "Women, shall we let our menfolk tear apart our country and our families? Shall we let them destroy everything we've built?" She hoped like hell her voice would last. More people were looking her way now, thinking she was part of the performance. Well, she was now—even if she was ad-libbing. "Or shall we be angels of peace and put an end to the strife before us?"

"Peace!" Olivia shouted, backing her up. "Angels of peace, unite!" She gestured for the women in the audience to join them. Most people looked baffled, but Mia ran onto the field to stand with them.

"Peace!" she shouted. "I'm an angel of peace, too!

Ella and Avery exchanged a look and a shrug and came to join them.

"I'm an angel of peace," Avery shouted, "And I

shall wreak vengeance on anyone disturbing the... peace." She made a face. "That's not right," Maya heard her mutter.

"Peace!" Ella grabbed a parasol off the ground and held it aloft like a sword. Tall, beautiful, with a voice that carried far better than the others', she got the audience's attention. "I am an angel of peace, and I will swoop in to restore order! Arm yourselves, ladies! Find weapons, angels! We go to war—for peace!"

Maya grabbed another parasol from the grass nearby and brandished it high. Mia found a serving tray from one of the earlier scenes. Avery grabbed a toy wooden sword from one of the kids in the audience. "I'll bring it right back!" she promised.

More women joined them, their skirts swirling, armed with everything from coolers to a folding chair. Others were getting to their feet, exchanging glances with friends and shrugging.

"I'll be an angel of peace," Maya heard one woman say. "Why not?"

Maya raised her parasol like Ella had a moment earlier and turned toward the battle raging behind them. "Peace!" she screamed. "Into the fray, angels!"

"Peace!" her followers echoed.

As they raced toward the melee, Maya hoped like hell she was doing the right thing.

Chapter Fifteen

"**I**'M GOING TO kill you, Cooper!"

Lance lunged to the side just in time to duck a broadside from the butt of Liam's rifle. Liam swung again, and the heavy wooden weapon glanced off Lance's shoulder.

He swore, swung his own rifle and clipped the side of Liam's head. "This is supposed to be a fucking re-enactment," he bellowed.

"This is supposed to be me putting you in your grave!" Liam came at him, his fury making him reckless. He swung too soon. Lance ducked again and hit him solidly in the ribs this time.

"This isn't the place. Get a grip, Turner!"

Out of his eye he noticed Steel close by, grappling with Noah. Both had lost their weapons, but they were going at it seriously. Hell, he hadn't meant to get his brother involved.

Liam jumped him, and Lance lurched forward, unprepared for the weight of the other man on his back. They both spilled to the ground, but Lance kept a grip on his weapon. Liam dropped his, reared up on his knees and fell on Lance, his hands searching for Lance's neck.

"Goddamn it, Liam—"

"Ow!" Liam fell sideways, clutching his head, and Lance looked up to see Maya brandishing a bent parasol.

"What the hell, Maya?" Liam growled.

"Back off, Liam—I'm here to dole out PEACE!" she hollered, wound up and accidentally smacked Steel, just lunging toward them. Her parasol glanced off his cheek, making him stumble.

"PEACE!" Avery raced by, whacking everyone within reach with a wooden sword.

"What are you—" Lance bellowed and fell forward when a searing blow connected with the back of his head.

"Whoops—hit you harder than I meant to." Ella Hall kept going. "Probably deserved it," he thought he heard her add as she was swallowed up in the crowd still raging around him.

Lance, on hands and knees, tried to grasp what was going on. All around him, women in Revolutionary War gowns were beating on unsuspecting soldiers on both sides, dashing them with serving trays, whacking them with umbrellas, tea kettles and even—hell, was that Olivia bashing one of Steel's shadowy friends with a folding chair?

"What the hell is going on?" Liam shouted from several feet away just as Maggie—little, timid Maggie— brought a thick book down on his head with all her might. "Ow—what the fuck, Maggie?"

"PEACE!" She ran off and hit someone else.

Was that Reverend Halpern?

It was.

Lance looked around him. Took in the pure chaos on the battle field. Now Maggie was helping Reverend Halpern to his feet.

This had all gone too far.

"Liam," he said. "We've got to stop this."

Liam looked around him, too. "You're the one who started it—"

"I might have gotten the re-enactment going, but I'm not the one who started this." He was pretty sure Liam knew he meant the feud between their families. "Tell you one thing, though. I'm sorry for how far it's gone. Sorry this is the kind of neighbors we are. We're tearing up this town. I never meant for this to happen."

Liam didn't look away. "Sure seemed like you meant it."

Lance sucked in a breath. They weren't talking about the re-enactment or the feud anymore. They were talking about football semifinals.

"I covered for you for years. Would have kept covering if I didn't think you'd get killed out there. Why couldn't you just stay sober for one game?"

Liam ducked his head. Shook it after a minute. "I... just couldn't," he said.

Lance waited for him to go on. There had to be more of an explanation than that. When Liam looked up again, there was anguish in his eyes.

"Every damn game got harder. Every time I had to

push myself to even walk out on the field. There was so much pressure. I couldn't screw up. My dad—he would have given me hell if I did. He was a hero. I just—"

Lance thought he understood. "You drank so you *could* play."

Liam nodded. "It was real bad that day. I had the shakes. A few beers, and at least that stopped. Guess I kept going, though. Switched to whiskey. Stupid move."

Lance closed his eyes. "I didn't get it back then—I was afraid you'd get hurt. The way the other team kept sacking you."

"I know." Liam rubbed a hand over his face. "As soon as I got kicked off the team, it all went away. Nothing's made me feel like that again." He shrugged. "Not until recently. I don't do much that puts me in the spotlight. Not usually." He looked away again. "And Dad's gone."

Lance wondered how William had reacted all those years ago. "When you got kicked off the team—"

"Dad chewed me out good," Liam said as if he understood what Lance was asking. "Hell, he swore he'd go to Coach and straighten him out—again. I told him no. Told him you'd screwed things for me good. Told him if he got you kicked off the team, everyone would hate me."

"And he bought that?" Lance thought William would have insisted on confronting Coach Andrews. He'd always been one to fight for his family.

"I think... I think he knew. I think he'd talked to Coach before. That's why I didn't get kicked off the team earlier." The pain in Liam's voice made Lance's stomach twist, and he realized this was why Liam hated him so much. Not losing his place on the team—he hadn't even wanted that in the end, had he? But Lance had helped him disappoint his father.

There was no forgiving that.

"I'm sorry." He meant it.

"I can't seem to move on," Liam said. All around them the battle still raged on, but they sat in an island of calm, as if the battlefield itself was conspiring to let them talk. "Can't get past Dad knowing what a loser I am."

"You're no loser," Lance said fiercely. "Look at what you've done at the Flying W, you and Noah—and Noah at our place half the time now. I heard you're getting your ranch certified organic. I wouldn't know how to start to do that. Your dad would be proud of you if he was here. He saw who you were. He'd never judge you for something as dumb as football."

"You don't think?" Liam asked so bitterly Lance knew William had.

"If he did, he doesn't deserve a son like you. Who the else would be so loyal to his family? His home? You stayed here, and now you stand in his footsteps, every bit as good as Noah," he added, heading off what he knew would be Liam's next objection. "So football wasn't your thing. The only question now is—what *is* your thing?"

Liam swallowed. Nodded. "Guess you're right."

"I know I'm right. And I'll tell you something else.

I'm not going to let my father's legacy control me anymore. You shouldn't either. I'm moving on. I'm going back to school. I'm going to work at the museum. And I'm going to be with Maya, whether you like it or not."

Liam met his gaze, a tired smile curling the corners of his mouth. "Of course you are."

"That's right; I am. So are we agreeing? Or are we going to fight some more?" Lance braced himself. Just for a second, he thought Liam might lunge at him again.

Then Liam laughed. "Hell, Cooper, you're relentless. Go ahead. Court my sister. Don't say I didn't try to warn you off. She's a scrapper, and she won't put up with any shit." He stood up before Lance could say anything, held out a hand and pulled Lance up, too. "Let's break up this shindig and go eat."

"Hell, yeah," Lance agreed. "PEACE," he shouted. "PEACE!"

"HOW THE HELL do we wrap this up in a way that makes sense?" Avery hissed when the fighting finally died out. The audience was sitting stunned on the grass. All around them, the combatants, including the female ones, were a bedraggled lot, their outfits battered and torn like so many trampled flags on the field.

Maya turned to Olivia. Olivia shrugged. They had all the follow-up scenes to do, Maya remembered. The ones that were supposed to take place after the war ended.

The Battle of Cowpens hadn't ended with a bunch

of angels of peace sweeping in.

The moment drew out. This was going to be a disaster if someone didn't say something.

Maya straightened and pitched her voice to carry. "The angels," she began haltingly, swallowed and forged on. "The angels of peace disappeared as quickly as they came, melting into the surrounding landscape until the combatants wondered if they'd ever been there at all."

The women took her cue and slunk away off the battlefield, putting down their makeshift weapons and sitting among the audience.

"The fog of war is a funny thing, after all," Maya went on, her self-confidence growing. "Often men at the same battle recall the things that happened differently."

A few people nodded in the audience. Maya took heart.

"The Revolutionary War raged on for two more years. When it was finally over, everything had changed."

At Avery's whispered prompting, the actors from the first scene of the re-enactment took the field again.

"My son came home a different man," Ella proclaimed. "Where once he loved to dance and play the fiddle, now he was apt to brood on long winter nights. At least he came back to us. So many people lost their loved ones."

The scenes continued until it was Maya's turn to step back out in front of the audience. "I'm still waiting," she said, and her voice broke because it occurred to her she *was* still waiting for her chance to love and be loved.

"Funny how we forget how precious peace is until it's gone," she went on. "Until our families are torn apart, our towns demolished, our country in fragments." She took a breath. "The soldiers are home or have been declared dead, and yet still I wait, in limbo. Where is the man I love?"

Lance stepped onto the field.

"Here I am."

Something gave in her heart, and Maya found she couldn't choke out the rest of her lines. As Lance moved toward her, she realized she'd been waiting for a man like him for years. Someone who understood her. Who loved her. Who saw her for what she was.

She fell into his arms and pressed kisses to his throat, jaw and cheek as fervently as if he'd been away waging a war. When he claimed her mouth with his own, she clung to him, long past caring what the script called for.

Cheers washed over them, and when she looked up, she saw the audience on its feet.

Lance chuckled. "We're bringing down the house."

"We did it," she whispered to him. "We pulled it off."

"Yes, we did. Together." He kissed her one last time and stepped back, then gestured for the rest of the cast and volunteers to join them on the field. The applause kept rolling as everyone took their bows. When they finally made their way to the sidelines again, Maya heard one man in the audience remark to his wife, "That wasn't like any re-enactment I've ever seen."

"I know," his wife said. "It was awesome."

Chapter Sixteen

"**W**ELL?" LANCE DEMANDED later that night when Warren had done a back-of-the-napkin calculation of their earnings. "Did we make enough money?" All around them, people visited the food tents and listened to a band making music as afternoon faded into evening.

"Looks like it. It'll be tight, though," Warren said. "We'll all have to work miracles with the new exhibits and get people through the door into the museum if we want to keep it running. I'll stay on until you two are ready to take over."

Lance met Maya's gaze. She nodded. She was up for the challenge if he was. He'd still need to explain to his family what his intentions were, and he'd have to work out with Steel—and Noah, too, probably, much as he hated to admit it—how to keep the ranch running while he went to school and worked. He was committed to trying it, though.

He was committed to being with Maya, too. He was done pretending he could live without her. He couldn't. She was all he could hope for from a partner in life.

"We'll get it done," he assured Warren.

"We will," Maya said.

Running footsteps behind him had Lance spinning around. Was there new trouble?

It was Bart... and Maggie, too, rushing toward them.

"What's wrong?" Lance asked them, getting to his feet.

"You mean, what's right?" Maggie laughed happily. She caught Bart around the middle and squeezed him. Bart grinned from ear to ear, his arm around her shoulders.

"We've had a brainstorm," he said. "Something that will help the museum—and us."

"What is it?" Maya asked.

"You know how wonderful I think it is that Bart wanted to make me a home from the warehouse he inherited," Maggie began.

Lance wondered if that was strictly true, but he didn't say anything out loud. Maggie certainly looked happy now.

"Thing is," Bart said, "I brought Katie to see it yesterday, and she didn't like it at all. She wants to be near her friends—not on the other side of town. The warehouse isn't exactly in a residential area."

Maya looked like she'd swallowed something wrong. Lance could guess why. How many times had he tried to tell Bart the same thing, after all?

"So I had a bright idea," Bart said. "We'll sell it to the museum! We can hold the mortgage ourselves. Instead of paying for the renovation, our savings can go to a down payment on a house, just like we planned, but the mortgage payments we get from the museum will go a long way to help cover our house mortgage payments. We'll actually be able to afford a home on the right side of town! What do you think?"

"Can the museum afford an arrangement like that?" Lance asked Warren.

"It'll hardly be more than the rent you paid before," Maggie assured him. "Bart and I did the math. Since we're the ones carrying it, we can decide on the down payment and the terms. We'll work it out."

"That's a very fair deal," Warren said. "Are you sure about that?"

"Positive." Maggie beamed at all of them. "We couldn't be happier to help."

"I think it's a great idea," Lance said. The warehouse would make an excellent museum. It already sat in the middle of a huge parking lot.

"I bet everyone who helped with the re-enactment would be glad to help out renovating the place, too," Warren mused. "We'd have a museum we could be proud of."

"And I think you'll find a wonderful house in town," Maya said to Maggie. "Megan is a realtor, and she's always looking for clients. You should go see her first thing tomorrow."

"I will. I can't wait to start looking for our new home."

"You know what this means?" Warren stood up and clapped Bart on the back. "You and Maggie just threw yourself into the running for the Founder's Prize. Maybe you should hold off buying anything until you see if you win the Ridley property."

Lance stiffened. Maya's eyebrows shot up. When their eyes met, however, he couldn't stop the smile that tugged one corner of his mouth.

"Damn," he said under his breath, edging closer to her so that only Maya could hear. "Who'd have thought Bart would be the one to outmaneuver me?"

"He outmaneuvered me, too," Maya said ruefully. "I guess I'm glad. I wouldn't want the Founder's Prize to come between us."

"You mean that?"

"Yep." She grinned, but her smile was lopsided as she shook her head at Bart and Maggie, who were too busy kissing again to notice. "But if we're going to be together, maybe we should join forces to make sure those sneaky Lawsons don't steal what should be ours."

"How are we going to stop them? Now each of our families has saved one of Chance Creek's landmarks— and Bart and Maggie did it without even meaning to."

"I'm not sure. It'll have to be some kind of team effort."

"I could get into that," Lance said. After seeing what they could accomplish when they worked together, he felt stupid for not trying it sooner. "Maybe we should throw in on more than the Founder's Prize." He glanced at Warren still talking with Maggie and Bart. "I think I need to talk to Noah about combining our cattle operations. It would free up enough time I could go back to school."

Maya raised her eyebrows. "Liam isn't going to like that."

"Liam will have to get over it." He lifted her chin and bent down to cover her mouth with his own. As they kissed, the Ridley property and all their troubles faded away. There was just him and Maya. Their own little world.

Just as it should be.

"I love you, Maya Turner," he murmured.

"I love you, Lance Cooper," she murmured back.

"Good."

WHEN LANCE EXCUSED himself to "go take care of something," Maya took the opportunity to find a table and take a seat. She felt light-headed and didn't think she could take much more today. The re-enactment had been a disaster, then a roaring success. Now it was all over—and the museum had been saved.

And Lance loved her.

The light was fading away. When it was fully dark, it would be time for fireworks. She tapped her foot to the beat of the country music. A band was playing, and couples were swaying around the outdoor dance floor.

When Jed approached and sat down unsteadily beside her, she smiled at him. "It's a lovely night, isn't it?"

"I saw you and Lance," he said gruffly.

Maya bit back a sharp retort. Not this again. "Don't even start," she warned him. "I'm going to be with him. I love Lance."

She thought he would yell at her. Instead, he sighed. "It's a difficult thing, loving a Cooper."

Jed should know, she supposed. When he and Virginia were young, he'd courted her for a little while.

It hadn't worked out.

"Why didn't you ever marry?" she asked him. "Surely you must have met someone who was right for you along the way." He'd been young when he and Virginia had broken things off. He could have had a dozen other paramours. He never talked about them, though.

"When you've had the right one, and then you've lost her, it's hard to settle for anything else."

Maya stilled. Had Virginia been the right one?

"Uncle Jed?"

"You've been cautious. You've worked hard. You always put the family first," he said tiredly. "Remember that sometimes life sticks you in an airplane, puts a parachute on your back, flies you up into the air and opens the hatch."

"That sounds dangerous," she joked.

"It is, but there's only one thing for it. Close your eyes and jump. And hope like hell that parachute opens. If it doesn't, enjoy the ride down as best you can."

She nodded. "I can do that."

"I hope so. Just make sure you win the Founder's Prize while you're at it." He got up again, looked around and spotted Stella. She waved and came to stand by his side.

"Ready to go home, Jed?"

"More than ready."

"Good night." Maya watched them go and wondered where Lance had gotten to. Should she wait for him, or—

A commotion at the far end of the field caught her attention.

Caught everyone's attention, actually. The music died, and there was the blare of a police siren. Pushing her way through the gathering crowd, Maya saw the sheriff's cruiser rolling onto the field. Its headlights cut through the gathering gloom.

When it came to a stop, Cab jumped out and jogged toward someone in the crowd. Maya looked past him to the figure in the back seat.

It couldn't be—

Cab returned, leading his wife, Rose. They spoke in hushed voices near the vehicle, but as Maya moved closer, she caught the tail end of the conversation.

"You broke into my store?"

"One, I'm the sheriff. Two, you gave me a key."

Rose looked like she would argue, but Cab pressed something into her palm, and Rose's fingers closed around it. A faraway look came into her eyes. Maya had seen that look before, when she'd accompanied a friend to Rose's jewelry store once. Rose had been helping a pair of customers shopping for an engagement ring. When they'd chosen one, she'd held it just like that—

Rose smiled and bent closer to the car. "It's perfect," she said loudly.

"Thank you, citizen," Cab said in an exaggerated cop voice. "That's all the evidence we needed."

Rose swatted at him as he opened the back door. Lance stepped out, grinning, and took whatever it was Rose had gripped in her hand.

Before Maya could go to ask him what was happening, Cab leaned in the front door and spoke into the cruiser's megaphone. "Can I have everyone's attention?"

He already had it, Maya thought with a shake of her head. What was going on?

"Please direct your attention to center stage," Cab went on. "It's time we gave this show a proper ending."

"We already gave the show a good ending," Avery said indignantly from a few feet away.

"Maya Turner, please step forward."

Cab flicked on the cruiser's high beams, and the bright light blinded Maya. She tried to block it with her hands, stepping through the parting crowd. When her eyes adjusted, Lance knelt before her.

Maya's breath caught in her throat.

Was he—?

He held up a ring.

"Maya Turner," Lance said. "When I first asked you to dance at my sister's wedding—"

A spate of fireworks shot up and exploded overhead, making the ring sparkle. The audience oohed.

"What?" Maya cried. She couldn't hear a thing Lance was saying.

"I always knew—" Lance said. Another volley of fireworks shot up into the night. Red, white and blue lights danced in the sky and drifted down.

"I can't hear you," Maya tried to say over the rat-atat sound.

"I—"

He was drowned out again.

Maya couldn't help but laugh, but at the same time she wanted to cry. She wanted to hear every single word—

"Damn it," Lance said over-loudly in a short gap between salvos. Another brace of fireworks shot up, and his evident frustration made her laugh again. They were doomed, weren't they? Fate was never going to smooth their path.

She didn't care. She'd take Lance easy or not.

"Yes!" she shouted when there was another pause between explosions. She wasn't sure if he'd asked the question or not yet, but she didn't care. She knew her answer. She needed him to know, too. "Yes, I'll marry you!"

For the third time that day, she was shocked how loud a crowd could be.

Chapter Seventeen

N OT EVEN THE heat could put a damper on Lance's mood as he stood at the end of the aisle in the Chance Creek reformed church and waited for Maya to appear.

It was long past the summer solstice, and the days were getting shorter, but the sun only seemed determined to shine brighter and hotter as July crept by. Even with the large fans they had set up in discreet places throughout the building, Lance's tuxedo was stifling.

He hardly noticed.

The bridal march started, his breathing hitched and he waited until Maya appeared, resplendent in her wedding dress, a simple, elegant gown that hugged her curves and brushed the floor as she walked.

He couldn't imagine being happier than he was already as she moved toward him on Noah's arm. When they reached him, Noah placed her hand in his. "Take care of her," he said.

"I will," Lance assured him. Noah was fast becoming a man whose good opinion he wanted to cultivate.

Maya took her place next to him while Reverend

Halpern began the ceremony. Looking over his shoulder at the congregation, Lance was struck by the realization that the Cooper and Turner sides of the aisle were beginning to blend: Olivia sat with Noah on the bride's side. Next time there was a wedding, he'd sit wherever Maya wanted to be.

Even more interesting, while Enid had refused to attend Olivia's wedding to Noah, she had come to his. He hadn't spoken more than a few words to her, and he wasn't sure what it would take to heal past hurts between them, but he had to admit he was glad she was here. Mary had come, too, at the last minute, perhaps spurred on by the news that Enid was coming. He knew Maya was happy to have her here, although the presence of Enid's stepchildren was a little awkward. Her new husband hadn't come with them. Lance thought Olivia was relieved.

He forgot all of that as Reverend Halpern began the words of the ceremony. He reached for Maya's hand, and when she curled her fingers around his, he squeezed them. He had no doubt that together they'd build a future and overcome any lingering hurts from the past. He didn't have to hide what he wanted anymore, which was the first step of making all his dreams come true.

MAYA COULD BARELY breathe as she said the words that would bind her to Lance forever. She hadn't known it was possible to be so happy, and she never would have dreamed she could find her partner in life so close to home. When Reverend Halpern told Lance he could kiss the bride, she tilted her face to him eagerly and relished the now-familiar feel of his mouth meeting hers.

Lance's kisses made her giddy, and the cheers of her friends and family underscored her belief that she was exactly where she was supposed to be. Their first dance affirmed that. Maya thought she'd always feel like she was floating in the clouds when Lance held her.

Hours later, after dinner, cake, dancing and congratulations, they finally stumbled out to the limousine that would take them home.

"I have a surprise for you," Stella said. She handed Maya a key. "It's in the cabin."

"I helped," Olivia said. Maya was happy to have her old friend back in her life.

Maya didn't have time to ask them what they meant before Lance bundled her into the vehicle. At the Flying W, they stumbled down the track to the cabin where Camila used to live, the location of their illicit rendezvous before Liam had intruded.

Maya fit the key in the lock and then shrieked when Lance scooped her up in his arms.

"Tradition," he told her and kissed her on the jaw, turning the handle and carrying her into the little house.

Maya gasped when she took in the interior.

It had been cleaned within an inch of its life. New rugs lay on the floor, and an L-shaped couch faced the fireplace. A beautiful dining room table and chairs stood opposite the kitchen, which had been spruced up with a new tile backsplash.

In the bedroom, the once-bare bed had been made up with new linens, a row of pillows lining the headboard.

"It's like a hotel," Maya breathed. Stella and Olivia had done a wonderful job.

"It's our new home," Lance told her.

"Did you make the table and chairs?"

He nodded. "And the end tables in the bedroom. And the dresser."

"You're amazing." She kissed him a half dozen times. "My husband."

"My wife," Lance growled, picked her up again and carried her over to the bed. She clung to him as he set her down, drawing him down on top of her, kissing him like she'd never stop.

She never wanted to.

"We'll make a life here, you and me," he said when they came up for air. "We'll go to school. I'll teach. We'll work at the museum."

"We'll have kids," she said.

"Yeah. Kids." His kisses trailed down her neck to the hollow between her breasts. "They'll love growing up on the ranches."

"They will." She arched back as his arms went around her and his fingers fumbled for a way to get her out of her dress. She helped him with the fastenings, wriggled out of the beautiful gown, set it carefully aside and lay back in her lacy bra and panties.

"You are a sight," he told her, stripping down quickly and lying next to her.

"So are you." She smoothed a hand down to rest on his hip. Every inch of him was amazing—and he was all hers. She arched back to let him undo the clasp of her bra, peeled it off and sighed when he cupped her breasts. When he touched her, all the world's troubles fell away and left her aching for him. Moments later, she lifted her hips and let him slide her panties off. She was more than ready for what would come next.

Lance settled between her legs, taking his time enjoying her breasts, teasing and caressing her, until Maya urged him to take things further. When he nudged against her and then pushed inside, she closed her eyes, wanting to savor every moment of their joining. He felt so good she thought she couldn't stand it, and when he began to move, Maya could only hold on and move with him.

They'd been together before, but this was different. This was a pledge they'd be together the rest of their lives. She gave herself to him whole-heartedly, clinging to him, moving with him, taking him in.

She loved this man. Now and forever. And as she came, she cried out, unwilling to hold back anything. Lance followed quickly, bucking against her with his release, his arms encircling her, his body tensing with his orgasm.

They collapsed together in a tangle of sheets, and all Maya could do was catch her breath.

"I love you," Lance whispered and kissed her temple. "I always will."

She kissed the underside of his chin. "I love you, too."

BACK AT THE reception, Liam had been holding a beer in his hand for an hour but hadn't had a single sip when he decided to throw caution to the wind.

"So, you're sticking around for a while?" he asked when he approached Tory.

"Looks that way," she said.

"Good. Then you'll have time for a dance." He took her hand and led her to the dance floor.

"You like making trouble, don't you?" she asked, allowing him to take her in his arms and begin to sway.

"You don't know the half of it."

To find out more, look for *The Cowboy's Stolen Bride*, Volume 4 in the *Turners v. Coopers* series.

Be the first to know about Cora Seton's new releases! Sign up for her newsletter here! www.coraseton.com/sign-up-for-my-newsletter

Other books in the Turners v. Coopers Series:

The Cowboy's Secret Bride (Volume 1)
The Cowboy's Outlaw Bride (Volume 2)
The Cowboy's Stolen Bride (Volume 4)
The Cowboy's Forbidden Bride (Volume 5)

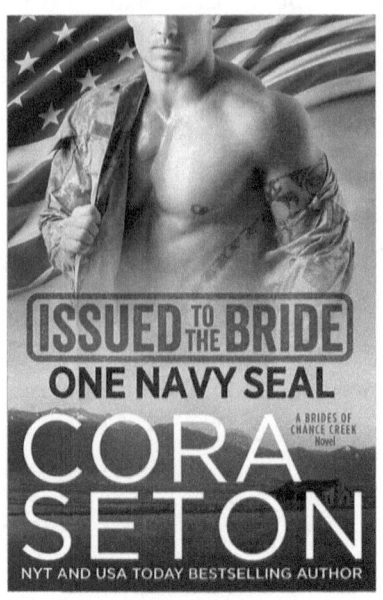

Read on for an excerpt of
Issued to the Bride One Navy SEAL.

Four months ago

O N THE FIRST of February, General Augustus Reed entered his office at USSOCOM at MacDill Air Force Base in Tampa, Florida, placed his battered leather briefcase on the floor, sat down at his wide, wooden desk and pulled a sealed envelope from a drawer. It bore the date written in his wife's beautiful script, and the General ran his thumb over the words before turning it over and opening the flap.

He pulled out a single page and began to read.

Dear Augustus,

It's time to think of our daughters' future, beginning with Cass.

The General nodded. Spot on, as usual; he'd been thinking about Cass a lot these days. Thinking about all the girls. They'd run yet another of his overseers off Two Willows, his wife's Montana ranch, several months ago, and he'd been forced to replace him with a man he didn't know. There was a long-standing feud between him and the girls over who should run the place, and the truth was, they were wearing him down. Ten overseers in eleven years; that had to be some kind of a record, and no ranch could function well under those circumstances. Still, he'd be damned if he was going to put a passel of rebellious daughters in charge, even if they were adults now. It took a man's steady hand to run such a large spread.

Unfortunately, it was beginning to come clear that Bob Finchley didn't possess that steady hand. Winter in Chance Creek was always a tricky time, but in the months since Finchley had taken the helm, they'd lost far too many cattle. The General's spies in the area reported the ranch was looking run-down, and his daughters hadn't been seen much in town. The worst were the rumors about Cass and Finchley—that they were dating. The General didn't like that at all—not if the man couldn't run the ranch competently—and he'd asked for confirmation, but so far it hadn't come. Finchley always had a rational explanation for the loss of cattle, and he never said a word about Cass, but the General knew something wasn't right and he was already looking for the man's replacement.

Our daughter runs a tight ship, and I'm sure she's been invaluable on the ranch.

He had to admit what Amelia wrote was true. Cass was an organizational wizard. She kept her sisters, the house and the family accounts in line, and not for the first time he wondered if he should have encouraged Cass to join the Army back when she had expressed interest. She'd mentioned the possibility once or twice as a teenager, but he'd discouraged her. Not that he didn't think she'd make a good soldier; she'd have made a fine one. It was the thought of his five daughters scattered to the wind that had guided his hand. He couldn't stomach that. He needed his family in one place, and he'd done what it took to keep her home. That wasn't much: a suggestion her sisters needed her to watch over them until they were of age, a mention of tasks undone on the ranch, a hint she and the others would inherit one day and shouldn't she watch over her inheritance? It had done the trick.

Maybe he'd been wrong.

But if Cass had gone, wouldn't the rest of them have followed her?

He'd been able to stop sending guardians for the girls when Cass turned twenty-one five years ago, much to everyone's relief. His daughters had liked those about as little as they liked the overseers. He'd hoped when he dispensed of the guardians, the girls would feel they had enough independence, but that wasn't the case; they still wanted control of the ranch.

Cass is a loving soul with a heart as big as Montana, but she's cautious, too. I'll wager she's beginning to think there isn't a man alive she can trust with it.

The General sighed. His girls hadn't confided in him in years—especially about matters of the heart—something he was glad Amelia couldn't know. The truth was his daughters had spent far too much time as teenagers hatching plots to cast off guardians and overseers to have much of a social life. They'd been obsessed with being independent, and there were stretches of time when they'd managed it—and managed to run the show with no one the wiser for months. In order to pull that off, they'd kept to themselves as much as possible. He'd only recently begun to hear rumblings about men and boyfriends. Unfortunately, none of the girls were picking hardworking men who might make a future at Two Willows; they were picking flashy, fly-by-night troublemakers.

Like Bob Finchley.

He couldn't understand it. He wanted that man out of there. Now. Trouble was, when your daughters ran off so many overseers it made it hard to get a new one to sign on. He had yet to find a suitable replacement.

Without a career off the ranch, Cass won't get out much. She might not ever meet the man who's right for her. I want you to step in. Send her a man, Augustus. A good man.

A good man. Those weren't easy to come by in this world. The right man for Cass would need to be strong to hold his own in a relationship with her. He'd need to be fair and true, or he wouldn't be worthy of her. He'd need some experience ranching.

A lot of experience ranching.

The General stopped to ponder that. He'd read something recently about a man with a lot of experience ranching. A good man who'd gotten into a spot of trouble. He remembered thinking he ought to get a second chance—with a stern warning not to screw up again. A Navy SEAL, wasn't it? He'd look up the document when he was done.

He returned to the letter.

> *Now here's the hard part, darling. You can't order him to marry Cass any more than you can order Cass to marry him. You're a cunning old codger when you want to be, and it'll take all your deviousness to pull this off. Set the stage. Introduce the players.*
>
> *Let fate do the rest.*

I love you and I always will,
Amelia

Set the stage. Introduce the players.

The General read through the letter a second time, folded it carefully, slid it back into the envelope and added it to the stack in his deep, right-hand bottom drawer. He steepled his hands and considered his options. Amelia was right; he needed to do something to make sure his daughters married well. But they'd rebelled against him for years, so he couldn't simply assign them husbands, as much as he'd like to. They'd never allow the interference.

But if he made them think they'd chosen the right men themselves...

He nodded. That was the way to go about it.

In fact...

The General chuckled. Sometime in the next six months, his daughters would stage another rebellion and evict Bob Finchley from the ranch. He could just about guarantee it, even if Cass was currently dating the man. Sooner or later he'd go too far trying to boss them around, and Cass and the others would flip their lids.

When they did, he'd be ready for them with a replacement they'd never be able to shake. One trained to combat enemy forces by good ol' Uncle Sam himself. A soldier in the Special Forces might do it. Or maybe even a Navy SEAL...

This wasn't the work of a moment, though. He'd need time to put the players in place. Cass wasn't the only one who'd need a man—a good man—to share her life.

Five daughters.

Five husbands.

Amelia would approve.

The General opened the bottom left-hand drawer of his desk, and mentally counted the remaining envelopes that sat unopened in another stack, all dated in his wife's beautiful script. Ten years ago, after Amelia passed away, Cass had forwarded him a plain brown box filled with envelopes she'd received from the family lawyer. The stack in this drawer had dwindled compared to the opened ones in the other drawer.

What on earth would he do when there were none left?

End of Excerpt

The Cowboys of Chance Creek Series:

The Cowboy Inherits a Bride (Volume 0)
The Cowboy's E-Mail Order Bride (Volume 1)
The Cowboy Wins a Bride (Volume 2)
The Cowboy Imports a Bride (Volume 3)
The Cowgirl Ropes a Billionaire (Volume 4)
The Sheriff Catches a Bride (Volume 5)
The Cowboy Lassos a Bride (Volume 6)
The Cowboy Rescues a Bride (Volume 7)
The Cowboy Earns a Bride (Volume 8)
The Cowboy's Christmas Bride (Volume 9)

The Heroes of Chance Creek Series:

The Navy SEAL's E-Mail Order Bride (Volume 1)
The Soldier's E-Mail Order Bride (Volume 2)
The Marine's E-Mail Order Bride (Volume 3)
The Navy SEAL's Christmas Bride (Volume 4)
The Airman's E-Mail Order Bride (Volume 5)

The SEALs of Chance Creek Series:

A SEAL's Oath
A SEAL's Vow
A SEAL's Pledge
A SEAL's Consent
A SEAL's Purpose
A SEAL's Resolve
A SEAL's Devotion
A SEAL's Desire
A SEAL's Struggle
A SEAL's Triumph

The Brides of Chance Creek Series:

Issued to the Bride One Navy SEAL
Issued to the Bride One Airman
Issued to the Bride One Sniper
Issued to the Bride One Marine
Issued to the Bride One Soldier

The Turners v. Coopers Series:

The Cowboy's Secret Bride (Volume 1)
The Cowboy's Outlaw Bride (Volume 2)
The Cowboy's Hidden Bride (Volume 3)
The Cowboy's Stolen Bride (Volume 4)
The Cowboy's Forbidden Bride (Volume 5)

About the Author

With over one million books sold, NYT and USA Today bestselling author Cora Seton has created a world readers love in Chance Creek, Montana. She has twenty-eight novels and novellas currently set in her fictional town, with many more in the works. Like her characters, Cora loves cowboys, military heroes, country life, gardening, bike-riding, binge-watching Jane Austen movies, keeping up with the latest technology and indulging in old-fashioned pursuits. Visit **www.coraseton.com** to read about new releases, contests and other cool events!

Blog:

www.coraseton.com

Facebook:

facebook.com/coraseton

Twitter:

twitter.com/coraseton

Newsletter:

www.coraseton.com/sign-up-for-my-newsletter